PRAISE FOR A LEGACY OF SILENCE

EARLY PRAISE FOR RIPPLE EFFECT

It's not easy to weave family drama and romance into a high-tension thriller about human trafficking, but Amy Rivers does it well in *Ripple Effect*, the third novel in the *A Legacy of Silence* trilogy. Highly recommended. - **Pat Stoltey, author of *In Defense of Delia***

PRAISE FOR COMPLICIT

2021 Pencraft Award Winner

A haunting deep dive into the demons all women must face. A brilliant masterpiece. - *Rea Frey, Author of Until I Find You*

Complicit is a rare powerhouse of a literary thriller with a profound moral compass. - *Joe Clifford, Author of Say My Name and the Jay Porter Series*

PRAISE FOR STUMBLE & FALL

2023 Firebird Award Winner

Part traditional crime story, part study in trauma recovery, STUMBLE AND FALL satisfies readers at both levels, offering a portrait of humanity at its best and worst. - *IndieReader Reviews*

This superior thriller finds as much suspense in sisters' relationships as in their efforts to stop sex traffickers. - *Booklife Reviews, Editor's Pick*

RIPPLE EFFECT

A LEGACY OF SILENCE

BOOK 3

AMY RIVERS

Compathy Press, LLC

Print ISBN: 978-1-7345160-8-1

Ebook ISBN: 978-1-7345160-9-8

Cover Design by Carl Graves | Extended Imagery

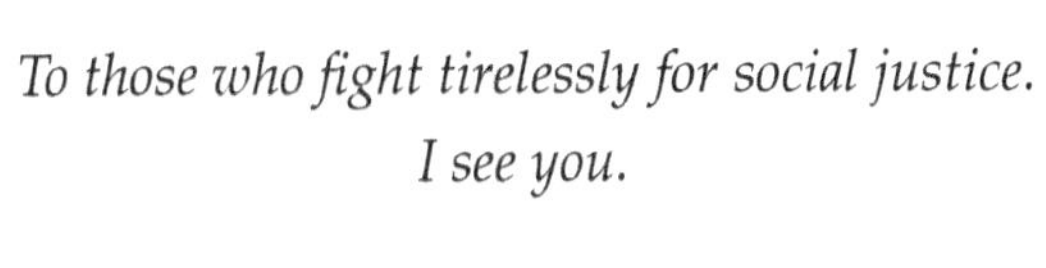

To those who fight tirelessly for social justice.
I see you.

PROLOGUE

It was the middle of summer, and the temperatures had been in the triple digits for days. Inside the office, with the air conditioning turned up to full blast, it was frigid. Ruth wrapped her mother's sweater tighter around her frame as she furiously sorted through invoices. Her boss, Mr. Flores, was at a lunch meeting, and she wanted to be done with her current task before he got back.

After her father died, Ruth became the sole financial support for her mother and younger siblings. With five children, Ruth's undocumented mother had resigned herself to cleaning work and other odd jobs that would pay under the table. There was never enough money, food, or attention. Ruth's childhood had been defined by poverty and all its aspects.

Having been born in the United States, Ruth's prospects were better than her mother's. From the age of fourteen, Ruth had worked any job that she could find—camp counselor, cashier, janitor. The job she now held had been a godsend. She worked in the office six days a week during regular business hours, and Mr. Flores had been kind enough to set her up on the cleaning crew on weekend nights. The pay was never quite enough, but there weren't a lot of options. Ruth was counting down the days until her brother was old enough to get a job.

She'd just finished the filing when she heard Mr. Flores out in the waiting room, giving her maybe three minutes before he entered his office. She closed the filing cabinet quietly and walked toward the door, taking off her sweater and dropping it on a visitor chair. She'd chosen a thin, lacy shirt that revealed more than her bare shoulders. Her hand was moving toward the doorknob when Mr. Flores walked in.

"Hello, Ruth," he said with a smile, not bothering to hide the way his eyes locked hungrily on her neckline.

"I was just leaving, sir," she said softly, but she made no move to exit. They'd been doing this dance for weeks, ever since Ruth noticed the way he looked at her. The way he looked at all the girls working for him.

There were several other teens in the office—all female, she'd noted—but none of them seemed to understand the power they held over their boss. Over men in general.

Ruth was different.

She knew how the world worked.

She'd watched her mother work tirelessly to take care of Ruth's father, cook, clean, raise children, and always be available for her husband when he needed her. Her father worked construction with a company that didn't ask a lot of questions as long as he was willing to work for whatever scraps they felt like throwing him. He went out drinking every night after work. Many nights he sent his children to bed right after supper, pushing Ruth's mother toward the bedroom.

Ruth could hear her parents' nighttime fumblings clearly through the wall. Sometimes her mother was quiet and all Ruth had to tune out were her father's ugly grunts. More often than not, her mother's cries penetrated the thin walls. Those nights were harder. Even in the heat of summer Ruth's mother often wore long sleeves and blouses that rode high on her neck, covering the evidence of her husband's frequent brutality.

It didn't take long for Ruth to understand that men made all the rules, and women just tried to survive them.

When Ruth turned thirteen, her father's best friend and drinking buddy had come for her. She knew he would. He'd been leering at her for as long as she could remember. As a young child, Ruth clung to her mother's skirts, knowing that proximity meant protection. But with each new baby, Ruth's mother had grown distracted. Tired. Empty.

But company didn't prevent Ruth's father from forcing her mother down the hallway, leaving her children at the mercy of his friend.

Ruth didn't blame her mother. She was simply doing what generations of women had done before. Enduring. Meanwhile, her husband's friend ripped away her daughter's innocence. It was inevitable. Or at least Ruth and her mother were built of the same stock. Flesh and bone without a shred of bodily autonomy.

Did her father know? Ruth never knew. She'd never asked him. And she did not shed a tear when he disappeared one night, despite the desperation she knew would follow for her and her family. Her father's friend also stopped visiting. A happy coincidence.

Ruth didn't blame her mother. But she refused to be like her.

"Ruth?"

Mr. Flores was watching her closely, and she turned her attention back to the present. Since starting this job, Ruth had observed a number of classmates come and go. Some served as interns. Some worked as paid employees. They never seemed to stay long, but Ruth often saw them in the halls at school, looking down at their shoes as if doing so would make them invisible.

She'd seen Mr. Flores look at them, too. She knew it was only a matter of time before his gaze shifted her way.

And when it had, she was ready.

Ruth stepped closer to Mr. Flores, a departure from their routine. She moved slowly, allowing him to back away if the timing wasn't right. He stayed still even as she slid her hand along his shirt sleeve, pulling him gently through the door and closing it. His eyes were wild with desire. Ruth pushed him against the office door, took his hands in hers, and placed them on her breasts.

Ruth knew how the world worked. You were either predator or prey. There was no question in her mind what she would be.

CHAPTER 1
TILLY

WHEN TILLY MEDINA stepped out of the courthouse for the Third Judicial District in Las Cruces, New Mexico, her whole body sagged with relief. She reached up to her head, unpinning her thick black curls and shaking the tension out of her head and neck.

"That was intense." Her friend and fellow forensic nurse, Jennifer Orozco, had fallen in step beside her. "How do you think it went?"

"It's always a mixed bag," Tilly said, taking off her suit jacket and folding it over her arm. The two nurses exited the courthouse and headed toward the parking lot. "Our case was strong, but you know how it goes. Blame the victim. Vilify the first responders. Sometimes it's hard to believe that anyone reports an assault in this area."

"And that Ken Johnson is a piece of work," Jennifer said, her expression souring at the mention of the defense attorney. "I know he's just doing his job, but he doesn't have to look so pleased with himself."

"I agree. It's hard not to get angry, especially when he made the 'false report' argument. Not unexpected, but did you see the look on that kid's mother's face? She absolutely believes that her son is an angel, despite the fact that he's been disciplined multiple times for harassment."

"I admit I'm not exactly looking forward to this part of the job." Jennifer winced. "He really went after you."

Tilly sighed. As a sexual assault nurse examiner (SANE), she'd testified in dozens of cases both in New Mexico and Colorado. She'd been on the stand for hours, and the cross-examination had been brutal. Not all defendants could afford to hire a defense attorney. This one could, and did. And though Tilly reminded herself that it was all part of the process, some of Johnson's insinuations had stung.

Thankfully, Tilly prided herself on being thorough, and in the end she was fairly confident that her testimony had been solid enough to reach the jury. She'd been a forensic nurse for over two decades—quite an accomplishment since the burnout rate for SANEs was very high.

"Here's my secret," Tilly said wearily. "I look at the victim while I'm testifying, so she knows I'm on her side. And then, under cross, I stare daggers at the defendant. It's funny how prolonged eye contact makes even the most arrogant dirtbags look away."

Jennifer laughed nervously. Sometimes Tilly could be too intense for her co-workers—she knew it. Jennifer was a newer nurse. She hadn't had the pleasure of testifying, but it was an inevitability in their line of work and an excruciating one. For victims and their loved ones, revictimization was a painful and long-lasting effect of participating in the criminal justice system. And for rapists, the system often failed to deliver real justice.

It could be demoralizing at times but it was a fight that Tilly believed in, heart and soul.

They arrived at Jennifer's car. Tilly was thankful that she wouldn't have to be behind the wheel as bone-tired and weary as she felt. As they made their way to Esperanza House, the clinic that housed the SANE program and other medical and mental health services for victims and their families, Tilly rested her head against the car seat and let her mind drift.

When they reached the clinic Jennifer put her hand on Tilly's arm, giving it a gentle shake.

"I'm awake." Tilly smiled but kept her eyes closed, enjoying a last moment of peace. With a sigh, she opened the door and stepped out. It was nearly summer and the days were already scorching. Tilly quickened her pace to catch up with Jennifer, who was already heading into the air-conditioned clinic.

"How'd it go?" Marie, the clinic director, asked as soon as they stepped in the door. When Tilly moved back to New Mexico the previous year, Marie had hired her on the spot. And with the addition of clinic coordinator duties to her nursing practice, Tilly was enjoying her work on the team.

"Good, I think. The DA's office will want to debrief, but not until tomorrow morning. I'm going home. I'm completely exhausted and I'm on call this week."

"I could take call tonight," Jennifer offered, but Tilly declined.

"It's okay. With Carmen on vacation, there's not much backup. If I'm lucky, it'll be a quiet night."

Marie smiled. "Get some rest. It's a good night for take-out and a bottle of wine."

Tilly dropped her briefcase in her office, locked the door, and headed home. An image of a nice big glass of wine poked at the edge of her thoughts, but Tilly knew better than to tempt fate. A year earlier, she'd been on the brink of having a real problem—maybe closer than she'd care to admit. The move to New Mexico and the subsequent death of her long-time boyfriend, Jim, had plunged her into a reckless, alcohol-fueled depression that had nearly cost her life. That demon had not been laid to rest, not entirely, but Tilly was determined to live her best life.

Besides, it was still early in the afternoon. What Tilly really needed was water. With the climbing temperatures and a sometimes erratic schedule, staying hydrated was a constant battle.

At home, Tilly warmed up some leftovers and sat down on the couch. Her phone pinged nearby, indicating an incoming text.

Probably Kate.

Tilly's sister Kate texted every day without fail. They had been through a lot in the last few years. Kate lived an hour away in their hometown of Alamogordo, New Mexico, where she ran a psychology practice for families. Kate seemed to be enjoying her work, but the income from her practice supported her real passion—the operation of a safe house for victims of a sex trafficking ring that she'd uncovered.

Kate lived in the house full-time; it was practically a fortress, complete with a state-of-the-art security system.

It wasn't Kate. It was Hannah Bross.

Can I come over?

Sure, I'm home, Tilly texted back. She cleaned up her dishes and was stretched out on the couch when her doorbell rang.

"Hi, Hannah," Tilly said, giving the teenage girl a hug. Hannah was the only child of Tilly's friend and Assistant District Attorney, Dan Bross. Dan's wife had passed away some time ago, and lately Hannah had been coming over to Tilly's to talk about topics that required a female ear. Having lost her own mother, Tilly had an especially soft place in her heart for Hannah. "What're you up to today?"

Hannah sank into an armchair with a dramatic sigh that only a sixteen-year-old could muster. "Dad is impossible," she moaned. "It's homecoming next week!"

Tilly smiled. Hannah had been through a lot in her short life and it was nice to see her acting her age, even if she was a little bit whiny now and again. "He's letting you go to the dance."

Hannah gave her an exasperated look. "Of course I'm going to the dance." Then she smiled. "The dress we picked out is amazing, by the way. Thank you for shopping with me!"

"So what's the problem?"

"Some of my friends are going to see a movie after the dance and then get some food at the 24-hour diner near the university. And he won't move my curfew at all! I never ask him for anything! Why is he being so overprotective?"

"What curfew do you want?"

Hannah grinned sheepishly. "Two a.m."

Tilly laughed out loud, which earned an instant frown

from her visitor. "Even I wouldn't let you stay out that late, Hannah. You're only sixteen."

Hannah was quiet for a moment. Tilly could practically see her gears shifting. "I know, but I'm responsible. You know I am!" Hannah looked at her pleadingly, her eyes wide, eyelashes fluttering.

Tilly realized she'd walked into a trap a moment too late. "No way. Whatever it is you think I can do to change your dad's mind, it's a hard pass for me."

"Oh, please! You know he listens to you. You can vouch for me." Hannah's eyes were brimming with hope and Tilly felt a small twinge of guilt about having to quell that spark, especially given what a wild child she'd been as a teen. But it was precisely her past that firmed her resolve. She sat down across from Hannah and put on her best "understanding adult" expression.

"Look, Hannah. I know it feels like the end of the world right now," Tilly said, noting the eye roll her words elicited. She held up a hand as if to fend off Hannah's next attack. "But I'm not being arbitrary, and I'm not just taking your dad's side."

Hannah sat up straighter in her chair to listen. Despite her adolescent angst, Hannah always listened when Tilly spoke, and Tilly honored that responsibility by trying to be honest with Hannah, even when it was awkward. *Almost like a parent*—a thought that never failed to create a rush of warmth through Tilly's core.

"I know I don't usually talk about my past, but when I was your age a lot of bad things happened to me. I was rebellious. My parents tried to get me to settle down, but I wasn't about to listen. And in the end my stubbornness got me into a situation that quite literally nearly ruined my life."

"What happened?" Hannah asked quietly. Tilly and Dan had talked at length about Kate's work to bring down the trafficking ring in Alamogordo, but they'd never told Hannah that Tilly had been a victim of the group in question. For a moment, Tilly wondered how Dan would feel about her sharing this information with his daughter, but she decided that honesty was the best policy.

"You know the stuff that's happening in Alamogordo? The stuff my sister is trying to stop?" Hannah's eyes grew wide with horror, and Tilly knew that she'd said enough.

Tilly sat in silence as Hannah considered this new piece of information.

"Do you think something like that could happen to me?" Hannah asked, unable to hide the hint of shakiness in her voice.

Tilly got up from where she sat and moved to the arm of Hannah's chair, where she could wrap her arms around the girl. "No, I don't. You're a very responsible girl, and you've got a lot of adults in your life, including me, who will do everything we can to help you have the happiest life possible. We can't protect you from every danger out there, but we can try to guide you as you make decisions. That's all your dad is trying to do here."

Hannah buried her face against Tilly's shoulder. A sense of calm and contentedness that Tilly had never felt before settled over her. She brushed a hand through Hannah's hair and just held the girl until finally Hannah pulled away.

"You know," Hannah said with a smirk, "he could've

avoided this whole mess if he just talked to me the way you do."

"Maybe," Tilly said ruefully. "But sometimes it's hard to listen to your parents the same way you listen to a friend."

Hannah smiled. "I love you, Tilly."

"I love you, too, kiddo."

———

Before going to bed, Tilly called Kate to check in.

"How'd it go in court?" Kate asked.

"As expected," Tilly said. "I held my own. I'll tell you about it this weekend. The more interesting part of my day was a visit from Hannah this afternoon."

"How's she doing?" Tilly could hear the amusement in Kate's voice. After a lifetime of swearing off parenting, Tilly's friendship with Dan had put her in a position to be one of the trusted adults in Hannah's life. A fact that Kate found endlessly entertaining.

"Homecoming drama," Tilly said. "But I got her straightened out. I know you think it's cute how she comes to me, but I just hope I'm not overstepping."

"I'm sure it's fine. You're practically her stepmother," Kate said.

Tilly felt warmth creeping up her neck. "I am not," she argued.

"Not because Dan doesn't want you to be." Kate knew how to push Tilly's buttons, and her aim was deadly. "You guys are together all the time. It's not like his interest is a secret."

Tilly sighed. Her first impression of Dan hadn't been very

positive, but as she'd gotten to know him she realized that his gruff exterior protected a heart of gold. They'd built a strong friendship, and he'd seen Tilly through one of the hardest years of her life.

She was in love with Dan. She knew it. Kate knew it. Even Dan knew it. But that was beside the point. It had been a year since Jim died, and Tilly's grief still felt too raw—too close to the surface. And thankfully Dan knew not to push.

"Not ready," Tilly muttered, hoping Kate would take the hint. A second or two of very awkward silence followed. Tilly jumped on the opportunity to change the subject. "How's my favorite future brother-in-law?"

Kate laughed. "He's fine. Loving every minute as an FBI agent. I keep thinking the novelty will wear off, but it's been nearly a year since he was accepted for training and he's still acting like he won the lottery."

"It's his dream job. And he managed to get that ring on your finger despite your best efforts to completely sabotage your own happiness. What more could a guy want?" Tilly teased.

The sisters shared a past riddled with grief. Both their parents were now deceased. For years the sisters had been estranged, largely due to the abuse Tilly suffered during her high school years. Neither sister felt entirely comfortable in romantic relationships, so there was a lot of back and forth as they navigated the ordinary parts of their lives.

Luckily, there were other areas where they felt more confident. Tilly and Kate shared a passion for forensics and criminal investigation. While Tilly had focused on forensic nursing, Kate had pursued psychology, working for many years in the prison system.

Though they both struggled with the personal sides of their lives, they made up for it by excelling in their professional pursuits.

Now Kate was engaged to her high school best friend, newly minted FBI agent Roman Aguilar. Roman had been in love with Kate since their teenage years, and it seemed like a small miracle that they were able to reconnect, especially given the circumstances—involvement in a murder investigation.

When one of the students at the high school was killed, Roman, then a detective in the local police force, reluctantly brought Kate in to consult. In the end, they'd uncovered a deep-rooted sex trafficking ring. Sending the murderer to prison was just the tip of the iceberg, and both Kate and Roman had ended up in the hospital for their roles in trying to unearth those responsible for the ongoing abuse.

Somehow, in the middle of all that chaos, Kate and Roman not only resurrected their friendship but had fallen in love as well. Again. At least Roman rediscovered the feelings he'd always held for Kate. As far as Tilly knew, Kate was still unwilling to admit that she'd buried her feelings for Roman deep since high school.

"He's gotten pretty lucky, hasn't he," Kate replied. "Speaking of whom, I agreed to do dishes tonight and I have an early client tomorrow, so I'd better let you go."

They said their goodbyes and Tilly settled down with a book, though she barely made it ten pages in before exhaustion took hold. She'd managed to sleep a few hours when her pager buzzed on her bedside table.

"Back to work," she groaned as she left the comfort of her bed to get back into her scrubs.

CHAPTER 2
KATE

"It's infuriating," Kate said as she paced the living room floor. Within the walls of her home—the hacienda she'd purchased as a safe house for abuse victims—she felt free to express all her frustrations.

For more than a year, Kate and Roman had been involved in the investigation of the trafficking operation that had been operating in their hometown for several decades. In the early days the struggle often felt insurmountable, but since the state police came onboard and several arrests had been made Kate's patience had grown thin.

Especially when none of the arrests had come close to the kingpins of the operation. Though Kate had her suspicions, the identity of whoever was running the operation remained unknown, at least in terms of evidence. She and Roman both saw Bill Gunnison, the Alamogordo Chief of Police, as the prime suspect. They just couldn't prove it.

Roman sat on the couch in front of her, listening patiently

as she verbally cycled through her frustration. She'd been at it for a good fifteen minutes and she knew she needed to wrap it up, but she was so angry she kept spiraling around in circles. She took a breath, making space for Roman to cut in—to reassure her.

"They're doing everything they can. When I spoke to Angie…"

"But there's nothing connecting these guys back to Chief Gunnison," Kate interrupted. "Or Ruth Flores. I mean, they've made three arrests already, not even counting Benny Parks. Three arrests! And nothing. Can you believe it?" She finally stopped her pacing and sank down onto the couch next to Roman.

He put his arm around her shoulders. "You know it's not that simple. Gunnison's been using the department as a shield for nearly two decades. And Ruth? She's been really smart. And really careful. We all see how well she's hidden her own involvement, but with so many people involved and so many years in operation I'm sure the State Police will find something."

Kate sighed. It had been nearly a year since she'd discovered Ruth Flores' ugly secret. It was a long time to be fighting a battle with no end in sight, and Kate was beginning to doubt. Though Ruth seemed to have inside knowledge about the trafficking ring, knowing something wasn't the same as participating. Maybe there was simply nothing to find.

Ruth had been one of the first people Kate connected with through the Chamber of Commerce, and for a while they'd enjoyed each other's company. Ruth had known both of Kate's parents, creating an almost instant bond. But Ruth had soon shown her true colors, lobbing some thinly veiled threats at Kate and hinting that she'd been involved in the death of Kate's mother, Addy.

Kate had already been disgusted by the situation, but the very idea that a woman had knowledge of the victimization of so many innocent girls—a woman who reminded Kate of her own abuela—made her want to throw up.

Once the shock wore off, Kate had doubled her efforts at breaking up the trafficking operation by taking a more public role in her fight. She'd begun speaking at community events and had created a youth program through the schools to prevent further victimization in their district. And on the surface it seemed to be working, but her friend, Angie— State Police Detective Angela Lopez—had yet to find anything tying Ruth to the vile practices taking place in their hometown.

That Chief Gunnison was using the police department to protect the abusers was equally abhorrent, but Ruth's betrayal felt personal for Kate. Ruth was covering for someone, and her complicity had Kate doubting so many of the things she thought she knew.

Kate's phone started buzzing on the coffee table. The caller ID read "Blocked", and for a moment she hesitated. It had been some months since she'd received any harassing calls, but she was still wary. Finally, she answered.

"Kate Medina?"

Kate couldn't immediately place the man's voice, though it was familiar.

"Who is this?"

"Sam Garrett." The City Manager's voice sounded pained, his breathing labored. "Don't hang up, please!"

"What do you want?" Kate sat up straight and looked at Roman, whose expression had become dark and serious. He knew better than to interrupt a call in case it was a client but she could see it was killing him to stay quiet.

"I need you to meet with me. Tonight."

"You must be joking," Kate replied, completely puzzled at the request. The City Manager had managed to avoid arrest, but Kate knew for a fact that he'd been a key player in the whole trafficking operation. "Or you think I'm crazy. I can assure you I'm not."

"Please," he pleaded. "There's something I need to give you. We can meet in public, but you have to hurry. It's not safe."

Kate had been ready to hang up, but something in his voice kept her on the line. Her work in the community was no secret, and she'd confronted Garrett directly, letting him know that he was in her sights. He'd seemed afraid even back then, but not afraid of her. Could he have information that would help her?

"Where?" she asked. Roman was already on his feet.

"The truck stop. I'll wait ten minutes and then I have to leave."

"Wait," she said, but he'd already disconnected.

Kate grabbed her purse and headed toward the front door, Roman and their dog Rusty on her heels.

"That was Sam Garrett," she said as she slid her tennis shoes on and disarmed the alarm system. "He says he has something to give me."

"And you believe him?" Roman put his hand on her arm. "Kate, you can't just go running off alone to meet this guy. He's a criminal."

Kate smiled nervously. "Who said anything about going alone? Might want to bring your gun. You know, just in case."

———

It took five minutes to get to the truck stop on the outskirts of town. Roman weaved through the busy parking lot to find a space. Kate was out of the car before he'd even turned off the engine. She sprinted into the store, earning suspicious looks from the cashier and a hostile glare from the trucker she nearly bowled over going through the door.

"Why don't you walk the perimeter. I'll check the bathrooms," Roman said, hot on her heels. They met back a few minutes later, empty-handed. "There's a payphone near the restrooms. No sign of him. Let's go check the parking lot and around the back."

Roman's expression was a mix of tension and concern. He let Kate walk out the door first, but stepped just ahead of her as they made their way through the parking lot and then to the back of the building.

"Oh no!" Kate gasped as she rounded the corner.

Near the dumpster a pair of legs were visible, though whoever's body they were attached to remained hidden behind the dumpster. Kate started to run forward, but Roman stopped her. Weapon drawn, he walked slowly to where Sam Garrett's body lay. When he looked up at Kate she knew that Garrett was dead, but when she approached his body she had to stifle a scream.

Someone had taken a blade to Garrett's handsome face and mutilated it savagely. But the wounds were older and already beginning to scar. The cause of his death was a bullet wound to the center of his forehead, fresh blood pooling beside him.

In the time it had taken Kate to get to the truck stop, someone had murdered Sam Garrett.

Roman, already on his cell phone with the sheriff's department, pushed Kate back toward the lights of the open parking lot. But Kate knew there would only be a few minutes before the scene was closed off to her. She looked around for Garrett's car, spotting it down the alley. In a moment of desperation she sprinted toward it, ignoring Roman's shouting.

She peered through the windows, careful not to touch anything.

"Are you nuts?" Roman had run up behind her and was now looking at her with a mix of horror and barely concealed fury.

"I thought maybe…"

"That what? You'd see an envelope with your name on it? What were you going to do, Kate? It's a crime scene. Sam Garrett was murdered not twenty feet from where you're standing. What if the killer is still here?"

Kate had been ready to argue, but Roman's words froze her in place. She hadn't been thinking straight and had run right into the path of danger. But she didn't feel like she was being watched. In fact she was quite sure whoever had killed

Garrett was long gone, though she knew Roman wasn't going to be satisfied with that hunch.

Roman turned toward the sound of approaching sirens and she fell in step beside him. Honestly, she'd had no idea what Sam Garrett wanted or what he might have had to show her. But she couldn't shake the feeling that something huge had just slipped through her fingers.

———

Kate watched from a distance as crime scene techs scurried around the parking lot. It had been hours since they'd arrived, but between talking with the responding officers and then waiting for State Police to show up neither Kate nor Roman had been eager to leave.

Their friend, Detective Angie Lopez, had been one of the last to arrive at the scene. As the lead detective on the trafficking case, she'd been an absolute beast in the fight to take down the traffickers one guilty party at a time. But so far, all her arrests had been dead ends in terms of dismantling the larger organization.

Kate watched as Roman and Angie talked with their heads close together. Roman and Angie had dated on and off over the years before Kate returned to town, and their relationship had been getting serious when Roman broke things off to be with Kate. It had taken most of the last year for Angie to begin talking to Kate again, and most of that progress had been engineered by Tilly. Both Angie and Kate's sister worked with the criminal justice system in Las Cruces, so they'd become friends, easing the way for Kate and Angie to make peace.

Not that long ago, seeing Roman and Angie together would have stirred up some insecurity in Kate, but tonight all she felt was despair. She'd been close to something—maybe a breakthrough—and now it was gone. She thought about Sam Garrett and wondered if their confrontation in his office had put a target on his back.

The conversation between Roman and Angie ended, and the detective made her way over to Kate.

"Here," Angie said. She handed Kate a steaming cup of coffee and took a seat next to her. "Roman took me through the basics, but I want to hear what you're thinking."

Kate sighed. "It took us about five minutes to get here, Angie. He said it wasn't safe, but I didn't realize he was talking about himself."

"What exactly did he say?"

"That he had something for me. That I had to meet him tonight."

"No hints about what it was?"

Kate shook her head. "He might have been setting me up, but something about how he sounded…I just don't think so. I keep having this terrible feeling that he was going to break things wide open, and now…" She slumped with the weight of disappointment and exhaustion. "Now what?"

"We investigate," Angie said as she got to her feet. "Maybe he left us some clues." She put a hand on Kate's shoulder. "I know this process is slow, and it doesn't always feel like we're making headway, but with every arrest we're making it a little bit safer."

Kate tried to smile, but the effort felt too great. "Thanks, Angie."

"Roman's heading this way," Angie said with a sigh that

may have been fatigue, or maybe something else. "I need you to give a statement. And then make sure you get some sleep."

As Angie walked away Kate noticed that her gait was uneven, her movements slow. It was a reminder to Kate that she wasn't the only one buckling under the weight of the investigation.

CHAPTER 3
TILLY

TILLY GRUMBLED to herself all the way from her car to the restaurant. She'd gotten home around four in the morning and had been on the verge of canceling her breakfast meeting with Angie. But the detective had been out on a call into the wee morning hours as well, so Tilly figured they'd both guzzle down coffee and commiserate. And she was grateful that she and Angie had become friends in their own right. At first Tilly had been guarded around Roman's ex-girlfriend, but in the past year Angie had become a regular fixture in Tilly's life.

Angie was sitting in a corner booth, looking like she might fall asleep in her cup. The string of a tea bag hung over the side of her mug.

"Tea?" Tilly said, sliding into the booth. "Hope it's black and loaded with caffeine. I'd go for an IV drip right about now."

Angie smiled. "Did you get any sleep?"

"Couple of hours. And Marie doesn't expect me in until

this afternoon, but I've got a pile of reports that need to be updated and filed. Putting all my faith in caffeine today."

While Angie sipped her tea, Tilly studied her friend. As a detective for the New Mexico State Police, Angie Lopez was involved in cases across the southern half of the state, which often kept her on the run. But today she looked unusually rough. The dark circles under her eyes looked like they were trying to take up permanent residence.

"Are you okay?" Tilly asked.

Angie sighed. "Is it that obvious?"

"You just looked more worn out than usual, which is totally expected after no sleep, but what kind of jerk would I be if I didn't ask?"

"You're absolutely right, of course. Ignoring it would be pretty heartless." Angie smiled sadly. "Long story short— I'm sick. It's chronic. Autoimmune. A vascular disorder. Diagnosed a few years ago. I'm having a pretty bad flare right now. The worst I've had. My doctor says stress isn't helping."

"Should you be working today?"

"No," Angie laughed. "But what am I going to do? Sit around my house all day feeling like shit when I have twenty active cases? Not to mention the trafficking investigation."

Tilly frowned. "You can't just ignore it, Angie."

"I know." The defeat in Angie's smile was heartbreaking. "I'm making it worse by not moving on with my life. I'm in a rut."

Tilly knew Angie was sidestepping any mention of Roman.

Since Kate and Roman announced their engagement, Angie

had been noticeably quiet about her personal life. She and Tilly had reached a comfortable place in their friendship, allowing Angie to talk more openly about her feelings as long as she tried not to attack Kate. Tilly understood the need to talk, so she'd learned to take off her sister-hat when she was with Angie. And when Angie found out that Roman was marrying Kate, Tilly was immediately aware of how quiet she'd been on the subject.

"You know I can't completely detach myself from Kate in this situation, but Angie, speaking only as your friend, you're going to have to let Roman go." At the dubious look on Angie's face, Tilly added, "I know I'm biased, but I'm also struggling with a similar problem, so chalk this up to a case of giving advice that I haven't figured out how to take myself."

Angie laughed, and a little bit of color returned to her cheeks. "Life really sucks sometimes."

The waitress approached, interrupting their conversation. Tilly ordered a pot of coffee and was making a good dent in the carafe, when Angie started coughing. She waved away Tilly's concern, but even after the fit subsided Tilly could see that Angie's breathing was more labored.

"You're looking awfully pale," Tilly noted, refilling Angie's water glass from the pitcher the waitress had left on the table. "Maybe you should go home and rest."

Angie was contemplative for a few moments, then she nodded. "Probably. I'm not going to be much use until I get some good sleep. Did you talk to Kate about what happened last night?"

"No, why would I?" Tilly asked warily. "Was she involved?"

"Indirectly. Sam Garrett—the City Manager in Alamogordo—was killed last night."

"What?!"

"He called Kate a few minutes before he was basically executed at a gas station outside of Tularosa. In the time it took Kate and Roman to get to the station someone shot Garrett in the forehead, but it looked like he'd been tortured —his face was all cut up and scarred. The ME said the scars were fairly recent, and it also looked like he'd been beaten up pretty badly before that. Lots of bruising and a few broken bones."

"Why did he call Kate?" Tilly's voice was becoming more shrill.

"He said he had something for her. She thought it might be evidence."

"Probably right since they killed him. Is Kate okay? I can't believe Roman let her go."

Angie chuckled. "Even you can't possibly believe he could have stopped her, though he did seem pretty unhappy about the whole situation."

Throughout the trafficking investigation, Kate had been in danger. She'd been attacked, run off the road, and threatened in her own home. And for some reason she ran toward the danger, taking risks that at times seemed uncalled for. Not that Tilly could fault her, since she'd done her own fair share of risk-taking.

"Yeah, I guess not," Tilly agreed. She put some cash on the table. "Listen, I need to call Kate and you need to go home and sleep, I'll check in with you later." As she prepared to walk away she added, "And please call me if you need anything, Angie. I know I'm Kate's sister, but I'm also your friend."

———

Later, sitting in her office, Tilly couldn't concentrate on her work. She'd called Kate and gotten a brief rundown on the shooting. Tilly insisted they meet up, and despite her assurances that she was all right Kate agreed too quickly for Tilly's comfort. A middle of the week get together usually spelled trouble. Tilly would have preferred to head over to Alamogordo the next morning, but she reluctantly agreed to wait a day, knowing it would be a juggling act for both of them.

A knock at her office door made Tilly jump.

Marie poked her head inside. "Do you have a minute?"

"Sure. What do you need?"

"I'm interviewing a new nurse and I wondered if you'd mind sitting in. She just moved to the area."

"Sounds good," Tilly said. As she followed Marie into the hall, she asked, "Anything specific you want me to address with her?"

"Not really." Marie paused. "I spoke with her earlier. She seems nice enough. I just got a feeling, you know? Wanted another opinion."

"Well, okay then. I'll keep an open mind."

They walked down to the small conference room, where a woman in black scrubs sat facing the door. She perked up when Tilly and Marie walked in.

"Heidi, this is our Clinical Coordinator, Tilly Medina. She'll be helping with today's interview."

"It's nice to meet you," Heidi said, standing to shake Tilly's hand.

"Heidi and I have gone over the basics," Marie said to Tilly, nodding to Heidi with a smile. "So I thought we could go over our basic operations, the call rotation, and whatever else seems pertinent."

"Are you currently working as a nurse here in town?" Tilly asked.

"Today's my first day in oncology at the hospital," Heidi replied. "My husband and I just moved here from Florida. I worked in the emergency room for the last seven years."

"Were you a SANE at your hospital?" Getting a trained nurse was always a huge win, so Tilly crossed her fingers.

"No. Our hospital was small and didn't have a program. We sent victims to the trauma center in the neighboring town." Heidi sighed. "One of my husband's frequent complaints."

Tilly cocked her head. "What do you mean?"

"Oh." Heidi's face flushed. "Sorry, my husband is in law enforcement. He was always annoyed at having to drive over to pick up evidence."

Marie was the next to speak. "Where is he working now that you're here?" The question struck Tilly as odd, maybe even inappropriate, but Marie seemed tense. She wondered what was going on.

"He took a position with the Border Patrol. He's really looking forward to helping keep our borders safe and secure." Heidi beamed with pride. "Florida has a lot of immigration problems, but it seems like this area is in real need of support."

"Immigration is definitely an issue over here," Tilly said

carefully. "But back to our clinic. In addition to sexual assault exams, which we do for both children and adults, we also provide follow-up medical and psychological support for our patients, many of whom are undocumented."

Heidi looked confused. "You serve illegals?"

"We serve anyone who's been assaulted regardless of nationality, gender identity, sexual orientation, race, religion...you name it," Marie said with a smile. Tilly understood the vibe Marie had picked up on. "Whether they decide to report their assault to law enforcement or not. Basically we're here to provide care and support for victims, but we also provide some medical services to people who can't afford a regular doctor's visit."

"Why wouldn't a person report their assault?" Now Heidi's tone held a hint of judgment. "I know if that ever happened to me, I'd want the police to know."

Tilly kept her voice neutral. "Forcing a victim to report the assault or to press charges can be harmful for a number of reasons. Unless a child is involved and we have a responsibility to report, we respect the victims' wishes. As Marie said, our main job is to provide medical care post-assault."

Heidi seemed to realize that things weren't going well. She smiled broadly and shifted gears. "No problem. I'm very professional, and I'll follow the protocols you've established to the letter."

"You seem like a very conscientious nurse, Heidi," Marie said. "We just want to make sure that this position is a good fit for you, too."

"So true," Tilly chimed in kindly. "For instance, we've had nurses who didn't feel comfortable dispensing Plan B to victims based on their religious beliefs."

"The abortion pill?"

"Plan B is a prophylactic intended to prevent conception," Tilly explained, wondering why it still surprised her when health professionals didn't understand these basic principles. "It can only be given within 72 hours of unprotected sex."

"How can you be sure that a woman hasn't already conceived?" Heidi's expression was one of genuine concern. While Tilly felt frustrated at the question, she also realized this nurse was truly misinformed. Luckily, Marie interjected before Tilly had a chance.

"Heidi, I really appreciate your interest in our clinic. However, respectfully, I don't think this would be a good fit for you. It's really important that we keep our personal and religious beliefs separate from the work we do in order not to further traumatize the victims we see. I hope you understand."

"Yes, thank you," Heidi said. She stood up and pulled her purse over her shoulder. "I wouldn't want to compromise my principles for any job." She smiled, but it didn't reach her eyes. Tilly noticed that she excused herself very quickly and was out the door of the clinic in record time.

Tilly turned to Marie. "What tipped you off?"

"I'm not sure. Something she said on the phone, or maybe just the way she said it. I thought maybe I was being too sensitive, given the politically charged society we're living in right now. But I don't want to bring someone on the team who might cause further harm, whether she means to or not. Especially given the population we serve."

"I agree with you one hundred percent. And it's not just immigrants, documented or otherwise. Just last year we did exams on almost a dozen Mexican citizens working legally on this side of the border." One of those cases had been part of a serial rape investigation that Tilly had gotten too involved with. To prevent reliving bad memories, Tilly refocused on her frustration with their interviewee.

"It's so hard to wrap my head around medical professionals who don't understand or support science. The rhetoric about Plan B and abortion and contraception and women's health care in general is just so dangerous." Tilly sighed. "My sister's doing a talk tomorrow about bystander intervention. How do we get regular people to intervene, when we have people who should know better walking around spouting nonsense?"

Marie patted Tilly's arm. "Thank you. I don't know what I'd do without you here."

"Lucky for you, you never have to find out," Tilly said with a chuckle, allowing Marie's praise to buoy her spirits.

CHAPTER 4
KATE

KATE DIDN'T WANT to leave her house the following day, but she was scheduled to give a presentation to the Rotary Club at noon. Besides seeing clients in her private practice, Kate had spent the last year giving talks and doing classes to educate the community about interpersonal violence and human trafficking.

Roman was already off to work, splitting his time between field work and the Las Cruces FBI office, though he was frequently able to work at home. He'd taken Rusty out for a walk before leaving, and the dog was napping contentedly on his dog bed. Kate could feel her restlessness churning toward anxiety so, hoping to self-soothe with distraction, she woke him up and took him into the yard to play. Kate envied his energy, transitioning to hyper play mode so fast it seemed like he'd been awake the whole time.

The wind was kicking up, sending dust flying into the air. Southern New Mexico was a dry, windy area, so the weather was annoying but not unusual. Kate pulled her hair back into a bun, hoping it would stay mostly put through her day.

She stalled a few minutes longer, telling herself that Rusty could use a little more outside time before the day started. He chased the ball she threw around the yard, his nap forgotten. Ever since her father died, Rusty had provided Kate with companionship and protection. He was a constant source of joy, and yet, today, his infectious energy couldn't break through Kate's malaise.

To the south, White Sands National Monument, which usually appeared as a white line on the horizon, was an ashen blur.

"The White Sands are in the air," Kate murmured. It was late spring. The temperatures were on the rise, and with monsoons still a month or two away the landscape was brown and inhospitable. She was thankful for the protection the tall adobe walls provided, and was glad she'd be inside most of the day.

Settling Rusty back inside with a treat, Kate headed out to her car with none of the enthusiasm that she usually felt on a speaking day.

———

Looking out into the crowd, Kate could see that most of the listeners were giving her their attention. A few people looked less than impressed. Kate felt that those were the people who needed her message most, and it took a lot not to sound preachy or condescending.

"While it's true that societal tolerance for certain behaviors has changed over time, I think it's important to remember that common human decency is at the root of everything I've been talking about today. For instance, we've always been taught to keep our hands to ourselves, to help if we see someone in pain, to tell someone in authority if we witness a crime."

Someone cleared their throat loudly, but Kate pressed on.

"Bystander intervention doesn't mean policing your friends or neighbors. It's more about being aware of your surroundings and choosing to step in when you see inappropriate behavior—so that we can work to build a community where we all feel safe and free to live our best lives."

Other than a few holdouts, the people in attendance gave Kate a nice round of applause. She took her notes back to her table and sipped some water while the group leader ended the meeting.

"Great information, Kate."

"Thank you," Kate said to the woman who'd spoken—a woman from her Thursday women's lunch group. "I appreciate you coming."

A line of people walked by her table, most thanking her politely for the presentation. A few asking more pointed questions.

As the crowd cleared, Kate saw Allen Parks and a few other men talking in hushed tones near the door. Parks glanced at her, making eye contact. He smiled.

Kate kept her expression neutral and went back to packing up her things. Allen Parks' nephew Benny had been convicted for the murder of Gabby Greene, a student at the school where Kate worked as a psychologist. She knew that Allen was just as entrenched in the trafficking ring as his nephew had been, but so far there had been nothing to tie him to the organization.

Thankfully, after threatening Kate, once outside the county jail and once in her office, he seemed to have taken seriously her demand that he stay away.

Maybe.

She looked up again and was relieved to see that the group of men had gone.

"Thanks for the talk, Kate." Judy Radcliffe, the current Rotary president, had invited Kate to speak and seemed quite pleased with the turnout. "I knew there would be a bit of grumbling, but it seemed like most of the group was listening. After you taught that class at the college, I knew this was something our group needed to hear."

Kate smiled. "I appreciate that, Judy. It's a lot to consider over lunch, but I hope it will help everyone be a bit more engaged in making the community safer."

Despite Judy's enthusiasm Kate was relieved when she excused herself, giving Kate the chance to duck back out to her car without more conversation.

Usually she left a presentation feeling invigorated. Or at least determined to continue to fight. Today, she just wanted to go home. Images of Sam Garrett's body haunted her, even in the daylight hours. She couldn't shake the feeling that he'd been ready to give her crucial information—something that could break the case wide open.

Now he was gone, and so was whatever evidence he might have had.

Kate headed over to her office, but she didn't stay long. Though the number of clients she saw regularly continued to grow, today was one of her quiet days. And that would have been great on any other day.

Today the quiet of the office felt oppressive, and her anxiety wouldn't let her settle in and concentrate on any one task. With images of Sam Garrett in her mind, and the sinister presence of Allen Parks and his ilk right there in plain sight, the possibility of making a difference seemed much more out of reach. How did you flush out the bad guys when they looked like everyone else? And when the whole town thinks they're good? After only a few futile minutes, she packed up her laptop and headed back out to her house.

———

Roman got home early. Kate was sitting on the couch reading when the gate alarm was disarmed. A few minutes later, he walked in the front door.

"Hey! You're home early." Kate put her book down and tilted her head to receive the kiss Roman bent down to offer.

"I've got a ton of paperwork, so I thought I'd do it here. No reason to hit the pass during rush hour if I don't have to."

The commute to Las Cruces took about an hour, and Kate was glad he didn't have to make the trip more often.

"I was going to start dinner in about half an hour," Kate said. "It's been a weird day and I'm feeling kind of off-kilter."

Roman sat down beside her. "I feel it, too. There are a lot of things I wish I could unsee in this job."

"How was your day?" Usually, asking Roman about his

day opened the floodgates for a long, detailed, and incredibly enthusiastic account of each and every thing he'd done —assuming it wasn't classified. Today, he was more subdued.

"My head wasn't in the game. I filled my lead in on what happened the other night. He knows State Police are involved, but you can see he's itching to swoop in. And I don't blame him. I get the feeling Angie doesn't want the interagency drama so she's been keeping my office at arm's length, mostly using us for areas where FBI resources can expedite something."

Kate frowned. "You'd think she'd want as much help as she could get."

"I kind of understand where she's coming from, though. It can be difficult to manage a case with too many jurisdictions involved. Since everyone involved thus far has been a New Mexico resident, it would be a stretch to take over." Roman's tone indicated that he'd been thinking this over, something that surprised Kate.

"Don't you think Angie is doing everything she can?" Hadn't he said as much just last night?

"Of course," Roman responded, but he had hesitated.

Kate scooted away a bit so she could look at his face. "What's going on, Roman? What aren't you telling me?"

Roman sighed. "It's nothing really. Angie's just been acting a little strange lately. Mercurial. Sometimes she's all forthcoming and collaborative. Other times she seems distant, and even combative."

"About the case?"

"Mostly. I called today to get some information and she didn't answer. Then when she called me back, she was evasive." He settled back into his chair. "She may just be tired. I know I am. And you. This case is really taking its toll."

"It is." Roman put his arm around Kate's shoulder, pulling her nearer. It was a comforting act, one that usually made her feel calm, but just like everything else that day it wasn't having the usual effect.

Kate didn't like to see Roman so down, and since his mood was related to Angie it put her on edge. What was going on with the detective? And was it something to do with the case, or something personal? In spite of herself, Kate still felt pangs of insecurity when it came to Angie Lopez.

CHAPTER 5
TILLY

SITTING across the table from Kate, Tilly felt her stomach roil. Her sister had just recounted the story of Sam Garrett's murder, and a voice in Tilly's head screamed for her to grab Kate and run far away. Not that Kate would go. Neither would Tilly for that matter, but the escalation in violence following the arrests was not a good sign.

"They're desperate," Kate said, voicing Tilly's own thoughts. It was hard to put words to all the thoughts and feelings swirling through Tilly's head. She cast her gaze around the restaurant, a favorite among Alamogordo locals.

The waitress who was assigned to Kate and Tilly's table was taking orders from a group of men. From the young woman's easy banter, the group were probably regulars. As Tilly watched, one of the men reached down and pinched the inside of the woman's leg. She yelped, and jumped, her cheeks turning bright red.

Recovering from the shock, the woman moved away from the man who'd pinched her, but smiled nervously and kept taking orders. As she made her way around the table, the man watched her with eagle eyes and a look that made Tilly's skin prickle.

"What are you doing?" Kate asked. Tilly realized that she was on her feet, her eyes laser-focused on the men at the table. Without a word to Kate, Tilly walked toward the table. As she approached, the waitress' eyes grew wide and fearful.

"You need to keep your hands to yourself and apologize to that young woman." Tilly's voice was shrill with rage. The whole restaurant grew quiet. The offending man turned toward Tilly, his expression full of indignation.

"Nobody asked for your opinion, sweetheart," the man said, sneering. He turned toward the front of the restaurant, summoning the owner who stood by the counter on high alert. The rest of his group looked slightly confused.

Tilly stepped right up to the man, close enough that he had to lean back in his chair to make eye contact. She leaned in a little closer. "How dare you!" she growled.

"It's all right, ma'am. I'm okay," the waitress mumbled from across the table.

"No," Tilly said, standing up straighter. "It's most definitely not okay." She turned to the rest of the group. "You understand that, don't you? That this girl is not here for you to touch. She's doing her job, you disgusting pigs." She spoke in a voice too loud for the room, making sure that every single person in the restaurant would hear. Turning back to her target, Tilly said, "Apologize."

The man glared at her, his eyes brimming with raw hatred. The person next to him cleared his throat, momentarily interrupting the standoff between him and Tilly. "We should get to work," he said under his breath.

At this point everyone at the table was on their feet, including Tilly's adversary, who was not even a foot away from her. Standing, he was more imposing, but Tilly stood her ground. The man's friend grabbed his arm. "Come on, Rob."

Shoving past Tilly, the man joined his friends, throwing cash onto the counter as they exited the restaurant. The owner was still in position, standing sentry near the register, as if paralyzed by the whole situation.

Tilly returned to her table, wondering for a moment if they were going to be asked to leave. But the buzz of conversation resumed without further interruption.

"Whoa," Kate said as Tilly took her seat. She leaned across the table toward Tilly and whispered, "That was crazy, Til. You could have gotten that girl fired. I'm surprised they haven't thrown us out." Kate's words were cross, but her expression was one of awe.

Tilly took a deep breath and sighed the tension out. "That's the problem," she said, feeling tired. "People worry about what other people will think or say. About who's going to lose their job or whether we'll be allowed to come back to the restaurant again."

Kate chuckled. "Well, the thought had crossed my mind."

"Exactly, and you're not most people, Kate. How many times do you think that man has assaulted someone right out in public and no has said a word. His friends didn't even bat an eye." Tilly could see the young waitress near the kitchen, rubbing her injured leg. "I should have called the police, but I figured shame was more likely to work. At least maybe he'll think twice before doing that again."

"Or he'll just do it more covertly," Kate said.

With another big sigh, Tilly said, "What makes you think he isn't already? He could be one of them, and even if he's not, he's the reason this has been allowed to continue for so long."

Having been a victim of sexual assault and trafficking, Tilly was well aware of the dangers in simply being a young woman. She shared Kate's determination to stop the traffickers, and since her own work put her in contact with victims every day she'd had enough of quietly sitting by.

"Here's to bystander intervention," Kate said, raising her glass of water in a toast. Tilly smiled at her sister, but in her heart she knew that her action, and every act like it, was just a drop in the bucket.

———

Tilly was still feeling a little bit rattled from her confrontation in Alamogordo when she agreed to join Dan and Hannah for a walk in the park Sunday afternoon. Hannah's constant stream of commentary on the upcoming dance was a wonderful distraction, but then her phone rang and she planted herself on a bench, staking out some privacy while Dan and Tilly continued on the path.

"Seems like you two are on better terms over homecoming," Tilly said casually, though she looked out of the side of her eye to see Dan's reaction. He smiled.

"She told me she had an epiphany and changed her mind." The look Dan gave Tilly made her laugh out loud.

"That's what I thought," he continued. "I'm glad she has you to talk to. I can't imagine being a teenage girl without a mom around."

Tilly winced, knowing that the death of Dan's wife had left a gaping hole in his world. When she'd first met him, his surly, combative attitude had put them at odds, but as she'd gotten to know him she realized that it was a coping mechanism. Between his job and the work of raising Hannah alone Dan had a lot on his plate, and found it hard to open up to people.

Sounds familiar, Tilly thought. That was one area where she and Dan had found common ground over the past year. She understood his need to compartmentalize and retain a professional distance. And he seemed to read Tilly in a way that even her former partner, Jim, hadn't.

That was another thing they'd bonded over: grief. Tilly knew what it meant to lose someone. A few months after moving to New Mexico her boyfriend Jim had died suddenly, turning her world upside-down. And given that Tilly was still mourning the deaths of both her parents, Jim's passing had sent her spiraling out of control.

"What are you thinking about?" Dan asked, startling Tilly back into the present moment.

"Jim," she said quietly. She looked at Dan, curious to see his reaction. She'd been attending a grief support group with Dan and Hannah for months, so they were all keenly aware of the other's feelings on the topic. Dan's face betrayed only the tiniest flash of sadness before he returned to neutral.

"I remember the first anniversary of Marcy's death," Dan said. Tilly had heard him speak about Marcy often, and with waves of emotion that seemed close to dragging him under. Today, his tone was more even. "It was pretty dark."

For a few minutes, they walked together in silence. Tilly looked over her shoulder and saw that Hannah was still glued to her seat, chatting happily on her phone. She thought about Kate and how much had changed for her over the past few years.

It was a perfect day, sunny but with a cool breeze, and for a moment Tilly felt bolder than she usually did with Dan. She decided to take a chance.

"Do you think you'll ever remarry?"

Dan stopped dead in his tracks, forcing Tilly to turn and face him. She couldn't read his expression, but felt her own cheeks burning with embarrassment. What had she been expecting? She took a breath and tried to salvage the conversation.

"Sorry, Dan. That was way too personal." She gave him a minute to compose himself, ready with a subject change as soon as he returned his attention to her. He seemed so far away.

Finally, he smiled. "I hope to," he said, giving her a look that she couldn't begin to decipher. Like he had a secret and she hadn't been clued in yet. It made her feel uncomfortable, and also a bit breathless.

Not knowing what to say, she began nervously rubbing her hands together. Dan's eyes sparkled. He seemed more relaxed then he had since she'd met him, as if a weight had been lifted. He leaned over and kissed her softly on the cheek.

Tilly knew how she felt about Dan, even if she wasn't ready to turn those feelings into action. But she realized at that moment, despite Kate's repeated teasing about any budding romance, that she'd been uncertain of Dan's feelings. Now she knew.

———

The conference room was empty following a staff meeting, but Tilly was in no hurry to move. She was nursing her coffee like a missed drop might make it impossible to continue to breathe. Marie was loitering near the door.

"Are you waiting for me?" Tilly asked.

"Yes, I have a huge favor to ask you," Marie said, taking a seat across from Tilly. Tilly smiled. "What's up?"

"The Advocacy conference starts this week and I have a conflict. My plan was to go and have you run the clinic, but I'm not going to be able to make it so I'm hoping you can cover for me."

"Sure," Tilly said. "Are you carpooling?"

"No, Meg is riding up with Susanne and Jennifer. I was planning on going up Thursday and coming back down Sunday. You can take my hotel room."

"Sounds great," Tilly said. "Marching orders?"

"I want to get some contact information from the trafficking commission and we need to upgrade the colposcope in room two, so if you see the reps you can let them know we need to get in touch."

"I'm on it," Tilly said with a smile. Marie got up and left and Tilly followed soon after, heading down the hall to her office. She had a stack of reports to complete, and she'd need to get them done before leaving Thursday.

Her phone rang.

"Hi, Hannah," she said. "Aren't you supposed to be at school?"

"I am," Hannah said. "Sheesh, you're as bad as my dad." She feigned irritation but started giggling almost immediately.

"What can I do for you?"

"Dad's going to be out of town this weekend, and I wondered if I could come crash at your place."

Tilly smiled. "Normally I'd be all over a slumber party, but I actually have to go to a conference this weekend. I'm covering for my boss."

"In Albuquerque?"

"Yes," Tilly said, sounding a bit suspicious.

"Must be the same one dad's going to," Hannah said. She paused for a moment, then said, "Hey! Maybe I could go with you guys!"

Tilly hadn't had time to think about the fact that she and Dan would be in the same place this weekend, together. She blushed, and was immediately glad that she was alone in her office. "You'd probably be bored. I'll be in sessions all day. And what about school?"

"Most of my work is online, so I think I could just hang out by the pool and still get work done."

Tilly could hear the excitement building in Hannah's voice. And honestly, Tilly thought it might be nice to have Hannah around to act as a buffer. Since their walk, Tilly hadn't been able to stop her mind from wandering to Dan, and she was feeling very conflicted—torn between this budding new relationship and the sadness and guilt she still felt over Jim's death.

When she'd told Kate she wasn't ready, she wasn't

kidding. And though she knew that Dan understood, her feelings and thoughts weren't exactly in alignment at the moment.

"Well, let me know what your dad says. Maybe we can try out that new Brazilian restaurant."

Hannah squeaked. "Yes! Okay, I'll talk to you soon." She disconnected before Tilly even had a chance to say goodbye.

CHAPTER 6
KATE

Kate had nothing to say, and wouldn't allow herself to be baited.

For weeks Ruth had inserted herself into Kate's conversations, into her space, at every women's luncheon. As if nothing had happened between them. It was a major shift from the avoidance and silence of the previous months.

The gathering had become unbearable. A storm raged inside Kate's body, anger and sadness and confusion all battling for position as she endured the invasion into what had begun to feel like a safe space. She was a fraud. She'd been preaching the need for community members to stand up for themselves and open their eyes to predatory behavior around them.

Ruth was a predator. It was clear to Kate that her old friend knew exactly how uncomfortable she was making Kate. That was the point, she figured. Kate knew that Ruth was somehow involved in the trafficking operation but had no idea what that role was, and with no proof she was in no position to make public accusations.

Worse, Ruth was a beloved member of the group, so snubbing her was likely to undermine the connections Kate had been making within the organization.

Kate was being neutralized, and it made her furious.

"I'm sorry, ladies, but I have an appointment right after lunch so I'm going to have to dash out early," Kate said, forcing a smile that she hoped resembled normal.

"Oh, that's too bad," Ruth purred. "But you're saving the world, Kate, so I suppose we'll let you go without a fight."

The other women laughed at Ruth's overly dramatic turn of phrase, but Kate startled. She made reluctant eye contact with Ruth and found not the hostile look she was expecting but a challenge, calling out Kate's powerlessness. Shaken, Kate said goodbye and left the event.

When she reached her office she let herself inside, locking the door behind her. Since she'd lied to her friends and had no appointments this afternoon, she should have just gone home. The office felt empty, or maybe it was just Kate herself.

Life was good. Her sister was only an hour away. She was going to marry the love of her life—something she never would have imagined just a few years earlier.

She loved her job. She felt like the work she was doing in the community was important. With every arrest, she felt like they were taking steps toward shutting down trafficking in the city.

But she missed her parents. And the strain of fighting against an enemy that still remained largely nebulous was taking its toll. Kate had seen the way that Angie's clothes hung from her frame. Kate had lost weight, too, and she couldn't remember the last time she slept through the night, especially since Sam Garrett's death. The panic attacks that had plagued Kate for years—since her own traumatic rape—were still making nightly rounds, but their tone had changed. Now, she saw the faces of girls who'd been saved. And those who hadn't.

Kate sat behind her desk, lost in thought, until her phone began ringing. She answered without checking the caller ID.

"Hello?"

"Kate?" Tilly's voice grounded her immediately. She looked at her watch and realized she'd been zoned out for nearly an hour.

"Hey," Kate replied. "What's up?"

"Are you all right? You sound tired."

"Weary is more like it. Just got back from my women's luncheon. Ruth is getting bolder. She called my work "saving the world" in front of the rest of the members. She wants a reaction, and I'll be damned if I'm going to give her one." Kate sighed. "Enough about that. How're things going for you?"

"I'm heading to Albuquerque for that conference tomorrow and I wondered if you had time to grab lunch when I pass through town."

Seeing Tilly was always a balm to Kate's weariness and fatigue.

"What time? I'm with a client until about 1:00."

"That should work fine, actually," Tilly said. "Hannah is riding up with me, but she's going in for her first few classes so we won't head out until 11:30. We can just meet you. Assuming you're okay with Hannah joining us."

Kate grinned. She loved the happy tone she always heard in Tilly's voice at the mention of Dan or his daughter. "You know I love hanging out with Hannah. I'm amazed she talked Dan into letting her come. Is she going to attend the conference?"

Tilly laughed. "No. She's going to do schoolwork pool-side, according to her."

"It'll be nice having her there," Kate hedged. She heard Tilly sigh loudly.

"Love you, Kate. I'll see you tomorrow,"

The promise of a mid-week lunch date with her sister propelled Kate out of her funk. She packed up and headed home.

———

Kate pushed her plate away, her appetite gone. She'd spent the afternoon trying to let go of the frustration she felt over her interaction with Ruth, only to come home to more bad news.

"I know," Roman said, reaching across the table to take Kate's hand. "It was a shock."

Roman had arrived home with the news that Angie was in the hospital. What Kate had chalked up to stress had turned out to be an autoimmune disorder affecting her vascular system, something she'd been battling for years but had kept quiet about. A flare-up landed her in the hospital and on paid leave until further notice, taking one of their biggest allies off the team.

A tear slipped down Roman's cheek, and for a moment Kate felt more responsibility for the situation than she was willing to admit. Even though Angie had seemingly made peace with it, Kate still couldn't help but harbor some guilt. Probably related to her own fears and feelings of inadequacy. A happy ending had never been something she'd anticipated for herself.

"Are you okay?" she asked, refocusing on Roman. He gave her a sad smile.

"Yeah. It's just hard to believe this is the first I'm hearing about it." Roman and Angie had dated on and off for years. Keeping her illness from him must have taken some effort, especially given Roman's caregiving nature.

"Can we visit her?"

"I'm going tomorrow," Roman said. Kate waited to see if he'd ask her to join him. Each moment that passed in silence made her uneasy.

"Tilly's stopping by for lunch on her way up to Albuquerque tomorrow." Kate's voice broke the uncomfortable silence, and she noticed a flush of red creep up Roman's neck. She couldn't deny that it hurt to see him so emotionally distraught over an ex-lover, no matter how fond Kate was of Angie. It had taken her so long to feel secure in her relationship with Roman. It took very little to rock that foundation.

"I'm sorry, Kate. It's not that I don't want you to come..."

"It's all right," Kate said, though she couldn't entirely hide the frustration in her voice. "I understand."

Roman nodded, but he didn't seem convinced. And honestly, she wasn't sure she was up to convincing him.

They'd already gone through a lot as a couple, and there was no doubt there would be more obstacles in their life together. Kate just hoped that they'd get to a point where every hiccup didn't make her feel the need to run.

———

Kate hated the stories she told herself. Despite every effort not to attach her own speculation to the news about Angie, she felt the distance between her and Roman expanding even as they sat watching television. She tried to pay attention to the show, but her mind kept creating scenarios—some realistic and some completely outlandish—most of which resulted in Kate ending up alone.

As they were getting ready for bed, Kate tried to make conversation. "Are you making any progress on the arson case?"

Roman was completely silent for a moment, and then, as if waking back up into the present moment, he replied. "What? Oh, yeah. Sorry." He paused. "We're close to making an arrest. I've got two new cases on my desk, so things are picking up."

Roman's role as the new agent at the Las Cruces FBI office had consisted mostly of paperwork, follow-up, and a lot of administrative work in the name of getting him acquainted with how the office worked. Kate figured he'd be annoyed, but the opposite had been true. He'd come home every day perfectly content, despite the hours of desk work and the long commute.

"That's great," Kate said, but it didn't seem like Roman was listening. "My afternoon client canceled tomorrow, so I'll probably come home early."

Silence.

"Roman?"

He looked at her, startled. "What?"

"Never mind," she said as she got settled and picked up the book she'd been reading.

Roman sat down beside her and sighed. "I'm sorry, Kate. I've just got a lot on my mind." He leaned over and kissed her, then settled into bed facing away from her. Shutting her out. Maybe he didn't intend to, but that's what it felt like to Kate. She read until she heard his breathing become regular, then turned off her lamp and lay down. A shaft of moonlight shone through the window. Rusty squirmed in his bed until he found the perfect spot, and before long he was snoring. Kate stared at the ceiling, wondering if her sleep would be plagued with nightmares.

CHAPTER 7
TILLY

Tilly was in Dan's kitchen, putting away the dinner dishes. She spent a lot of time at Dan's house—enough that the space was beginning to feel familiar. The kitchen was Tilly's favorite room. It was warm and sunny, with beautiful tile backsplashes that reminded Tilly of her grandmother's house.

"Need any help?" Hannah put the last of the leftovers in the refrigerator.

"Nope, I'm done." Tilly closed the cabinet and pulled the damp dish towel from her shoulder, hanging it over the oven handle. "I think your dad's putting on a movie. Want to join us?"

Hannah rolled her eyes. "Um, no. I've got to call Suzi. We're getting a group together for homecoming and I said I'd help make plans. Since I'm leaving tomorrow, I need to make sure she doesn't need me to do anything this weekend."

"No date?"

Hannah shook her head, but averted her eyes momentarily. When she met Tilly's gaze again, she blushed. "No date. But there's a guy in my lit class who might join us."

"I don't suppose he's the motivation behind the curfew argument, is he?"

Hannah grinned. "Believe it or not, no. Actually, that plan fell apart. Seems that my dad isn't the only overprotective parent. Which is totally fine, because we're going out before to eat and play games. It's going to be epic!"

Tilly laughed. "Sounds like a much better plan." Then she wrinkled her nose. "I'm really starting to sound like an old woman." Hannah walked over to Tilly and gave her a hug, giggling. Tilly threw up her hands in mock disgust. "Oh, thanks a lot. You're supposed to argue. I'm the cool one, remember?"

"I'm going to go pack." Hannah practically skipped out of the room. Tilly chuckled. Over dinner, they'd discussed Hannah's proposal to join them at the conference. Dan was planning to drive up after work, so Hannah launched into an enthusiastic pitch for riding up with Tilly, leaving Dan exasperated and Tilly giggling uncontrollably.

Tilly poured two glasses of wine and walked into the living room where Dan sat on the sofa, tapping away on his laptop. She sat down beside him, placing his glass nearby before taking a sip of her own. He spent a few more minutes typing and then closed the lid to his computer.

"You're sure it's not too much, taking Hannah tomorrow?"

Tilly smiled. "We'll be fine, Dan. She'll probably be under her headphones the whole way up anyway."

"Yeah, right. She may ignore me like any normal

teenager, but something about you perks her right up. It's been nice hearing her talk when you're here—seems to be coming out of her shell." Whenever the conversation touched on Dan's dearly departed wife, Tilly noticed the sadness that creeped into his expression no matter how hard he tried to hide it.

"Are you sure *you're* okay with her riding up with me?" she asked kindly, knowing these last few years had been hard on him. They'd been hard on everyone, but it was hard to imagine raising a child alone—especially a teenager. Tilly wondered what her own mother and father would have done under those circumstances.

Dan smiled broadly, the warmth returning to his eyes. "Of course. Not that she'd let me change the plans on her at this point. The promise of a girls' trip is too inviting, I think. Hanging out with her friends' moms isn't the same."

"Did Marcy like to travel?" Tilly had been making a point of asking about Hannah's mother, and she appreciated that Dan didn't avoid answering her questions, though she knew it sometimes hurt.

"We did a few family trips when Hannah was younger, but Marcy liked being at home. And when I took the ADA position, our adventures were mostly confined to road trips and camping. What about your parents?"

"My mother was a homebody, just like her mother. If we went anywhere it was with our father," Tilly said. She paused to gauge Dan's reaction, but he seemed engaged, so she continued. "He loved to hike. So did Kate and I. When I was really small, I remember him carrying me in a camping backpack while he and Kate picked their way along the trails. We spent half our weekends in the mountains—at least when we were younger."

"Something tells me that the teenage years were another story."

Tilly laughed. "True." Then her smile faltered. Her teenage years had started out happily enough, but they hadn't stayed that way. "I hardly spoke to my parents the last two years of high school."

"I'm sorry, Tilly," Dan backtracked. "I didn't mean to bring that up."

Tilly put her hand over his, feeling a thrill of intimacy that scared her. "It's okay, Dan. It's actually nice to talk about the happy parts of my past. I've tried to avoid that whole part of my life for way too long."

He turned his hand over in hers, and for a moment she felt like she couldn't breathe. Then he gave it a gentle squeeze and let go. Her heart fluttered and her stomach ached with guilt. Seeming to sense her uneasiness, Dan reached for the remote and turned on the television. They watched a sitcom, and by the end Tilly almost felt comfortable sitting there beside him.

———

At home, Tilly felt restless. She laid her suitcase out on her bed, but by midnight she hadn't packed anything, busying herself with deep-cleaning the kitchen. If she thought about it, she knew exactly where all her nervous energy was coming from. She'd come home from Dan's house feeling like a schoolgirl with a crush. A serious crush. And no matter how many times she told herself she was not ready for a relationship, her heart was turning traitor.

The weekend loomed. The advocacy conference was one of her all-time favorite professional gatherings. She'd attended every year for more than a decade, even when living in Colorado. It kept her tied in to her home state even if she couldn't bring herself to live there or even visit much. In her new role, she and Marie would be alternating years, so getting to attend unexpectedly was a welcome surprise.

She'd always loved the drive from Colorado Springs to Albuquerque, coming over Raton Pass and the vast expanses of desert with nothing cluttering the landscape for miles. The peaks of the Sandia Mountains to the east. Crossing over the Rio Grande. Colorado was a beautiful place, but New Mexico spoke to Tilly's soul in a way that its northern neighbor never had.

But it wasn't the anticipation of the conference that was keeping Tilly's nerves on edge. Anytime she stopped moving, her thoughts went to Dan. To the feel of his hand over hers. How solid he felt sitting next to her on the sofa. Since Jim's death, Dan had become the person that Tilly confided in. Other than Kate, he was her best friend. She'd never felt that strongly about Jim, and the guilt was crushing.

Finally she plopped down on the foot of her bed, exhausted.

Because she hadn't been planning to go to the conference, she hadn't considered the possibility of alone time with Dan. When Hannah asked to go along, Tilly was initially grateful that she wouldn't have to think about it anymore. But the relief was short-lived. Tilly loved Hannah, but she felt a pang of regret at the missed opportunity. And that regret was fueling a torrent of guilty thoughts that wouldn't give her a moment's peace.

Tilly stood up and walked over to the dresser. She opened one of the top drawers slowly and pulled out a framed picture of her and Jim. Seeing their smiling faces reminded her that this had been a happy time in her life. When he died, Tilly had tried to remove all the things that reminded her of him from her line of sight. It was just too painful. But as she looked at the image, something clicked in her mind. She'd been working through her grief with Dan and Hannah and the rest of her support group, but the clean break she'd made by moving out of the house she'd shared with Jim and into this apartment was keeping her from having real closure. An ending made all the more final when she didn't make room for any of the things that reminded her of their relationship.

Hence the guilt.

Tilly closed the drawer, setting the frame on top of the chest. With a loud sigh, she started packing her suitcase. As she moved around the room, her eyes frequently crept over to the picture. It had taken a lot of hard work to process her grief up to this moment, and it looked like she still had a lot of work to do.

CHAPTER 8
KATE

IN THE MORNING, Kate woke to an empty bed. The evening had been tense and Kate had gone up to bed early, falling asleep before Roman made it upstairs.

Now she wondered if he'd ever been in bed with her at all.

She got up, put on her robe, and walked downstairs to the kitchen. Rusty followed her, padding along quietly like he was reading her mood.

There was coffee in the pot. Rusty had clearly been fed. But no Roman.

A peek at the gate camera app revealed what she already knew to be true—Roman had gone, left early without saying goodbye.

Kate tried not to let it bother her. She had lunch with Tilly and Hannah to look forward to. Whatever was going on with Angie—and however Roman was feeling about it— would have to wait until later, when they had a chance to talk. Still, the idea of his hasty departure and visit to the hospital weighed heavily on her mind.

Kate picked up her phone and called her friend Kathleen. She and Kathleen met at the women's group Kate attended along with Ruth Flores. Kate had seen Kathleen's daughter as a client for several months, but they'd developed a friendship outside of their professional roles.

"Hey, Kate! I hope you're calling to schedule lunch sometime soon. It's been ages."

Kate chuckled. "Next week? Maybe we can skip the Thursday luncheon."

"Is it just me, or has Ruth been particularly obnoxious lately? I know you guys are friends, but she just drives me crazy." Kathleen and Ruth had never gotten along, which worked out well for Kate as she tried to avoid contact with Ruth. But Kathleen didn't know the reason Kate was distancing herself from Ruth.

"She's definitely been over the top," Kate replied noncommittally. "Do you have a few minutes now to chat?"

"Of course. Is everything okay?"

Kathleen's immediate shift from playful to concerned was soothing. Kate's social circle was very small, and she was grateful for Kathleen's friendship.

"Yeah, everything's fine." Kate considered her words carefully. "You know Roman's ex, Angie?"

"Yeah. Why?" Kathleen was the one person Kate could talk openly with about her feelings over Roman and Angie. "I still can't believe you guys all get along so well." Kathleen paused. "Wait, please tell me she's not trying something with Roman."

"No, it's not that." Kate was finding it hard to say what she was thinking. "She's in the hospital with a chronic illness. Roman didn't know about it, and he's really upset."

"I guess that makes sense. They were together for a long time. Seems like something she would have told him."

"That's what he said, too."

"How did he find out?"

Kate paused. "You know, he didn't say. He was so upset when he came home last night, I didn't think to ask."

"I guess the real question is, how are you feeling about it?"

"Sad. Conflicted." Kate sighed. "Worried."

"Worried about Angie?"

"Not really, and I feel kind of terrible about it. I'm worried about what this means for me and Roman."

"Why would it change anything for you and Roman?"

Kate thought for a moment. "It shouldn't." Another moment passed. "It won't."

"What aren't you telling me, Kate?"

"He's going to see her today and didn't want me to go with him. He left before I even got up. No goodbye."

"Oh, Kate," Kathleen said. "Men like Roman aren't always good at dealing with big emotions. You know that. My husband practically goes off the grid when something really troubling happens. I've gotten used to just giving him space. He always comes around eventually, and I'm sure Roman will, too."

"I know you're right. I feel like an idiot, still getting jealous of Angie. Tilly reminds me that Roman is all in, and I know that's true. Why can't I just accept that things are good?"

Kathleen laughed. "Listen, Kate. You spend every day helping people with their problems and trying to educate the community about really horrible crimes. You tell people all the time that they shouldn't take anything at face value. If you're in the habit of scrutinizing everything, it's probably just a byproduct of your work. And that's okay, because Roman knows who you are and that's what he loves about you."

"Well, maybe not only that," Kate added begrudgingly, and was rewarded with another laugh from Kathleen. She smiled. Some of the weight lifted from her shoulders. "Thanks for listening."

"Anytime. And I'm putting you down for Thursday lunch. We'll go somewhere fancy. A break from the usual stuff, that's what we both need."

———

Kate's second morning appointment was a new client, Christina, who was feeling depressed. When she arrived, Kate handed her a clipboard with intake paperwork and then sat down at her desk and observed her new patient. Christina's curly dark hair reminded Kate of her own, though Christina's was heavily peppered with gray.

When Christina looked up, she smiled wearily. "All done." She handed Kate the clipboard and then returned to her seat.

Kate put the information aside. "I try to keep the paperwork light so you don't have to repeat yourself a million times." She took out her own notebook. "What brought you in to see me?"

"Well, I'm having a hard time wanting to do things." Christina hesitated. "This is the first time I've left my house this week. Everything just feels like too much trouble. And yesterday, my husband told me I was letting myself go."

Kate cringed. "I bet that didn't feel great. How long have you been feeling this way?"

"I think it started when my youngest left home."

"How long ago was that?"

"Almost a year. I know what you're thinking. Empty nest. And that might be true, though maybe not for the reason you're thinking."

"What do you mean?" Kate asked.

Christina sighed heavily. "My husband is having an affair."

"Are you sure?"

"Yes, and I think it's been going on for a long time. But when my kids were home, I didn't think about it much. Now that they're gone, it's pretty obvious that he doesn't love me. And to be honest, I'm not sure I love him either. In fact, when I look back, I can't remember the last time I felt much for him."

The situation tugged at Kate's heart. "How long have you been married?"

"Twenty-three years."

"Are you worried about being on your own?"

"A little, but I think what's really gotten to me is how he acts around me. When he told me I was letting myself go, I realized he's been criticizing how I look for as long as we've been together. He's just doing it more now."

Kate bristled. "That's definitely not okay. Have you talked to him about it?"

Chrstina laughed. "We don't talk. We never have."

"You don't sound terribly conflicted. Are you planning on divorcing him?"

"No," Christina said. "At least not right away. I realize I've become one of those middle-aged women whose husband is sleeping around. No job skills. Nowhere to go. I think that's what's making me so depressed. I get out of bed every morning and just don't really see the point of making an effort."

Kate nodded. "I understand. As women, we're often led to believe that being a wife and mother is the most important thing."

"Don't get me wrong," Christina interjected. "I wouldn't trade being a mother for the world. My kids are my life. So much so that I guess I put up with a lot of poor treatment over the years." She smiled sadly. "I'm kind of envious of this new generation. They seem to have so many options."

"True, although they have a whole new array of problems to deal with as well." Kate thought about her teenage years. They seemed so simple compared with what kids dealt with in the age of social media. "What does your support system look like?"

Christina frowned. "Not great. I mean, they love me. But my family thinks my husband Kyle hung the moon. He's a respected member of the community. Everyone loves him. I have a few friends who know how bad our marriage has been, but they're very traditionally-minded. They don't see divorce as an option. Actually, that's why I came in. I don't really want to focus on leaving. I want to focus on myself. On figuring out what makes me happy and how to cope with my depression."

"I'll do my best to help," Kate said. She felt sad for Christina, but it reminded her how much she appreciated Roman. If she could get out of her own way, she'd be married to a man who loved and supported her exactly as she was.

CHAPTER 9
TILLY

"I'M SO EXCITED!" Hannah was bouncing on her toes waiting for Tilly to get to her car. The teen had already thrown her bag into the backseat, and she was so eager to get on the road that Tilly laughed out loud.

"Yes, all right. Let's go," she said, a big smile on her face. Dan's work day had been extended, so Tilly and Hannah would be hanging out for most of the day without him. Though Tilly had agreed to the plan, she wasn't entirely sure she'd survive four hours in the car with Hannah at this energy level. Tilly hoped maybe after lunch she'd talk Hannah into listening to some music that might put her guest to sleep for the remainder of the trip. After a long and restless night with little sleep, it was going to take more than coffee to get Tilly through the day.

As they made their way over the pass, Hannah jabbered continuously about the homecoming celebrations the following week. Tilly remembered her own excitement over her first homecoming dance. Her mother had bought her a brand new dress—emerald green satin that fell just below her knee. By today's standards the dress would be horribly outdated, but Tilly remembered feeling so grown up that day.

She and her friends had gone together, dancing in a group while most of the boys in their grade stood awkwardly around the punch bowl or slumped in the bleachers. It was a wonderful night. Before boys were really in the picture. Before Jacob Copeland and the beginning of the end for Tilly.

That night seemed so far in the past it felt more like a dream, blurry around the edges. But as Hannah chattered on, Tilly was reminded of some of her happiest memories as a teenager. She'd been reminiscing a lot lately. Something about being with Hannah—and Dan—made her think about her family and a childhood that for much of her adult life had seemed better left behind. By the time they reached Alamogordo, Tilly was feeling more content than she had been in a long time.

They met Kate at a local pizza place and ordered a pie to share, salad, and enormous hand-spun milkshakes.

"Hanging out by the pool sounds pretty great," Kate said as she and Hannah chatted. "Though, not gonna lie, the conference sounds even better." She gave Tilly a rueful look.

"You could come," Tilly offered.

"Nope. My next two days are packed with client work, so no can do. Maybe next year." Kate's expression darkened.

"Hannah, will you go get a couple of to-go cups? There's no way I'm going to make it through this shake before we have to hit the road."

Hannah gave Tilly a knowing look. "Sure. I'm going to

visit the restroom first. That'll give you time to talk." She gave an exaggerated wink and walked away.

Kate laughed. "She doesn't miss a thing, does she?"

"Nope, which ought to make for an interesting weekend," Tilly said sheepishly. Hannah was the perfect buffer between Tilly and any possible romantic moments with Dan, which she found both frustrating and relieving in turns. "So what's with the doom and gloom expression?"

Kate sighed. "Angie's sick."

"As in the flu?" Tilly felt her stomach tighten, wondering why Angie had chosen this particular moment to reveal her illness to Roman.

"She's in the hospital. Roman's going to see her today."

"In the hospital?" Now it made sense, though Tilly still worried about the implications. "Is she going to be okay?"

"Depends on your definition of okay I guess," Kate replied wearily. "It's something chronic. Roman didn't have all the details. I'm sure I'll hear more tonight." Then her expression changed. "You knew."

"She told me a little bit yesterday." Tilly hesitated. "How's this sitting with you?"

Kate frowned, then she shrugged. "Doesn't really matter, does it? I mean, it's terrible. I wish she'd told us before so we could have helped her."

"And," Tilly added, "you're worried. Probably about you and Roman and how this is going to affect your relationship. Which…" she held up a hand to stop Kate from protesting. "Which is both expected and normal, given their history, but also unwarranted because you know that Roman is all in. Both feet across the threshold."

"He didn't want me to go with him today," Kate said

sulkily, though she smiled a little which Tilly took as a good sign.

"I'm sure it's just as confusing sometimes for him as it is for you." Tilly put her arm through Kate's and rested her head on her sister's shoulder. When she sat back up, she smiled. "It's going to be okay, Kate."

Kate smiled, too. And then Hannah bounced back to the table.

"That guy behind the counter is hot," she whispered, gesturing over her shoulder. The guy in question looked to be about Hannah's age, with curly hair pulled back in a bun and the haphazard facial hair of someone who was still trying to work out his own sense of style.

"Pretty cute," Tilly said, earning an eye roll from Hannah. "What? I'm an old woman."

Hannah laughed. "You are not!" Then she smiled mischievously. "But my dad might get jealous."

Tilly felt her face turning bright red, and both Hannah and Kate laughed. Maybe Hannah wouldn't be a good barrier between her and Dan after all, though she was glad the girl didn't hate her. That would have made it much too scary for Tilly to even think about a possible future with Dan.

The pizza arrived and they dug in, enjoying the food and the company. The restaurant's jukebox poured out a stream of hits from the '80s and '90s. Hannah pretended to be horrified when Kate and Tilly sang along, but it was clear she was amused. Tilly's embarrassment faded as the time went by, and soon it was time to go.

She wrapped Kate in a big hug and whispered, "I love you, Kate. Don't worry so much."

Kate squeezed Tilly tighter. "You, too, sister. Don't be afraid to let Dan love you. It's pretty clear his daughter already does."

Tilly could feel her eyes mist a little. "It's hard, but I'm working on it." She turned to Hannah. "Let's go, kiddo."

———

They were ten miles west of Carrizozo when Tilly's car started making a funny noise—a sort of rattle. One that she'd never heard before.

She groaned. Her car was less than a year old.

"There's smoke," Hannah said, pointing to the hood where a thin, steady stream of black smoke rose near the driver's side.

"Shit." Tilly pulled over and turned the car off. "Sit tight," she said to Hannah as she climbed out.

She walked around to face the car and popped the hood, releasing a puff of smoke that sent her coughing. She wanted to scream. A car flew by every few minutes, but she wasn't ready to start flagging down help. She got back behind the wheel and grabbed for her cell phone, which was missing from its usual spot in the console.

"Shit!" Tilly rifled around in her purse and then, coming up empty, she reached under the front seats.

"What's wrong?" Hannah asked.

"My phone's gone. I think I forgot it at the restaurant."

"Should we go back?"

Tilly sighed. "Probably." She turned the key, and the car made a weak sound as the engine did its best to turn over. Nothing.

"Ugh." Tilly rested her head on the wheel. "I don't think we're going anywhere. Can I borrow your phone?"

Hannah grimaced. "My battery's dead. I meant to charge it last night but I fell asleep."

Tilly sighed. "I'm going to go see if I can flag someone down. Otherwise, we may have to walk back to town."

"I'll come, too." Hannah popped her door open.

"It's hot already. Hopefully this won't take too long."

Tilly leaned against the driver's side door and Hannah took up a post nearby. A few minutes in the sun and both women were starting to sweat. Tilly was thankful she'd taken after her father in terms of complexion—Kate's lighter skin tone would have been sizzling in the sun.

"You'd think there'd be more traffic right now," Tilly mumbled grumpily. A few more minutes passed without a single car going by and Tilly was beginning to worry.

"There's someone," Hannah said, pointing to the west, where a dark shape was encased in a dust cloud, a common sight in the dry Southwest. As the vehicle appeared, Tilly straightened up and waved her arms frantically. She took a step away from the car and continued her movements.

"Hey!" she shouted. "Hey, stop!"

Much to Tilly's relief the SUV began to slow, coming into focus as the dust settled around it. It drove by Tilly and Hannah, then made a U-turn and eased up behind Tilly's car. She fought back irritation. They'd have to pull around again if she needed a jump. But she tried to stay grateful.

The vehicle's windshield was dirty. Tilly could make out a driver and passenger, but not well enough to see their faces. She'd been ready to walk toward the driver, but a prickle of fear made her stop in her tracks. Another car raced past, but there were no other vehicles in sight.

The driver's door opened slowly and a man stepped out, his cowboy boots hitting the ground hard. He didn't close the door behind him.

"Do you need some help?" He wore a baseball cap pulled low over his eyes, and in the afternoon sun it did a remarkable job of obscuring his features.

"Hannah, get in the car," Tilly whispered. For a moment, the teen stayed frozen in place. "Now, Hannah."

Hannah walked around the front of Tilly's car stiffly while Tilly kept her eyes trained on the approaching stranger.

"Car broke down. Do you have a cell phone I can use?" Tilly kept her voice calm, hoping that this man really was trying to help, but her whole body was on high alert. "My boyfriend is headed this way. I just want to let him know where we are."

The man smiled. "Sure. You can use my phone." He reached into his back pocket. As he did, the passenger door opened and another pair of boots hit the ground. Hannah had just reached the passenger door, but when Tilly looked over she'd stopped, and Tilly could see her arms trembling where she'd crossed them.

Tilly cursed herself for letting fear get the better of her, knowing she'd passed it on to Hannah. She returned her attention to the driver, forcing a smile. A lone truck rolled by before Tilly had a chance to react, leaving the road empty again.

"Thanks. He's only a few minutes behind us, so we don't

need you guys to do anything." Keeping her voice level. "I just want to check and see how long he'll be."

The passenger took another step forward, his eyes locked on Hannah. "She's not supposed to be here."

They were in trouble.

"Get in the car!" Tilly shouted, and turned to open her door. Both men bolted forward. Hannah made it into her seat, but before she could lock her door it swung open and gloved hands reached in to grab her.

"Tilly!" She flung out her arms in Tilly's direction, but Tilly's attacker had gotten hold of her before she'd had a chance to even close her door. Tilly watched in horror as Hannah tried to grab on to anything within reach, sending her water bottle and their leftovers to the ground. Tilly tried to turn toward Hannah but was wrenched backward, her head slamming hard into the car door.

She saw stars, and pain shot through the back of her head like lightning. She could hear Hannah crying somewhere nearby. A dirty rag was pushed against her mouth and nose. Soon, the world began to fade.

CHAPTER 10
KATE

THE HOUSE SECURITY SYSTEM CHIMED, the perimeter sensor signaling that someone was at the front door. Kate had been sitting in the living room trying to read, but all she could think about was Roman, who was still not home from his trip to Las Cruces. Startled by the sound, she reached for her phone, pulling up the camera app.

Dan Bross stood by the door, nervously shifting from one foot to the other. He looked up at the camera and his distress was plain.

Kate rushed to the front gate to let him in, Rusty at her heels.

"Dan? What's wrong?" She stepped aside to let him through.

"Have you heard from your sister?"

"Not since lunchtime. She and Hannah met me for pizza. Is something wrong?"

Dan nodded but didn't say anything, making Kate's

nerves tingle. "What's going on, Dan? Did you call Hannah?"

Kate pulled out her phone and dialed her sister's number. It went to voicemail. "Tilly, call me when you get this, okay? It's urgent." She was about to question Dan again, when he finally snapped out of his daze.

"I got out of the office late. When I called to let them know I was going to miss dinner, no one answered. I kept calling all the way over the pass. Hannah's phone is going straight to voicemail—like the battery is dead or it's turned off."

Kate's heart was racing, panic creeping perilously close to the surface. She was probably overreacting but, given all the horrible things that had happened to both her and her sister, it was hard not to. "Maybe they had car trouble."

"Maybe," Dan said, but they both knew Tilly's car was new and in perfect condition. "I'm going to get back on the road."

"I'll come with you," Kate said, grabbing her purse from the table and locking Rusty inside as she hurried behind Dan.

"Is Roman working?" Dan asked.

"No, but he should be on his way back from Cruces anytime now." She sent Roman a text but left the details vague, telling herself she had nothing to worry about.

As they passed through the village of Tularosa on their way to Carrizozo, Kate remembered that she and Tilly had both set up a tracking app on their phones. After all the things they'd been through it had seemed like a reasonable thing to do, and now Kate was glad they'd been cautious. She pinged Tilly's phone.

"Oh no."

"What?" Dan's voice held a frantic edge.

"I pinged Tilly's phone. It's in Alamogordo at the pizza place. She must have forgotten it at lunch."

"I guess that explains why she's not answering," Dan muttered.

"Do you have a tracker on Hannah's phone?"

"Yeah, I do. It was the first thing I checked, but nothing registered." He handed Kate his phone. "Here. Check again."

Kate found the app and pinged Hannah's phone. "No signal." Kate laughed uneasily. Dan had been right—Hannah's phone was most likely dead. "You know, they're probably having dinner, and since neither one has their phone they won't see we were trying to call until they're finished."

"Maybe," Dan replied, but he still sounded strained. "If that's the case, I'm going to ground Hannah until she's 18. She knows better. We have a system. She wants more freedom, she has to make sure her phone is charged and on."

Dan's rant began to sound like a recycled argument, but Kate let him continue. She felt like her heart was going to burst. The idea that something, anything, had happened to Tilly stabbed at her heart. She couldn't imagine the agony Dan must be feeling.

As they reached Carrizozo, Kate's phone began to ring.

"It's Roman," she said quickly, in response to the hopeful look on Dan's face. He pulled into a gas station to fill up the tank.

"What's going on?" Roman sounded tired and maybe a little bit annoyed. Kate had left him a cryptic text.

"Are you home now?"

"Yes, just got here. Rusty's a little manic. Has he had dinner? When are you getting here?"

"I forgot to feed him before I left." Kate buried the twinge of guilt she felt. "Listen, Roman. I'm on my way to Albuquerque with Dan."

"Why?" The shift in Roman's tone was immediate—all sounds of exhaustion replaced by concern.

"Tilly and Hannah headed up earlier, but now they're not answering their phones."

"Did you call the hotel?"

"Dan did before we left the house. They hadn't arrived. Or at least Tilly hadn't checked in yet."

"Call again. I'll feed Rusty and head your way."

Kate hesitated. "They might just be having dinner. Tilly's phone is back in Alamo. I think she left it at the restaurant. And the battery on Hannah's might be dead. It keeps going straight to voicemail." She was rambling.

"Call me if you hear something. I'll text you when I'm on the road." He disconnected, leaving no room for further discussion.

———

The sun was beginning to set, casting vivid bands of orange and red across the horizon. Dan turned west from Carrizozo, joining a steady stream of traffic heading toward the freeway. A few minutes outside of town they drove past the jagged black rocks of the Valley of Fires, a long stretch of lava flows that had become a recreational area.

In the dimming daylight, the desolate area seemed

ominous. As a kid, she'd loved coming here with her parents to picnic and hike. Now, the darkness and isolation was giving her the creeps. Kate rested her head against the passenger window and watched the painted lines of the highway go by.

"Stop!" She bolted upright in her seat and pointed to the side of the road. "Pull over there."

As Dan brought the car to a stop Kate jumped out, ignoring the honks of cars that'd been blindsided by their sudden maneuver. She heard Dan's door shut and he was beside her.

"What is it?" His voice was barely a whisper above the ringing in Kate's ears, her anxiety in full swing though she fought against it.

A Styrofoam container with its contents spilled across the desert floor and a discarded water bottle featuring the Las Cruces High School mascot lay in the dirt. Kate knelt on the ground and brushed dirt away from a cell phone, its screen shattered.

"Call the police," she said. Dan reached down to touch the phone. "Don't."

"It's Hannah's," Dan said, his voice strangled with fear and grief.

"Right now, Dan. Call 911," Kate repeated more forcefully this time. She picked up her own phone, thankful she still had a signal, and called Roman.

CHAPTER 11
TILLY

WHEN TILLY OPENED HER EYES, her vision was blurry and distorted. Light attacked her senses, causing her head to throb painfully. The smell of sweat and dust and something else—something sour and foul—filled her nose, completing the assault.

Her hands were bound behind her and one side of her face was smashed into musty-smelling fabric. Soon, the floor beneath her started to bounce, causing pain every time a body part connected with the hard floor. As her vision started to clear she thrashed, trying to loosen the ties on her wrist. She wasn't sure where she was, but her fight or flight response was fully activated.

"She's waking up." A gruff male voice several feet away. She heard a metallic click and two thumps that sounded like footsteps on metal. She realized she was in a vehicle just as a rag came down hard over her nose. The sickly smell twisted her stomach in knots. She retched violently, emptying the contents of her stomach, before a chemical drowsiness pulled her under.

The last thing heard were the angry curses of her captor.

———

Tilly ran down the street, crying out for help. She heard footsteps behind, but she knew if she stopped to look back they'd have her. Her whole body ached, and something warm and sticky slid down her legs. She looked down long enough to see a stream of red flowing from somewhere deep in her core.

Suddenly, her foot hit a rut in the road and she went flying. She braced herself for the pain she would feel when she hit the asphalt, but it never came.

Instead, she woke up in her bed. The bed she'd slept in as a child.

"You have to get up, mijita," her mother said, pulling the comforter off from her. A chill swept over her body, and she tried to tuck her arms and legs into the oversized hoodie she wore to bed just for this reason. She was horrified to find that she was naked. She scrambled to cover her body as she looked over to where her mother stood.

But it wasn't her mother. A row of men stood along the wall of her room, examining her like she was a slave up for auction. She screamed for her mother, and one of the men shook his head.

"I'm looking for something easier to handle."

A mumbled conversation ensued between the men. No matter how hard she struggled, or how loudly she screamed, they ignored her. She tried to sit up, but something held her down. Her arms were pinned underneath her body, and nothing she could do would free them.

As terror took hold, her ability to move disappeared. She was as still as stone. The men were gone. She was lying on a cold, hard floor in a pool of her own vomit. Opening her eyes wide, she saw someone lying beside her. As her eyes adjusted she saw Hannah's beautiful face, pale and unmoving.

Once again, she started to scream.

Tilly woke from the nightmarish images to the feel of rough hands lifting her off a putrid-smelling surface. She felt a hot wind across her face, and then she was being carried. Every jostle was painful. The wind disappeared. So did the light. Then she was lying on a cold, hard floor, wondering if the nightmare would ever end. When the rag was placed over her nose again, she was almost grateful for the darkness.

CHAPTER 12
KATE

FOR THE SECOND time in a week, Kate sat on the hood of a car, watching helplessly as the police conducted a search of the area. A road block had been erected to make room for the search along the narrow stretch of highway. A long line of headlights stretched back behind the barrier as far as Kate could see.

"Tell me one more time how you located the phone?" A sheriff's deputy was taking Kate's statement, and he couldn't seem to wrap his mind around her spotting Hannah's phone in the dirt along the road. His suspicious tone made her angry.

Kate sighed heavily. "As I've told you, I was looking at the side of the road as we drove through. I saw the take-out container and then the sun glinting off of something. I'm not sure if it was the phone or the water bottle, but I wanted to check it out. Honestly, if the traffic hadn't been slowing things down, I'm not sure I would have even noticed.

There's a lot of trash along the road, and Hannah's phone was nearly covered with dirt."

"And your sister's phone is back in Alamogordo?"

"Yes," Kate groaned, knowing where this line of questioning was headed.

"How can you be sure she didn't go back to get it?"

"I can't," Kate said, unable to hide the frustration in her voice. "However, since the restaurant still has her phone and we found Hannah's phone here, it seems pretty clear that something happened to them."

She'd avoided speculation up to this point, but her exhaustion and an overload of emotions were wearing her thin. The expression on the deputy's face changed in an instant, and she knew she'd lost him.

"I'm sure we'll find her."

His patronizing dismissal was more than Kate could stand. She hopped to her feet, pushing past the officer, and walked over to Roman who was deep in conversation with the sheriff. Roman looked up as she approached. The intensity in his gaze radiated throughout his body.

"What's the plan?" As she spoke she locked eyes with the sheriff, hoping he would understand that she was in no mood to be placated.

"Kate, this is Sheriff Brown."

The sheriff offered his hand. "You can call me Steve, ma'am." He had a faint Southern accent. "Given what Agent Aguilar has told me about your situation, I'm inclined to escalate things quickly."

Kate scrunched her nose suspiciously. The sheriff laughed.

"I can understand that look," he said. "You'll be happy to

know that Roman grilled me thoroughly before telling me anything. I just moved here a few years ago and I haven't really had a chance to establish any strong ties to law enforcement in your area. In fact, they've been a little standoffish."

Roman added, "One of the men arrested a few weeks ago was from Carrizozo. Steve's been in touch with the State Police regarding our trafficking investigation, so he actually knew a lot already."

"So, you think this is related?" she asked, though there was no doubt in her mind.

"I'm not sure what this is yet," Steve replied, choosing his words carefully. "Based on what you've told me, it seems reasonable to assume that something happened to your sister and Miss Bross. Normally I'd get a lot of resistance to pursuing this as a missing persons case, given your sister is an adult and we can't even technically declare her missing at this point." He held up a hand before Kate could interject. "But, with a minor involved, I've got a lot more leeway in how we proceed."

"Sheriff, we got a call." Another deputy had approached from the roadblock, his phone in hand. "Dispatch got a call from a gentleman who drove through here this afternoon. He said he noticed a car pulled over to the side with the hood up. Metallic brown newer model Toyota. Two women standing by the passenger door. He only saw them briefly, but they fit the descriptions of Ms. Medina and Miss Bross."

Kate's heart pounded hard against her chest. "That's Tilly's car." She looked at Roman, whose demeanor remained stoic. It was Tilly's first brand new car and she'd only had it about a year.

The sheriff took the call and walked away to talk.

"She must've had car trouble," Kate said quietly, despite the absurdity. Tilly had never mentioned having any problems with it, and the evidence pointed in a different direction, but Kate was afraid to let her mind go there. Not yet.

Roman seemed to be thinking the same thing. "I don't buy it."

"Neither do I."

"Neither do I," the sheriff said, returning to the conversation. "The caller said he saw a vehicle pulling up behind your sister's car. He says he didn't think anything of it, but when he got home to Socorro he was telling his wife about it, and something she said made him rethink things."

"What did she say?" Kate asked. She curled her fingers into fists and ran her thumbs across the knuckles back and forth.

"He realized that neither of the women moved when the vehicle pulled up behind them. He described the woman, your sister I assume, as standing with her arms crossed, and in his rearview mirror he saw the younger woman walking around the front of the car to the passenger side. Then he lost sight of them." Steve took a breath. "Looking back, he says the older woman looked unhappy. At the time he thought it was because of the breakdown, but now he's not sure."

"You keep saying 'vehicle'," Kate noted.

Steve frowned. "Yes, the caller said the vehicle was either a dark van or SUV, but he couldn't remember which. I don't think he would have called in if his wife hadn't made him feel guilty about not stopping."

"That's not much to go on," Roman said, glancing

wearily at Kate. She realized he was running on fumes and wondered just how long this endless day would last.

"No, but at least it answers a few questions. It looks like your sister drove through here with Hannah Bross. And they didn't make it to their destination, so we can put out a BOLO for your sister's car. We can also issue an Amber Alert."

"Will the investigation stay in your jurisdiction?" Kate asked.

"For the moment. As we receive information from the alerts, we may have to call in the State Police."

"What can we do to help?" The idea of going home and facing a whole night of not knowing what was going on made Kate sweat.

"We can't," Roman said with a sigh. Any fight Kate might have put up died when she saw how badly fatigued Roman appeared. The shadows beneath his eyes were cavernous, and she wondered if he'd had any sleep at all last night. She wasn't sure he should drive himself home. With reluctant acceptance, she asked the sheriff, "You'll notify us immediately if you find anything?"

He nodded. "It'll probably be a few hours before we start getting responses, so I suggest getting some sleep while you can. Make sure your alarms are armed," he said gravely. "If this is related to the trafficking case, I think we have to assume that you're both at risk."

Kate offered Dan a room at their house, but he wasn't willing to leave the scene no matter how valid the arguments. As she drove home Roman snored quietly in the passenger seat, leaving her plenty of time to think. She couldn't shake the image of Sam Garrett's mangled body from her mind, making the trip absolute agony. Thankfully, the nap seemed to have done Roman a world of good. When they arrived home, he ran interference with Rusty while Kate made some tea.

She settled onto the couch, allowing the warmth of the steam rising off her cup to relax her, even if only for a moment. When Roman joined her, she was collected enough for the conversation she knew they needed to have.

"How's Angie?"

Roman's shoulders sagged a bit, reminding Kate just how complicated the situation was becoming. Angie, their biggest ally on the trafficking case, was out of commission. Despite all the precautions they'd taken and the fact that Tilly lived in a different town, whoever was gunning for Kate had finally found a way to get to her.

"She's not well, but it seems like they're able to treat her. If I understand correctly, she'd been asymptomatic for a long time. But she knew this could happen." He gritted his teeth and Kate heard the unspoken words. The rawness of Angie's betrayal was evident in his voice.

"I'm sorry," Kate said softly, but she didn't reach for his hand. She was holding herself together, but only just. Any tenderness might break her down, and she needed to get through this now. Before the next round of bad news. "Are you okay?"

It was a loaded question. Despite their devotion to one another, Kate and Roman's relationship had been an uphill battle. Kate's trust issues had been a constant companion, and though she'd come a long way in coping with her irrational fears the jealousy she still felt over Roman's relationship with his ex was always just below the surface. With everything going on, she couldn't afford to be distracted by it.

Roman seemed to understand all the nuances of her question. He remained silent for an uncomfortably long time and then exhaled long and slow. "No, I'm not okay," he said simply. Kate's chest contracted painfully as she endured the next long pause.

"I'm angry," he continued. "We were together for years and she never told me about this. I deserved to know. She should have told me." The last statement was muttered and barely audible.

Kate resisted the urge to reassure him, knowing that he couldn't work through this without feeling his way through. It was a hard lesson, and one that Kate struggled with all the time.

"What if we'd been married? And had kids." His voice was growing louder. Rusty, who'd been curled up in his bed near the couch, perked his ears up as if preparing for action. Kate reached down and rubbed the soft fur between his ears, but he stayed alert.

"I'm…" His struggle to find the right words twisted Kate's stomach in knots. "I don't know, Kate. I don't know what I feel or what I'm supposed to do." He stood up. "I'm just…tired. I think I have to go sleep."

He walked away from her without another word, and she heard the bedroom door close down the hall.

Roman's departure left Kate feeling empty. She sank down to the floor and leaned down so that her head rested on the pillow next to Rusty. He rested his head against hers, sensing that she needed comfort.

And she did need comfort, because the moment her mind wandered back to Tilly all she could see was her sister's beautiful face, bloodied and bruised—disfigured the way Sam Garrett's had been. She fought hard to keep that image in mind, knowing that her imagination could take her to much darker places if she let it.

CHAPTER 13
TILLY

As Tilly woke, her head pounded angrily, sending shooting pains down into her neck and back. The very thought of moving was too much, so she remained still and tried to breathe calmly. She remembered the attack, and she knew that she needed to make sure Hannah was alive, but the pain in her head was overwhelming, insurmountable. Being awake took more energy than she had.

She groaned involuntarily.

A deep voice chuckled nearby and she heard heavy footsteps coming toward her. Fear rippled through her body as fabric was pressed against her nose and mouth, robbing her of her consciousness once again.

———

The next time she woke, Tilly heard muffled sobs. It took a moment to realize that they weren't coming from her. She tried opening her eyes slowly, wincing as they adjusted to the light in the room. Every movement hurt, causing tears to form in the corners of her eyes. She was lying on her side on a hard surface, and as she scanned the area, careful not to move her head, she saw nothing but a dirty concrete floor and stucco walls in a state of disrepair.

Gathering her courage, she whispered, "Hannah." Her voice was ragged, her throat dry with thirst. The whisper caused her to cough, her vision blurring as pain wracked her body. When she settled, she realized the crying had stopped.

"Hannah?" This time she forced more air out of her lungs, projecting her voice as loudly as she dared. Another coughing fit ensued, leaving her breathless. She was facing the wall, and had yet to attempt to turn over. The anticipation of more pain was stronger than her desire to learn about her surroundings.

She heard something soft sliding over the floor in spurts. Suddenly, cold fingers grabbed her arm. Tilly stifled the scream that threatened to escape.

"Tilly?" Hannah's voice sent immediate relief through Tilly, followed quickly with dread at the weakness in the young woman's voice. "I thought you were dead." Hannah's voice broke at the end and she began to sob again.

Tilly reached up to put her hand on Hannah's and began the agonizing act of turning toward the girl. As her body shifted, Hannah scooted back a bit to make room. When Tilly was facing away from the wall she closed her eyes and panted, trying to ignore the faintness the motion had caused. She was fairly certain she had a concussion, but she had to be strong. For Hannah.

Her gaze moved past Hannah's kneeling form. Light from a small window high up in the wall shone down into the room, casting shadows in the corners and revealing their sparse surroundings. In the far corner, a thin mat covered in threadbare blankets lay abandoned. A door along the far wall was the only exit.

As Tilly became more aware, the stench of human waste and sweat accosted her senses. She gagged.

"Where are we?" Tilly groaned as she pressed her arm against her nose. Between the pain and the smell, she wished she had never woken up.

Hannah's frame shook with silent grief, but the teen seemed incapable of making a sound. Tilly put her hand on the floor and tried to push herself into a sitting position, letting a cry escape as the world spun. With the last of her strength she pushed herself back against the wall, slumping against it while her vision began to darken.

Before Tilly passed out Hannah moved to sit beside her, giving her a place to lean as her consciousness faded.

———

"Let me go!" Hannah screamed.

Tilly jerked awake, opening her eyes to a new horror. Two men with baseball caps and scarves tied across their faces were pulling Hannah to her feet. The girl was fighting like a wildcat, but her slight frame was no match for her attackers.

"Stop," Tilly croaked. Then, with everything she had, she yelled, "Stop! Leave her alone!" She reached out to grab Hannah's flailing arm, tugging hard. She felt a pop and her stomach roiled, but she managed to hang on, using Hannah to leverage herself to her feet. Overcome by dizziness, she staggered forward, wrapping her arms around Hannah and putting her full weight into dragging the girl to the ground with her.

"Fuck!" The taller man looked down at jagged, oozing scratches running the length of his forearm where Hannah's nails had left their mark. He turned a murderous gaze on both women and kicked hard into Tilly's exposed side. A burst of pain took her breath away and she rolled into a ball.

"Leave her alone!" Hannah screamed again, but Tilly could hear the change in her tone as terror turned to rage. Hannah launched herself at her attackers, clawing at their faces with a fury. Both men seemed thrown off guard by the change in her demeanor. They stepped back several paces to avoid her attack.

Hannah dropped back down to Tilly's side, placing herself as a barrier.

For a moment, all was quiet and still. Then a low chuckle rose from the shorter of the two men. It was the sound that had been haunting Tilly every time she lost consciousness.

"Dumb bitch." His voice was ragged and cruel. He reached down and grabbed Hannah's shoulder hard, roughly lifting her off her feet. His partner stepped up and quickly pulled Hannah's arms behind her. He reached into his pocket and retrieved a zip tie which he used to bind her wrists.

Tilly struggled to her feet but her side cramped hard, making it impossible to straighten. She glared at the men, pouring all her anger and hatred into her stare. "If you hurt her, I will kill you." Her voice was a growl, low and deadly serious. The tall man blinked as though unnerved, but the other man just laughed.

"Don't worry, *puta*." He made a show of running his hand over Hannah's chest as the girl continued to struggle, her screams echoing in Tilly's head. "We won't break her." He hit Hannah hard upside the head. The girl slumped in his arms.

And as they exited the room, he turned and Tilly could hear the smile on his face. "Yet."

———

Hours passed. The room grew dark.

As Tilly pulled herself up to standing her stomach revolted. She leaned over, bracing herself against the wall as she vomited. With every convulsion, the pain in her side and in her head resulted in spots across her vision. When she'd reached the point of painful dry heaves that brought her to knees, she begged silently for the oblivion of unconsciousness, but it never came.

Instead, she waited for the pain to subside and tried again to stand. This time, dizziness washed over her, robbing her of her equilibrium. She clung doggedly to the wall, closing her eyes and hoping that this too would pass. When it became manageable, she started to walk.

Tilly staggered around the perimeter of the room, her hand trailing along the wall for support. With each revolution her vision cleared, though the pounding in her head hindered her concentration.

Tilly waited anxiously for Hannah to be returned. Needing an outlet for her anxiety, she began the work of reorienting herself. The man's boot had caused damage—a broken rib or two at the very least—but she was determined to fight back when the men returned. Hannah needed her. They needed to find a way to escape.

When no light remained and Tilly was weak with dehydration and exertion, she collapsed onto the mat. Resting against the wall, she dozed on and off. Each time she woke she sat very still, listening for anything that might give her a clue about their location. There was nothing but the sounds of the desert—the wind, crickets chirping, coyotes howling.

But no sounds of traffic. Tilly began to worry about what they would face when they did escape. How far had they been taken? She had no concept of time.

The sound of the door being unlocked woke her. No light came through the door, but she heard footsteps across the floor and then a warm body was thrown into her lap. She could almost make out the shape of the man as he walked out the door, locking it behind him.

Tilly's voice shook. "Hannah?" She could feel the rise and fall of Hannah's chest. Not knowing what state the girl was in, she was afraid to move her. So she cradled Hannah as best she could. "Hannah? Wake up."

She repeated her request over and over until sleep finally took her.

CHAPTER 14
KATE

KATE WOKE to the smell of coffee. She opened her eyes, surprised to find herself lying on the couch. She was covered in her favorite quilt. As she sat up, her back and neck ached in protest. She groaned dramatically.

"I made breakfast," Roman called out from the kitchen. Kate stumbled in that direction, mostly relying on her sense of smell. The room was still very dark and her eyes were bleary from sleep.

"What time is it?" she whispered as she took a seat at the table. Roman put a cup of coffee in front of her, along with a plate of eggs and toast.

"Just after five." He sat down beside her, reaching over to take her hand. "Kate, I'm sorry about yesterday."

"I know," she murmured. She picked up the cup of coffee and closed her eyes, trying to focus only on the aroma. *One thing at a time*, she thought.

"It wasn't fair." Roman sounded more like himself this

morning, and she hoped whatever space he'd needed to wrestle with his feelings had been enough.

"No, it wasn't. But it's okay." There was really nothing for Kate to say. Roman and Angie would always have their past, and she could either have faith in the fact that he was committed to their life together or she could spend her whole life looking over her shoulder, wondering when the other shoe would drop.

Intellectually speaking, she knew it wasn't the way she wanted to live. Just like she knew she had to let herself feel the pain, the jealousy, and whatever other emotions washed through her body, and then let them go. But it was so hard at the moment.

"Sheriff Brown called," Roman said, moving away from one painful topic to another. "They found Tilly's car."

Kate felt the blood drain from her face.

"She wasn't in it," Roman added quickly. He was looking at Kate like he was worried she might pass out. "It was parked in a shopping center in Albuquerque. It had been wiped down with bleach. Brown thinks someone drove it there and cleaned it up, hoping it wouldn't be noticed for a while. Which might have been the case, except security at the shopping center records the license plate numbers for all cars parked overnight."

"Who has her?" Knowing that Kate and Hannah had been abducted, not outright killed, was only a slight comfort —they might still be alive. Most of the known players in the trafficking ring had been arrested, except Sam Garrett.

"I don't know," Roman said, his expression dark. "Brown asked the same thing. I walked him through everything, even back when I was with Alamogordo PD. So far we haven't been able to directly tie the police chief to the operation. We know Allen Parks is involved, but again, no evidence. I've given both their names to the sheriff, so if anything at all comes up he'll be able to move."

"What about Ruth?" Kate's voice was so soft she wondered if Roman had heard her. But the look on his face confirmed that he had.

"I don't know if she'll talk to me," Roman said. "And I'm not sure that sending you to talk to her is the best idea."

Kate nodded. "What choice do we have? I know she's involved. I've been able to avoid her for a long time, but maybe that was wrong. I need to know what she knows."

It was the only thing Kate could think of that might give them a clue about Tilly's whereabouts. But the idea of having a conversation with Ruth made her stomach turn. Ruth was a predator, and Kate didn't want to play games with Tilly's life in the balance.

––––––––

In the months that they'd been friends, Kate had never been to Ruth's house. The older woman had popped up at Kate's on several occasions, unannounced. During the last visit, Ruth had warned Kate that her continued involvement in the trafficking investigation would put her in danger. Well, more danger, since Kate had been run off the road only a few weeks prior.

Up to that point, there had been signs that Ruth wasn't being entirely honest with Kate, but after that visit it was crystal clear that Ruth had connections with the trafficking ring. Kate had launched a very aggressive public education campaign to try and flush out the traffickers, knowing that the only reason the operation had been able to hide for so long was a lack of awareness in the community. She'd made it her personal mission to give each and every resident the tools to intervene, to report, to end the violence.

And for a while, it seemed that her efforts were making Ruth uncomfortable. In their shared group, Ruth kept her distance. In fact, her waning participation in the group had become a topic of gossip among some of the women.

Then, in the last few weeks, Ruth had reemerged with a vengeance, inserting herself directly into Kate's conversations and being outwardly friendly every time they crossed paths in public. The amusement and satisfaction in Ruth's expressions were barely concealed, but if you didn't know the whole story it all looked innocuous.

The uneasiness Kate felt was fully present as she approached the front door of Ruth's house, a beautiful Southwestern-style villa in the foothills of the mountains. The house had been through a number of renovations, but it was easy to see the original beams and adobe walls, giving it a timeless charm.

Kate rang the bell and readied herself for a confrontation. When the door opened, Kate was surprised to see Ruth dressed down and looking every bit her age. The sight made her gasp.

Ruth smiled. "Hello, Kate." She opened the door and gestured for Kate to come inside. "I suppose I'm not surprised to see you, but I didn't think it would be quite this soon."

Kate frowned. "I don't know what you mean."

Ruth led Kate into a sitting room with a huge window

facing the mountain. She shakily lowered herself onto one couch and Kate sat across from her, noting just how unstable the woman seemed.

Ruth searched Kate's face curiously. "Maybe you don't." She sighed heavily. "I know why you're here."

Kate had to fight to keep from arguing and offering more information than she wanted to divulge. "And why is that, Ruth?"

"There's no need to be childish," Ruth chided, her tone full of disappointment. "I know your sister has been taken. And the girl. I warned you that this might happen."

Ruth's scolding tone chipped away at Kate's control. "Where are they?"

"I don't know," Ruth answered, and to Kate's astonishment her answer sounded sincere.

"How is that possible?" Kate finally exploded. "How can you know they've been taken, when it only happened 12 hours ago and in another county? How can you know that but not know where they are?" Kate's hands were shaking, anger coursing through her in waves. She fought to keep her voice level. "I know you were involved in my mother's death. You know more about what's going on in this town than most people. What are you playing at, Ruth?"

"Sometimes you do what you have to do to survive."

"Why would you have anything to do with something so vile?" Kate's voice was growing shrill and desperate. "You're responsible for my mother's death. Now my sister is gone. And the girls? Jesus, Ruth. All these girls. You have to help me! You owe it to my mother."

Ruth's eyes looked sad. "Things have changed over the years." She looked off into the distance, as if her mind had wandered away from the room, from the present. "I've known for some time that the end was near. And I've made my peace. I was ready to let it all go. I've been making decisions for such a long time, and I thought I was in control. But I've been a fool."

"What are you talking about?" As Ruth spoke, Kate became more agitated, more uncertain. She wasn't sure exactly what she'd expected to learn during this visit, but suddenly she was terribly afraid. "Ruth? Please. I don't understand."

A single tear slid down Ruth's cheek. "I never meant to be in this position. Prey. Now look at me."

In the moment of silence that followed, the pieces fell into place. "It was you," Kate whispered. "It was always you. The girls. The way you've kept it hidden so long."

"It was a means to an end." Ruth's detachment made Kate want to vomit. "Women today don't understand. Sex is power, a way to control the men who run everything. To make them vulnerable. When I worked for my husband, I saw the way he looked at me. He was going to take what he wanted, one way or the other. I simply took control of the situation. And after we married, I turned his sick hobby into something that would guarantee my future."

"Trafficking girls for sex," Kate said, swallowing bile.

"Oh, please. I've provided these girls with something valuable. I've shown them the power that they hold. I've given them something they'll be able to use in their lives—to succeed."

"What about Gabby Greene?" Kate was finding it harder to breathe. With every new revelation, every new moment of understanding, her chest became heavier and all she wanted to do was leave this horrid human being behind.

Ruth looked down solemnly. "What happened to Gabby Greene should not have happened." When she looked up at Kate, more tears welled up in her eyes. "After that girl in the '90s, I made sure that we rotated the girls more quickly. Kept tabs on the men so that they didn't begin to think the girls were theirs. I provided a service, nothing more."

"You served those girls up." Kate gritted her teeth so hard that her jaw began to throb. "You gave them drugs and alcohol. You threatened their families. And you let men rape them, repeatedly."

"I lived through it. They will, too." The cold, impersonal tone was more than Kate could take.

"You know that's not true."

Ruth sighed, dabbing at her eyes with a tissue. When she spoke, her voice was contemplative and distant. "I've been running this enterprise for more than 30 years. Like any business, we've had to correct problems to ensure things run smoothly. Other than a few instances, I've sent all the girls out into the world to live their lives. Now it's all over."

"You're a monster," Kate said. Then she stood and walked out of Ruth's house without another word.

CHAPTER 15
TILLY

It was mid-morning, maybe later, when Hannah finally woke up. Her face was bruised, and one eye was swollen shut. When she spoke, her voice was hoarse and her jaw seemed stiff on one side. Tilly hoped it wasn't broken.

During the night, their captors had come into the room and left drinking water and a bag of food. Unwilling to move out from underneath Hannah, Tilly had to focus on the opposite wall to keep from looking at water. Her throat ached and she felt faint, but the sight of the supplies made her both ecstatic and scared.

The appearance of food and water was a sign. A sign that they weren't going anywhere anytime soon.

Hannah sat up sorely and Tilly helped her sit back against the wall. She started to speak, but Tilly quieted her. "We need to drink some water first. We'll talk after."

She walked over to the tray that had been set just inside the door and grabbed two bottles of water. Despite her stomach's protests she left the bare-bones sandwiches, knowing that it would be better to drink some water and see how everything settled. No use throwing up the meager food they'd been provided, and quite frankly she didn't want to add any more vomit to the putrid smell of the room.

"Here." She handed Hannah a bottle and sat down beside her. "Take small sips. Otherwise it'll make you sick."

The girl nodded, and Tilly felt a small twinge of pain in her stomach each time Hannah winced when she swallowed. Her own throat burned uncomfortably with the first few sips, then began to ease as she continued drinking. She took calming breaths in between, praying that the water would stay down.

The water break provided a few moments of peace before Hannah talked about where they'd taken her. Tilly could see the physical damage that had been done to her face, but was relieved not to see any obvious marks on her neck, which meant the pain in swallowing was probably just thirst, same as Tilly.

Of course, Tilly knew that the injuries you could see were often the easiest to overcome. She was thankful for the pause, because she wasn't sure if she was ready to hear what Hannah had to say. Despite her best efforts to detach emotionally from the situation, Tilly was struggling with an enormous amount of anger.

Her whole adult life had been spent helping victims, and despite all the danger that might have put her in it wasn't until she came back to New Mexico and reconnected with her sister that danger had been brought to her doorstep.

That's not fair, she thought. *Blaming Kate for what's happening right now is like blaming the victim. She didn't ask for this to happen.*

But the rational side of her brain was not in charge. The abduction had been planned. They knew she'd be on that highway at that time. How? Tilly was still working on that part, but the implications were horrifying. She knew that the traffickers were watching Kate. She knew what they were capable of, but she'd been complacent, thinking that living away from Alamogordo would keep her out of it. It was hard enough worrying about Kate's safety. She'd never dreamed she'd have to worry about her own Or Hannah's.

"We need to get out here," Hannah said quietly, echoing Tilly's own thoughts. "I heard them talking when they thought I was still passed out. They're freaking out because they didn't know I'd be with you and they figured out who my dad is."

"Start from the beginning," Tilly said, focusing her mind entirely on the present.

Hannah took a slow breath in and then exhaled just as slowly, forcing Tilly to practice her own breathing to keep the panic at bay.

"There were at least four of them." A tear slid down Hannah's cheek, but her voice was eerily calm. An emotionless tone that shook Tilly to the core. The panicked teenager from yesterday was gone.

"They asked me a lot of questions about my dad, and about your sister. The short one hit me even when I answered," she continued. "The rest of the men seemed kind of reluctant. Not him. He liked hurting me."

For a moment, Hannah seemed lost in thought. Tilly watched Hannah breathe, readying herself for whatever was coming, knowing that it had to be bad if it was taking this much effort for Hannah to tell it.

"He…" Tears were streaming down her face now. Tilly's heart broke in two. The grief she felt for Hannah pressed at her chest, making every breath painful. "He…"

"It's okay, Hannah," Tilly said, her voice choked with emotion. "You don't have to say it. Not right now."

Hannah nodded. Her hands were shaking where she held them in her lap. She began to rub them together, pressing harder until Tilly could see the skin turning pink. Then she stopped, letting her whole body go completely still.

"He kept hitting me. Even while he was… I blacked out at some point. I don't know how long, but I woke up a few times. Someone came in and put a blanket over me. I laid really still, and then they got into a fight right outside the room I was in. They were trying to be quiet."

She took another sip of water. The pace of the story was eating away at Tilly, heightening her anxiety and fueling her anger.

"His name is Rick. The one who hurt me. One of them is called Mark. That's the one who was arguing with Rick. I'm not sure if he was the other one who was in here with us. It was too dark to tell."

"What were they fighting about?" Tilly asked.

"About me." Hannah's hands began to shake again, but she pressed them into her legs. "Mark said that now, after what Rick did to me—after he, um, raped me—there was no letting us go."

Time stood still for a moment as Tilly's fears were realized. If there had been a way out—a resolution that meant Tilly and Hannah would walk out of this alive——it was off the table. Rick had made sure of that.

Was this the same man who'd attacked Kate in her home?

The way Kate had described him, it fit. He'd been more than happy to do Benny Parks' dirty work for him, and neither Tilly nor Kate had any doubt that he would have made good on his threats.

Now he had. And Tilly would make sure he suffered for it.

CHAPTER 16
KATE

When Kate returned home, Roman met her at the door. One look and the color drained from his face.

"What happened?"

Kate stepped toward him, resting her forehead on his chest, and let the tears she'd been holding in on the drive home flow freely. To Roman's credit, he wrapped his arms around her and let her cry. It was one of the things she loved most about him. He let her fall apart without trying to fix her, without offering a solution, until she was ready.

When she began to calm down, she followed him to the sofa and sat down. Rusty curled up at her feet. He'd been dancing around her, waiting to be petted, but she'd hardly noticed.

Ruth's words rang in her ears, blurring her vision, upending everything she'd believed about the world, her community, her family, her life.

"Ruth was home," she said, preparing herself to tell the story, though she hadn't even begun to unpack the implications of Ruth's confession. Roman sat beside her, offering her a glass of water that she hadn't noticed him pour.

"She told you something," he said encouragingly when a few moments had passed.

"I wish I'd never gone there. I wish I could unhear it." Kate knew it was selfish. She'd gone to see Ruth hoping that she'd learn something that might lead them to Tilly. And Hannah. She hadn't gotten what she was looking for, and the overwhelming truth that Ruth had delivered was suffocating.

Roman waited for her to continue, but the tension in the room was pressing down on them both. Kate could see him crumpling under the weight. She felt it, too. An oppressive force that would bury her if she let it.

She couldn't let it.

Firming her resolve, she took a breath and continued, trying to keep her voice steady. "She's not just involved, Roman. She's in charge. She's been running it the whole time"

"Oh my God." His voice was just a whisper, but she could see him putting the pieces together. The horrid realization that this woman had been at the root of so much violence against young women was incomprehensible.

A woman Kate had called friend. Who had been friends with her mother and father. The realization that Ruth had known about—had been responsible for—the abuse Tilly suffered as a teenager and the death of their mother.

"She tore my family apart," Kate said, putting voice to the thought that had threatened to consume her all the way home.

"Did she say anything about Tilly?"

Kate nodded. "She said she'd warned me that this would happen."

"She knows where she is?" Roman's voice had gone cold with anger. He straightened up, but curled his fingers tangled up with Kate's as they sat, side-by-side, trying to make sense of it all.

"I'm not sure," Kate admitted. "She says no, but she was strange—the way she talked was vague. More about the organization than anything. She wasn't specific, but she says she's lost control. She may not have been involved in Tilly's disappearance directly, but I'm sure she knows who was."

Roman's face was an impassive mask, but Kate knew that expression hid raging emotions. For years, that mask had hidden his true feelings for her. She squeezed his hand to help ground him. His jaw relaxed, but she could feel tension radiating from him.

"We need to call Angie," Kate said, wincing as Roman clenched his jaw again. "I can call her."

"I think that would be best," he said. "Dan is coming by in a while to shower. No new updates, but I think I finally convinced him that this is a good base of operations."

Kate knew firsthand how hard it was to pry yourself away from ground zero, even when there was nothing you could do. "That's good. I know this is killing him."

Finally, Roman let down his guard. His shoulders sagged and he leaned against Kate. She realized how much tension she'd been holding when she was able to relax back into him. Unfortunately, the momentary relief led to another flood of tears.

"I'm having a hard time seeing how this is going to work out," Kate whispered, feeling guilty for giving in to despair.

She didn't want to give up hope, but every hour Tilly and Hannah were missing made the outcome more and more grim.

"I have no idea how to feel about Ruth," Roman admitted. "But that's more information than we had last night. There's nothing to do but push forward."

"I know." Intellectually, Kate agreed. But emotionally and psychologically, she felt like she was playing a game without knowing the rules. She didn't know what the next step should be. How could they ever expect to win?

———

Dan looked like he'd aged about ten years. Kate ushered him inside and upstairs to the spare room. She could tell he needed sleep just as sure as she knew that he wouldn't be able to get any. Not yet.

Downstairs, Roman was on his laptop, under headphones, listening in on some kind of work meeting. He'd taken a few days off, but as the newest agent in his office he was still trying to prove himself. Luckily his office knew what was going on, and Kate was thankful for their flexibility.

Kate took Rusty outside, dialing Angie's number while he ran around the courtyard.

"Hi, Kate." Angie's voice was weak, but she sounded upbeat. Kate's emotions were all over the place, but she took a calming breath.

"How are you feeling?"

"I'll live." Angie sighed. "Can't imagine that's why you're calling."

"No," Kate admitted. "But I have been thinking about you." She recounted the events surrounding Tilly and Hannah's disappearance, as well as her visit with Ruth.

"This is a nightmare," Angie said. "I'm being discharged today. I need to speak to one of the other detectives about the case. I'll do that as soon as I get home."

"I'm sorry to lay this on you right now."

"As if you had a choice," Angie said. Kate knew she was teasing, but she couldn't help feeling guilty. Guilty that her involvement in the investigation was impacting everyone she loved.

An image of Tilly flashed through her mind, but she pushed it aside. "What can I do?"

"I don't know," Angie said. "But you need to stay away from Ruth. And stay safe. This doesn't feel methodical or organized. It's desperate, and desperation breeds unpredictability. We need to focus on finding your sister without any more casualties."

Kate felt the word like a knife to her heart. She pictured Hannah's sweet face, and the way this situation had already aged Dan. Angie and Dan had been working together for years. The reminder gave Kate's guilt more mass.

Would any of them ever be the same?

CHAPTER 17
TILLY

"I'm not leaving without you," Hannah protested.

Tilly had spent time examining the door, but with no tools to work with, and given their weakened conditions, attempting to break through the door and overpower their captors seemed like a fool's errand. Hannah had barely kept the food down, and Tilly's stomach roiled, threatening to betray her at any moment. Between the heat, the putrid smell, and the physical injuries they'd both endured, nausea was a constant.

The door wasn't an option. Instead, they had turned their attention to the window. It was high up in the wall—Tilly could just curl her fingertips over the ledge. Even if they got up to it Tilly wasn't sure she could fit through it, but it seemed their only option.

"I'm going to sit against the wall. I want you to step up on my shoulders and see how close you can get." Seeing the panicked look on Hannah's face, Tilly added, "We're just looking."

Hannah reluctantly hoisted herself onto Tilly's shoulders, doing her best to put as little weight on Tilly as possible. Tilly bit her bottom lip, holding back the grunts and groans that wanted to escape under the pressure.

"I'm about two or three inches away from the windowsill. There's nothing to hold on to up here," Hannah said. She stepped back down.

"Okay, let's try this." Tilly positioned herself in a wall-sit and put her hands together to boost Hannah. "Step up using my hands and then up onto my shoulders."

"I don't want to hurt you," Hannah whimpered. Tilly felt a surge of love, but the situation was dire and they didn't have time for comfort right now.

"It's fine," she said, her voice firm, though her legs burned and wobbled. "Come on now."

Hannah's foot was in Tilly's hand when the doorknob rattled. Hannah jumped down and both women scrambled to the mat, huddling together just as the door opened. Tilly's chest heaved and she kept her head down, trying to calm her breathing so the intruders wouldn't notice and become suspicious.

The same two men entered the room. The tall one, Mark —the one who'd kicked Tilly in the side. And the short one, Rick. Their faces were covered and they wore baseball caps. When Rick stepped forward, it was all Tilly could do to keep from tackling him. But her fury would have to wait until Hannah was safe.

"Stay put," Mark said. His voice was gruff, but held none of the venom she'd witnessed the day before. He took the bucket they used for waste and placed it outside the door, replacing it with a clean pail.

Rick stood by, watching them while his partner did all the work. Mark put down a paper bag, which Tilly assumed contained more food.

Rick moved closer to the mat. Hannah cowered behind Tilly.

"Don't be shy, girl. We're friends now, right?"

"Leave her alone," Mark snapped. Rick sneered and emitted a low, angry growl, but he turned and followed Mark out the door. Both Tilly and Hannah stayed frozen in place until the lock clicked and the noise of receding footsteps disappeared.

Tilly could feel Hannah shaking beside her. "Let's see what they brought us. Hopefully more water." She took Hannah's hand and hauled her to her feet. The bag contained several bottles of water, a loaf of bread, and some bologna.

Time passed. They sipped the water, but it took a while—maybe an hour or more—to start nibbling at the food. Hannah tried to refuse the bologna, but Tilly made her take some anyway.

They ate in silence. Tilly remembered hating bologna as a child, but the sustenance was absolutely necessary. She divided the food up, giving Hannah a larger portion and wrapping several slices of bread in some of the paper from the bag.

Then she walked over to the wall under the window. "Okay, let's try again."

After a few attempts, Hannah managed to get up onto Tilly's shoulders.

"Can you see out?"

"Yeah. I see desert. Not much else."

"That's good. Hopefully we're away from the front of the house. Can you reach the window?"

Hannah's toes dug into Tilly's shoulders. She stifled a cry, knowing that her distress would stop Hannah in her tracks. That simply was not an option.

The weight on Tilly's shoulders lightened slightly. "The window is locked, but I think I can knock it loose." She bounced, sending shooting pain down Tilly's right arm.

"Almost…" Hannah's voice was strained with effort. "Shit!"

"What happened?"

"My finger slipped on the latch. I'm bleeding. There must have been something sharp."

"Come down. Let me take a look." An injury in a filthy place like this could become serious fast.

"Just give me one more minute." Hannah pushed hard off of Tilly's shoulders. A bolt of pain shot through her back. Tilly bit hard on her lip, tasting blood. A click echoed off the walls. "Got it."

Tilly wanted to celebrate, but she was worried they'd been making too much noise. Hannah seemed to feel the same. She stayed very quiet as she continued to work. Tilly barely heard the creaking of a hinge that hadn't been used in a while—blood pounded in her ears and every muscle in her body screamed out for relief.

"It opens out from the bottom, and not very far," Hannah said, looking down at Tilly. The shift in weight provided both relief and anguish. "I'm not sure if there's enough room for us to slip under. I'm afraid to push it harder. It's loud."

"Come down. We'll figure something out."

Hannah slowly lowered herself to the floor. Tilly's body

ached in protest as she straightened. Her chest heaved and dark spots flitted around her visual field. *Stay calm. Breathe.*

"Are you okay?" Hannah asked. The concern on her face made Tilly's heart ache right along with the rest of her. She shoved every emotion down as far into the recesses of her mind as possible, knowing that the next few minutes would be impossible if she wasn't completely detached.

"Here's what I'm thinking. Let's put the water and whatever food is left over up on the ledge. We don't know how far we are from anything, and we may have to walk a long way. Getting dehydrated will slow us down."

They readied their supplies. It took several tries to get the rations up onto the windowsill. Hoisting Hannah up was becoming harder as Tilly's strength quickly dwindled. Her whole body shook, making it difficult for Hannah to keep her balance.

Each effort left Tilly panting for breath and wondering if she would simply collapse before the task was done. She would push through one more lift, and then, hopefully, she could rest.

"Okay, I'm going to send you through first. You have to go slowly. Make sure there's no one watching."

"You should go, Tilly. I know you're exhausted."

Tilly smiled. "I am. But you're smaller than me and it would be pretty disastrous if I got stuck, right? You have a better chance of making it through."

Hannah hesitated. "My arms aren't very strong. What if I can't pull you up?"

"One step at a time." Tilly mustered as much confidence as she could. "If you can't fit through, then we're back at square one anyway, right?"

"Okay," Hannah said.

Tilly took her place against the wall, a little higher up this time. The plan would only work if Tilly could raise herself into a standing position, pushing Hannah high enough to climb up and through the window. She wasn't confident, but she was determined to put everything she had left into it.

The task was grueling. Tilly could feel sweat dripping down her back as Hannah made her ascent. Standing upright was so much harder than she'd anticipated. She felt the rough texture of the wall scraping against her back as she slid, fighting for every inch, until her knees locked into place.

"I'm going to pull myself part way through."

"I've got you." When Hannah's feet left Tilly's shoulders, Tilly turned and put her hands under Hannah's feet to help boost her if needed. She rested her chest against the dusty wall, locking her knees again for one last push. "Can you fit?"

Hannah's voice was so soft Tilly had to strain to hear. "Yes, I think so." Tilly watched Hannah's upper half disappear out the window. "It's the back of the house. I don't see anything out here. No cars. No road."

"Can you see anywhere to hide?" Tilly said a silent prayer.

"The bushes are pretty thick. I think if we make it far enough out into the desert, it wouldn't be hard to stay hidden if we stay low."

So many things could go wrong. Images flashed through Tilly's mind. Hannah taking a few steps and then being recaptured. Maybe brutalized as punishment for her escape attempt. Or maybe she would make it just far enough to get away, but they were so far from civilization that she would die of exposure before anyone could find her. It happened all the time out in the open desert.

Tilly shook her head hard, clearing away the doubt. Either they went forward, or they waited here and accepted whatever fate awaited.

"Not a chance," Tilly muttered.

"What?" Hannah was more than halfway out, making slow, deliberate movements.

"Take your time," Tilly whispered as loudly as she dared. Hope warred with anxiety as she watched Hannah's feet disappear over the ledge.

For a moment, all was quiet. And the quiet was ominous. But soon, Hannah peeked back over the edge.

"Take the supplies outside."

Hannah did as she was told and then looked back over the edge. "Okay, let me see if I can hook my feet on the wall. Then I can try to reach you."

Tilly looked up, and as she met Hannah's gaze she saw the girl's face go from determined to stricken. The betrayal on Hannah's face branded itself on Tilly's heart. "No, no, no. Tilly."

Tilly put up her hand. "Stop. Listen to me. You can't reach me. And I'm too tired to pull myself up. You have to go. Now."

Tears began to pour down Hannah's face as she shook her head. "I can't."

"Yes, you can." Tilly's stomach twisted into knots. "You have to, Hannah. I have no idea how long it's going to be before they come back, and you have to be a long way from here."

The look of absolute despair on Hannah's face threatened to dissolve Tilly's painfully constructed emotional walls. It was a horrible thing she'd done, and she wasn't sure it was something that Hannah would be able to forgive. None of that mattered if Hannah got away. And nothing mattered if she didn't—they both knew what these men were capable of.

"Stay away from the driveway. Go into the desert. Stay low, but keep moving. If you see a road or a building with a lot of cars, go that way."

Hannah was still sobbing softly, but she nodded in acknowledgement of each instruction Tilly gave her.

"Hannah," Tilly said, knowing that she needed to hurry the girl along, but not wanting to abandon her either. "I love you. Now go."

Hannah disappeared and the window shut behind her. Tilly listened intently, hoping not to hear anything. But with each passing moment, she felt the darkness close in on her. With the last of her strength she hobbled to the mat and curled into a fetal position, allowing exhaustion to drag her into oblivion.

CHAPTER 18
KATE

KATE DRUMMED her fingers against the table. She, Dan, and Roman had been sitting in the kitchen for an hour in a silence loaded with tension and laced with occasional nervous small talk. Each of their cell phones lay on the table, screens facing up.

The waiting was killing them.

Kate looked around and saw agony that mirrored her own on both men's faces. It had been thirty hours since lunch at the pizza place. Thirty hours since Tilly or Hannah had been in contact with anyone. And it had been hours since the last update from the sheriff's office.

"I'm going for a walk," Kate said. She reached for her phone and then hesitated, her fingertips lingering just above the screen. She pulled her hand away. "I'll only be gone a few minutes."

Roman shifted as he started to accompany her, but when his eyes met Kate's he seemed to change his mind. She hoped he saw how badly she needed to be on her own. Just for a moment. She turned and walked out the door, Rusty on her heels.

Leaving the hacienda behind, she walked down the road toward the mountains. Her house was the last on a dirt road that ended a hundred yards away. Kate picked up a rock and threw it hard. Rusty barked happily and took off after his perceived toy.

While he ran around, Kate kicked rocks from the road into the desert.

Angie had called the abduction desperate, and it was, but Kate couldn't stop thinking about how much planning had gone into it. They'd known where Tilly would break down. In fact, Kate was starting to wonder if they'd sabotaged Tilly's car somehow. The timing was too coincidental.

Kate had parked right outside the pizza parlor at lunch, but Tilly had parked around the corner. A call to the restaurant confirmed that there were no cameras on that side of the building. Plenty of time and access to have messed with Tilly's vehicle.

If they'd been following Kate, they may not have seen Tilly and Hannah arrive. They might not have realized that Tilly had a guest with her in the car.

They.

That one word caused Kate so much pain and anguish. How could *they* be this organized and still fly under the radar?

I warned you this would happen.

Ruth's voice sliced into Kate's consciousness like a razor. It was the only thing she'd been able to think about. Every minute that Tilly was gone, Kate replayed the words over and over as she tried to think of anything, anything at all, that would lead her to where Tilly and Hannah had been taken.

Kate blamed herself. Ruth was right. She'd warned Kate, but Kate's overinflated sense of duty had taken it as a challenge. Despite all the attempts to scare her away, to threaten her, to hurt her, Kate persisted, and now look where it had gotten her. Kate's dogged pursuit of justice would likely destroy everything she'd ever loved.

With every hour that passed, she felt dread permeate her heart. Her senses. She realized she'd been waiting for the phone to ring, and dreading it at the same time. No news was good news, right?

"Kate?" Dan's voice startled her out of her thoughts.

"Did they call?"

"Yeah. Nothing to report."

Rusty ran up between them and nudged at Dan's leg until he finally relented and scratched behind Rusty's ears.

"I wish there was something I could do," Dan said, his voice stretched thin. "I feel so helpless."

"I know," Kate whispered. She was glad Dan had spoken the words. It was better supporting him in his grief and anger than it was to feel her own.

"Roman told me about what that woman said." The way he gritted his teeth on the words echoed her own emotions. It was hard to picture Ruth as anything but a monster.

Kate's eyes filled with tears. "I'm so sorry, Dan. I'm so sorry."

"I know," he said. "Just like you know that it's not your fault. Or mine. Or Tilly's. Or Hannah's."

His words should have been a balm to her soul, but the

guilt she felt was so solid, so impenetrable, it couldn't be moved. She smiled weakly and headed back to the house.

————

When the call finally came, it was dark outside. Kate sat up, disoriented. She was lying in bed, alone. She remembered going to bed after Dan left. She wondered if Roman had gotten any sleep.

"Roman?"

"I'm here." He was standing in the doorway, a glass of water in his hand.

Kate flipped on the lamp and reached for the phone, her heart in her throat.

"Hello?"

"Kate. It's Dan. I'm driving out toward Socorro. They have Hannah at the hospital." Kate's heart leapt into her throat.

"We'll meet you there."

She disconnected and hurried out of bed. "Hannah's at the hospital."

"Is she okay?" Roman pulled on a sweatshirt and sat down to put on his shoes.

"He didn't say. I don't think he knows." The truth was, she hadn't asked. Fear had both prompted her to action and kept her silent. She needed time to try and come to terms with whatever news might meet them at the hospital.

A few minutes later they were on the road. Sunrise was still a few hours away, and the blackness of the landscape was nearly absolute as they sped past the place where Hannah's cell phone was found and on toward Socorro.

"Did you get some sleep?" Roman had been making attempts at small talk. Kate knew he was just as anxious as she was, but she couldn't muster the energy to talk much.

"A little bit. Did you?"

She hoped she sounded interested, though her mind was far from the car. She gripped her phone tightly, hoping Dan would call with good news—and praying it would stay silent equally hard. She wasn't even sure if Roman answered her.

"I wish I could say something that would make you feel better." Roman reached over to take her hand. "I love you."

"I love you, too," she murmured, wishing that they could suffer the ride in silence. She knew Roman would stand by her no matter what, but sometimes she felt suffocated by his affection. Usually when she was angry or upset with herself. Or guilty.

She sighed, aware of the cycle she was entering into. It was something she'd been working dutifully on breaking since reuniting with Roman. But old habits died hard.

"Sorry, Roman. We have no idea what we're about to find out. I'm scared and I'm so angry."

"With who?" Roman said quietly. They both knew the answer, and she was irritated that he felt the need to poke at her. To call her out and force her to own up to her self-destructive behavior.

"Why are you baiting me?"

"Because I've been watching you withdraw into yourself for the last few days, and I know what happens when you start beating yourself up."

"Just like you know that I'll figure it out," Kate snapped back.

"True." Roman's voice was sad. "I just wanted to remind you that we're in this together."

Given the current situation, it was hard to imagine even thinking about anything but Tilly and Hannah and hoping they were going to be all right. But Roman's words hit their mark. Kate had her insecurities and Roman had his, too. And, given Kate's tendency to push him away when she was feeling overwhelmed, it wasn't a mystery why they were suddenly having this discussion.

The temptation to retreat into her own misery was strong, but her love for Roman was stronger.

"You're right," she said, glad that she hadn't pulled her hand away from his. It was a new skill, learning to stay present in their relationship when her natural inclination was to detach from everything. To solve problems on her own.

"Dan didn't say anything about Tilly," she whispered, holding on to Roman's hand now for dear life.

The question that had been gnawing at her since she hung up the phone rang loudly in her mind. Hannah was at the hospital. Where was Tilly?

CHAPTER 19
TILLY

TILLY WOKE to the sound of raised voices and then she was yanked into a sitting position and shoved against the wall, her head bouncing off the hard concrete with an audible thud. Her body screamed in protest, taking her breath away.

"Where is she?"

It took a moment for her eyes to adjust to the early morning light coming through the window. Her captors seemed frantic. She wasn't sure who had grabbed her, but since Rick was pacing nervously near the door she assumed it was Mark. He stood closer, scanning the room as if Hannah might appear in a dark corner somewhere.

Without warning, Rick bolted across the room and was in her face, squatting just inches away from her. His face covering hid most of his features, but he was close enough that she could see his eyes. In the dim light, they looked black.

"Where the fuck is she!" His scream seemed to reverberate through her skull, and she could smell his foul breath as it was forced through the flimsy cloth covering his mouth.

"Who?"

The punch came quickly, but Tilly had been expecting it. He hit her hard on the cheek, sending her sprawling sideways on the mat. The weight of his body as he straddled her was unexpected, compressing her chest and making it nearly impossible to breathe. Frenzied blows rained down on her until Mark pulled him off of her.

"Get off of me!" Rick shouted angrily. Having his weight off of her was an instant relief, but he'd done a lot of damage during the assault.

Tilly's vision was blurry. She didn't bother trying to sit back up. If they were going to kill her, let them do it.

"Get out of here!" Mark shouted as he shoved Rick toward the door.

"I'm gonna kill her!" Rick screamed again as he retreated, leaving the door open. From the mat, Tilly could see beyond the doorway. A stairway led up to a lighted landing, and she could hear more voices coming from that direction.

There are four of them, Hannah had said. Tilly wondered if the other two men were thugs like Mark and Rick, and if whoever was in charge was just up those stairs.

Mark had moved away from where Tilly sat. He was standing by the window, looking up. There was only one way out of the room, so it wasn't a mystery how Hannah had escaped, but Mark seemed to be puzzling it out anyway. Finally he walked over to the mat and squatted down next to Tilly, taking a decidedly less aggressive stance than his partner.

"How long has she been gone?" All the malice had gone

from his voice. Now he spoke to Tilly like she was his ally, which just made her angry.

"I don't know. I passed out." Lying seemed pointless. They were either going to catch Hannah or they weren't. The fact that they were down here asking gave Tilly some small hope.

"Stupid," he muttered. "We're miles away from anything. She's going to die out there."

"Better than in here," Tilly hissed.

Mark was quiet for a moment. He seemed to be debating what he was going to say next. "We weren't going to hurt you," he said lamely.

"Right," Tilly responded. "You were just going to kidnap and rape a teenage girl and then let her go."

She closed her eyes, waiting for the blow she knew would come. Instead, she heard Mark sigh. "She wasn't supposed to be with you."

"Are you looking for sympathy?" Tilly was a little surprised at the power of her hatred and how strongly it came out in her voice. She'd just taken a beating, but none of the fight had gone out of her. She looked at where Mark was squatting and then at the open door.

Watching her, Mark said, "You can't just walk out of here."

"I wasn't planning on it." From the moment Hannah was returned to the room and Tilly had seen that look in her eyes, she'd known she wouldn't leave this place without making sure that Rick never harmed another girl again.

Mark's eyes were wide with understanding. He stood slowly, keeping Tilly in his line of sight as he backed toward the door where a new paper bag had been set. As he exited he reached down, and for a second Tilly thought he was going to take the bag with him, leaving her with nothing.

He didn't.

The door closed. The lock engaged. Tilly shut her eyes and focused on the pressure in her head and the pain of each breath until she gave in to sleep.

———

Tilly woke in a panic.

She had no idea how much time she had before they came back, but she couldn't waste another second sleeping. Struggling to her feet, stiff and aching from Rick's assault, she was grateful to find her vision had cleared.

She staggered over to the door and pulled a bottle of water out of the paper bag. Having sent Hannah with the last of their water, it had been a long time since she'd had anything to drink and she was thirsty. She drank the whole bottle, ignoring the nauseating sloshing in her stomach as she examined the rest of the contents in the bag.

"Damn," she whispered. It was surreal to see the pocket knife at the bottom of the bag. It wasn't big, but it was more than she'd had before.

A bright ray of sunshine shone through the window and onto the basement floor. Hannah had been gone for hours and now Tilly had a weapon, a tool she could use.

Hannah had escaped. That was all that mattered now.

Tilly allowed herself to think of Dan, to imagine for one moment what it might have felt like to have a family of her own. A husband. And a daughter. A daughter she would have done anything to protect. Had done everything she could to protect.

It didn't take long for her chest to constrict with grief. For a little while that dream had almost been hers, but she'd always known she wasn't meant for that kind of happiness.

From the moment Jacob Copeland entered her life, she'd known that this day would come. That she was destined to lose everything that meant anything to her. That she would die alone. Still, she sometimes allowed herself to hope.

She'd dedicated her life to helping other victims. Every conviction felt like a victory, however small. She'd even allowed herself to fall in love—twice. A miracle in its own right, given how hard it was for her to trust anyone much less form such an intimate bond.

She'd lost her mother. Her father. Her family. She's lost her first love and now her last. The daughter she'd never known she wanted. The family she'd never known she needed.

But she'd be damned if she wouldn't go down fighting.

The last person she allowed herself to think about was Kate. For so many years, she'd kept Kate at arm's length. She longed for her sister, but more than that she was grateful that they'd found each other again. Kate would be horrified by her current plan, but she would also understand. She would forgive Tilly. Hold her. Console her.

Just imagining Kate's face gave Tilly strength. She savored the feeling, let it take root and grow inside her. Then she locked that vision of Kate away and embraced the raw power of her rage.

Leaning her back against the door, Tilly extended the knife blade, pleased to find that the blade and tip were sharp. While she rested her body, her mind sifted through a dozen scenarios.

She looked up at the window, imagining what might have happened if she'd managed to escape with Hannah. But that kind of thinking wouldn't serve her, and she refocused on the task at hand.

She left the second sandwich and took the remaining water to her mat, wondering how long it would be before she ran out of time to plan. She was thankful she'd slept through the night—that she'd allowed herself more sleep after this morning—because she couldn't afford to sleep again. Not until her task was done.

CHAPTER 20
KATE

Kate and Roman arrived at the hospital a few minutes behind Dan, who was standing at the registration desk.

"I'm Daniel Bross. My daughter Hannah was brought in earlier tonight."

"Mr. Bross?" A sheriff's deputy walked over from a seat in the corner. "I'm with the Socorro County Sheriff's Office. Sheriff Brown asked me to wait out here for you." He eyed Kate and Roman suspiciously.

"They're with me," Dan said. They followed the deputy into the Emergency Department.

"How is she?" Dan asked. The strain in his voice was evident.

"The sheriff will brief you." The man's voice was formal and he looked uncomfortable. Kate wondered how long he'd been with the office, or with law enforcement in general. She didn't recognize him from the other night.

Dan's posture and stiff movements radiated the agony he

was feeling. It seemed so heartless not to tell him more—to let him know what he was about to walk into.

When the deputy didn't offer more information, Kate's impatience forced its way to the surface, "Was anyone with Hannah when she got here?"

"No ma'am," the deputy said. He didn't elaborate, but it didn't really matter. Kate's hope for Tilly deflated. Dan's footsteps faltered momentarily, like he'd hit a sticky patch of tile and almost tripped. He didn't look back at Kate—he didn't need to.

Roman took her hand and whispered, "We'll find her."

Kate hoped he was right.

———

Kate had been inside much bigger hospitals, but the department corridors were sterile and labyrinthine so she lost track of where she was. They passed a nurse's station and entered a longer hallway.

They were taken to a room at the far end of the hall. Another deputy sat beside the door, but he stood as they approached and opened the door, nodding to his colleague who turned on his heel and walked briskly away, his relief almost palpable. Kate envied him and despised him all at once.

Dan walked straight to the bed where Hannah lay sleeping. Kate, Roman, and the deputy who'd been standing guard followed him into the room. This officer was older and took charge of the room right away, closing the door behind him.

"The sheriff will be in soon, but he asked me to brief

you." When Dan didn't reply, refusing to take his gaze away from Hannah, the deputy continued. "Your daughter was picked up on the highway about 20 miles south of town by a truck driver on his way to Albuquerque. She was huddled on the side of the road. If it had been any darker, I'm not sure he would have seen her. She was barely responsive. He brought her straight to the Emergency Room."

"How can you be sure he isn't the one who took her?" Roman asked.

"His boss verified his pickup time. They have cameras at the depot, so we know he was there this morning. His alibi for the last few days is solid."

"Did she say what happened?" Dan asked quietly.

"She's been asleep most of the time. I'll send the doctor in to talk to you, but from what I gather she's mostly dehydrated and hypothermic. I'm sure they'll do more tests and imaging, but right now she's stable."

Dan nodded and the deputy left.

"Hey, sweetie," Dan said softly. He put his hand over Hannah's. "I'm here."

Kate's heart broke for Dan. Hannah's face told the story of at least one beating, and a brutal one at that. One eye was swollen shut and turning purple. There were bruises and abrasions everywhere, including a number of bruises on her neck. Kate wondered what other trauma the girl had been subjected to.

They all jumped when the door opened. A doctor and nurse walked in.

"Mr. Bross?" The doctor shook Dan's hand and introduced herself to Kate and Roman while the nurse busied himself with Hannah's IVs.

"We've given her two liters of IV fluids since she arrived, as well as a course of antibiotics. Her blood pressure was low when she arrived, but her vitals are stable now that she's got some fluids and is warming up."

"But she hasn't woken up?" Dan asked.

"She's been in and out of consciousness. No signs of concussion thus far, so I think she's just exhausted. Her injuries are minor but still look pretty bad. We haven't done much with the cuts and bruises."

Kate knew what was coming, and apparently so did Dan. His hand began to shake when he'd laid it on top of Hannah's. Kate moved over to him, putting her hand on his shoulder, hoping to give him some comfort.

"I'd like to order a rape kit, now that you're here. We'll wait until she wakes up for the majority of the exam, but the sheriff would like to document the injuries on her face and neck before we clean them up. The rest of the exam can wait a while. And we need to get her in for some x-rays." The doctor looked sympathetically at Dan. "We can start with photos for now. The nurse is waiting."

"Okay," he said, his voice barely audible.

"We'll wait in the lobby," Kate said, leading Roman into the hallway, wanting to give Dan a few minutes alone with his daughter.

"There's a waiting room for family around the corner," the nurse said, pointing the way. "It's a little more private."

"Thank you." When they arrived the room was empty, and Kate collapsed into a chair in the far corner. Roman sat down beside her. The silence stretched out for a long time. After a long while, Dan walked into the room and joined them.

"How is she?" Roman asked. Dan's eyes were red and puffy, and his voice was shaky when he answered.

"Still asleep, thankfully. As much as I want her to wake up, I hope she's at least getting some rest. She'll be waking up to a nightmare." He ran his fingers through his hair and sighed. "I stayed while the nurse took pictures and started the paperwork. The sheriff is heading this way, so I figured we should all talk to him." He gave Kate a meaningful look.

Neither of them said Tilly's name, as if by some unspoken agreement. Kate sat in silence, trying to clear her mind. It would be too easy to let panic set in. It was exhausting holding it at bay.

When the sheriff walked in a few minutes later, he was carrying a tray of coffee cups. They each took one, murmuring thanks.

"The deputy briefed us," Roman said. "What's going on with the investigation?"

The sheriff shifted his focus to Dan, whose face was becoming more pale by the moment. Roman shot Kate a concerned look, but she felt as drained as she suspected Dan did. She nodded, a signal to continue, while she rested her hand again on Dan's shoulder.

"I spoke with the doctor. Now it's just a waiting game until she wakes up. I know you've been brought up to speed, but I wanted to go over what we know so we have all the facts."

The sheriff repeated what the deputy had already shared. "We took a statement from the driver and I have the crime scene crew out there now. From what we can tell, she walked right out of the desert. We just don't know how far. But I have officers canvassing every house within a five-mile radius and I've ordered a K-9 unit. They'll be here in the morning to retrace her steps. We'll expand that if necessary."

"No sign of my sister?" Kate finally asked, knowing it would never be the right time to ask. She looked at Dan, who seemed just as interested in the answer as she was.

"No ma'am. Hannah was carrying an empty water bottle. We took it into evidence and are running it for prints." He took a seat next to Kate. "She hasn't been coherent enough to question, so we'll know more when she wakes up."

"What do we do now?" Kate hated the sound of desperation in her voice, but she couldn't mask it.

"I'll notify you if we make any headway," the sheriff replied, with a look that acknowledged how hard the statement would be to hear. She admired his compassion, though it did little to ease the waves of sadness and guilt that crashed into her.

While maintaining contact with Dan, Kate rested her head against Roman's shoulder and closed her eyes. She needed comfort as much as she wanted to give it, but she couldn't look at Dan, knowing that both his daughter and the woman he loved were in peril because of her.

CHAPTER 21
TILLY

TILLY'S MIND was beginning to play tricks on her. She'd been sitting for hours, knife clenched firmly in her hand, waiting. After a while every noise made her startle and soon, the ebb and flow of adrenaline making her sleepy. She nodded off, waking each time her head sank down to her chest.

Sometimes the knife was still in her hand. Other times, it lay on the mat beside her, having slid free of her grip while she slept. Each time, she grabbed it again, clenching her fist tightly around the handle as if it held the key to her survival.

In a half-lucid moment, Tilly swore that she saw Hannah's face in the window. She cried out, "Run!" but then the image faded. She got up to stretch, walking to the window just to be sure Hannah wasn't there, and then scolded herself for letting her imagination get away from her.

She kept telling herself she had to stay awake, stay alert, because at any moment she might have the only opportunity to take revenge on Rick. But every time she woke up with a start, she was more disoriented.

When she finally heard the door being unlocked, she was too slow to react. Mark walked in alone, bent to retrieve the bag and to give her a clean bucket, and then walked out without a word.

At that moment, Tilly realized she was going to die. Not that she had been deluding herself into thinking she'd make it out in one piece, but the inevitability of her death—the reality that she would be leaving Kate behind, leaving her life and her work behind—came crashing down on her.

She collapsed onto the mat and curled into a ball as wave upon wave of unfettered sorrow and grief came pouring out of her. She didn't care if she ever rose from this position again. In fact, she was beginning to hope the door would stay locked, that no more food and water would be forth-coming—that she would be abandoned. She could lie there and wither away with thoughts of her family, Jim, Dan, and Hannah, held close to her heart.

The knife forgotten, Tilly lay still and silent through two more visits from Mark. If he brought her food and water, she didn't look—didn't acknowledge his presence. If he had someone with him, she didn't know. All the fight had gone from her and she was left with a hollow feeling that her entire life, from the moment she was born, had been a sad waste of breath.

———

"Hey." Someone was shaking Tilly's shoulder, but she didn't bother moving or responding. She hoped the movement would stop, allowing her to slip back into sleep "Hey, wake up."

She could hear the frantic scuffle of shoes on the concrete floor near her head. A breeze drifted across her face, carrying the musty and putrid odors that she'd almost become immune to.

"Goddammit!" Someone kicked the wall. "Fuck!" She heard hopping sounds. She tried to be amused. Tried to hope that whoever was throwing such a tantrum hurt themselves in the process. The sensory input was beginning to bring her mind back to the present.

"Wake up!"

The voice was familiar.

It was Mark's.

"Leave me alone," Tilly muttered, trying her hardest to ignore the intrusion. As the hours passed, her dreams had become more gentle. Instead of being plagued by nightmarish images, her mind served up happy memories—or better, dreamlessness. She wanted to stay asleep, and she'd be damned if she was going to be dragged back into reality by this asshole.

"You need to drink some water," he said, putting a bottle near her hand. When she didn't make a move to grab it, he took her hand and tried to force her to hold the bottle.

"What the fuck?" His voice sounded desperate. She felt a tiny spark of amusement at the distress she was causing, but she smothered it, refusing to be drawn back into a game she knew she couldn't win.

"You have to drink. It's been a whole day."

Tilly couldn't decide whether to laugh or cry. Ultimately, she didn't have the energy for either.

"Why do you care?" she croaked, resenting the pain in her throat as it brought her back to reality.

"Dammit, just take the water. What is wrong with you?" He tried once again to force the bottle into her hand, then he grabbed it, ripped off the lid, and dumped the contents over her head. The cold of the liquid shocked her out of her apathy, but only for a moment.

Tilly felt a spark of anger. She'd finally resigned herself to her fate. Why couldn't Mark just let her die? True, he'd given her the knife, but did he really expect her to use it? Did she?

She honestly had no idea how much time had passed since Hannah escaped, but thirst seared her throat, and when she opened her eyes even for a moment she felt off-kilter, dizzy, and weak.

"Leave me alone," she said, this time with an edge. "I'm not getting out of here alive. We both know it. Leave me alone."

He stood up and walked out of the room, closing the door behind him. She waited for the sound of the lock, but it never came. This confused her, but she was much too tired to care. She closed her eyes and went back to sleep.

CHAPTER 22
KATE

KATE SAT in the hospital cafeteria, picking at some eggs. The antiseptic smell of hospital cleaning fluids mixed with cafeteria food brought Kate back to the final days of her father's life, when she'd spent many similar mornings pretending to be strong. The thought killed her appetite, so she'd turned her breakfast into a tool for calming her nerves. She raked her eggs back and forth like sand in a Zen garden, but the desired effect was just out of her reach.

"You need to eat," Roman said, though his own plate was barely touched. It was a reminder for them both—one that would be disregarded on each side of the table.

"I know." Kate put down her fork and took a sip of her lukewarm coffee, tepid evidence that time was passing. "Where's Dan?"

"He went back up to Hannah's room." In the early morning hours, Hannah had been transferred to a private room. She'd woken briefly—long enough to consent to the SANE exam. Dan had gotten a few moments with her, but after the exam she was exhausted. She didn't wake up during the transfer, and Dan was determined not to leave her alone. "The nurse said she'd make sure he got something to eat."

"That's good." Kate closed her eyes and tried to release the tension in her neck. She'd fallen asleep in one of the waiting room chairs, and her body was protesting. Between stress and lack of sleep, Kate knew they were all headed for trouble if they couldn't keep their strength up, but knowing that didn't make the eggs look any more appetizing.

Finally she pushed the plate away. "I can't."

Roman nodded. "I'll grab some muffins. We'll take them back up to the room."

They threw away their plates and Kate waited near the exit while Roman filled a bag with muffins and bagels. Then they made their way across the hospital and up to Hannah's floor.

Dan was dozing in an armchair, lightly snoring. Roman quietly set the bag of baked goods on the table and then took a seat beside Kate on the couch.

"Why don't you try to get a little more sleep," Kate said, offering her lap as a pillow.

"I'm good for now. I want to make a few calls. Why don't you rest. I'll go down the hall."

She nodded wearily. Roman folded up the sweatshirt he'd been wearing so she could rest her head against it. Lulled by the machines recording Hannah's vitals and Dan's snoring, it took no time at all for Kate to fall asleep.

———

Kate woke to a commotion. Bolting upright, she struggled to make sense of where she was, but Hannah's cries brought her back to her senses.

Dan sat on the edge of the bed, cradling Hannah against him. What had started as a guttural cry had become more of a prolonged wail. Hannah's face was streaked with tears, but the look of terror was something Kate knew all too well.

"She had a nightmare," Dan whispered in confirmation. He stroked Hannah's hair and cooed into her ear. Kate couldn't make out what he was saying, but the sound of his voice was clearly soothing to his daughter. Soon, she was calmer.

Hannah looked up and seemed confused to see Kate in the room. "Kate? What are you doing here?"

"Just making sure you're okay," Kate said softly. She looked at Dan, but his expression was unreadable. "How are you feeling?"

Hannah seemed puzzled by this question.

"My head hurts." She reached up and touched the swollen flesh around her eye. "Guess that explains why."

"Do you remember what happened?" Dan asked, surprising Kate. Her own instinct was to give Hannah time before asking her questions that would bring her trauma to the surface again. Still, she held her breath in anticipation.

Hannah nodded. "I wish I didn't." A few more tears slipped down her cheeks. She grabbed the remote control for her bed and moved the back up high so she could sit.

"You should probably get more rest," Kate said, feeling the now all too familiar tug between needing to know and not wanting to hear.

"No thank you," Hannah responded. "I'm not going to sleep again. Maybe ever."

Kate smiled sadly. "I know the feeling."

Hannah looked between her dad and Kate. "Last night, the nurse told me that I'd have to repeat everything to the sheriff. Can I do that now? Can you call him?"

"You sure you're ready for that?" Dan asked. It was clear from his expression that he had no desire to make Hannah rehash what had happened, even though he'd started the conversation. Kate wondered if he would be able to handle hearing it.

"Call him, please," Hannah said, agitation making her voice thin. "Can I talk to Kate alone?"

Dan nodded. He picked up his cell phone and headed out the door to make the call.

"I am so mad at Tilly," Hannah burst out as the door closed. As she said the words, her whole body began to relax. "I needed to say that out loud and I didn't think Dad needed to hear it, but I needed someone to hear it. I'm sorry it had to be you. I can't imagine how you must be feeling."

"No need to apologize," Kate said. "I've been mad at Tilly a time or two in my life."

Hannah smiled, though it looked painful. "I was such an idiot. She knew the whole time that she wasn't going to come with me. I believed her, I guess because I wanted to. If I'd thought about it, I would have realized sooner what she was planning."

"What happened, Hannah?"

"They took us to a house. I only saw the outside for a few minutes. I had to stay out of sight, but we were in a basement. There was a window, and I guess they didn't realize we could reach it. Tilly boosted me up."

Kate tried to picture it. Why would they keep them in a place that was so easy to escape from?

"It wasn't easy," Hannah said, as if reading Kate's thoughts. "We were both so thirsty. They gave us water, but it wasn't enough. Tilly looked like she was going to drop from exhaustion, and she may have had some bruises. Maybe a broken rib. It took everything she had to boost me up."

"She knew she couldn't get you both out," Kate said, understanding. Tilly had made a choice—the same choice Kate would have made under the circumstance—but it would take time for Hannah to forgive.

Hannah nodded. "After Rick raped me…"

"Rick?" Kate shuddered.

"I heard some of their names," Hannah said. She looked at Kate with concern. "Do you know him?"

"I don't know," Kate murmured. "Maybe. If it's the same person who attacked me."

Hannah covered her mouth with her hand. Kate wasn't sure if she was shocked or trying to stop herself from screaming. Kate felt a surge of raw fury sweep through her.

"Tilly had that look, too, when I told her." Hannah's voice shook.

Despite her best efforts, Kate felt the sting of tears as she saw Rick's face inches from her own, his hands wandering over her body as he told her exactly what he would do to her. At the time, his words were just a threat issued on behalf of Benny Parks, but the thought of him touching her still gave her nightmares.

And now he'd carried out his threats. On Hannah.

Kate could only imagine how Tilly must have felt hearing his name out of Hannah's mouth. If her own reaction was any indication, Tilly would have been livid.

The door opened and Dan walked in, followed by the sheriff and Roman. The three men paused, taking in the scene. Kate realized she was sitting on the edge of her seat, leaning toward Hannah, her whole body rigid. Hannah looked just as tense.

"Everything okay?" Roman asked tentatively, searching Kate's face as if trying to understand what had taken place based on her expression.

Hannah nodded and Kate sat back in her seat, trying to regain her composure. She'd tell Roman, but right now she was grateful for the interruption.

"Do you want to sit down?" Dan asked the sheriff.

"No. You all make yourselves comfortable." He walked over to the sink area and leaned against the counter. "How are you feeling, Hannah?"

"I'm fine," she replied. "I have some pain and I'm still feeling super tired, but I'll live." Her expression turned intense. "We have to find Tilly. Right now!"

"That's the plan," the sheriff said, pulling out a notebook. "Let's start from the beginning."

Hannah took them through the abduction and waking up in the basement. "Tilly was unconscious for a long time. And when they came in the first time, the short guy, Rick, kicked her really hard in the side."

"Did they tell you their names?"

"No. After they took me upstairs..." Hannah took a deep breath. "Rick beat me up and raped me, and then I passed out. I woke up a few times. I heard them talking, arguing, about me. I heard at least four men's voices, but the only ones we ever saw were Rick and Mark. They argued in front of me, that's how I knew those two."

She described them as best she could, but since both men had worn face coverings and hats she didn't have many details to share.

"I told Tilly what happened, and that's when we started planning to escape."

Hannah described the room, its meager contents, and the window. "I took two water bottles and some bread. So Tilly wouldn't have had anything left in the room with her. She'd already been giving me bigger portions. God, why didn't I see what she was doing?" Her voice became more of a mutter, directed at herself.

"You didn't see anyone as you were leaving?"

Hannah shook her head. "I looked, but the window was on the back of the house. It was small, the house. The paint was peeling from the siding and it didn't really look like anyone was living there. The desert plants were growing right up to the back wall."

"Okay, tell me about your walk."

"The sun was starting to go down when I started, and it was really dark. I walked straight away from the house. There were mountains in the distance, but it was mostly flat."

"Did you walk all night?"

"Yes, but not very fast. I fell down a few times, but I kept getting back up. I was so scared they were going to find me and take me back."

"Did you hear or see anyone, any cars?"

"No, nothing until the sky started getting a little bit light and I realized I could see a clearing in the distance. I started walking toward it and then I saw some headlights. Just a few, and there were long stretches in between them. But I ran out of water while it was still dark and was starting to feel like I couldn't walk anymore. I was afraid to fall asleep in the middle of the desert, so I walked toward the road."

"Do you remember the truck driver who stopped for you?"

Hannah made a face. "Kind of. He asked me a bunch of questions, but I couldn't really figure out how to answer. It was like my brain was really slow. I remember he picked me up, and I thought he might be taking me back to the house. I almost tried to fight, but then I thought he might take me back to Tilly."

Hannah had managed to keep herself calm up to that moment, but the mention of Tilly seemed to break her resolve. She began to weep quietly.

Dan returned to the side of her bed and let her lean against him while she cried. His expression was so anguished, Kate couldn't look at him for long without feeling suffocated by his grief.

"Roman, can I see you for a minute?" the sheriff asked, gesturing toward the door.

When they'd gone, Kate rested her head against the back of the couch and mulled over Hannah's story, imagining what might have happened to her sister when they found Hannah missing.

CHAPTER 23
TILLY

Tilly dreamed of her mother braiding her hair. As Addy's fingers worked Tilly's curly locks into a tight, perfect braid, she hummed a song.

"Was your abuela nice?" Tilly asked.

"She was." Tilly could hear the smile in her mother's voice. "I spent a lot of time at her house when I was little. She was always busy doing something. I loved when she made tortillas. Her whole house smelled like warm flour."

"I like when you make tortillas," Tilly said with a giggle. "Did your abuela serve yours with butter?"

"With honey," Addy replied. "And she used to crochet dresses for all my dolls. And slippers for the grandchildren at Christmas."

"Do you think she was happy?"

Addy's fingers paused in this task. "Sometimes. Life was hard back then, mijita. Abuela didn't get to go to school. She had to help raise her brothers and sisters. She didn't have a lot of choices—women didn't have many choices. That's why your father and I are always on you about your school work."

"Was your abuelo nice?" Tilly asked.

Addy sighed. "My abuelo was a good provider, but he wasn't always nice. Life isn't easy, Tilly. Good people sometimes do bad things. It's not black and white."

Tilly woke up wondering if her mother had actually said those things. She couldn't remember having conversations like that with her mother, but the feeling of warmth and comfort the dream left her with was familiar.

She opened her eyes and looked around her. Same mat. Same cold walls. But something was different. When she turned her head, her face pressed against the wet mat where Mark had doused her with water.

Not much time had passed.

"Yuck," she groaned, pushing herself into a sitting position. Her body resisted, stiff from lying on the mat for so long. Her throat raged with thirst.

Beside the door was the usual paper bag. Tilly got to her feet and carefully walked to it, reaching inside and grabbing a bottle of water. One of two. Enough to survive, but never enough to quench her thirst. She twisted the lid, noting how every single movement felt dull and painful.

When she took a drink the water burned her dry throat, making her wince. She took another sip and then another, until finally the burning turned to a dull ache. She felt her legs weaken with fatigue, so she sank down beside the door and drank in small bursts until the bottle was gone.

Her stomach roiled, and for a moment she thought she'd lose the water. She closed her eyes and focused on each inhale and exhale, emptying her mind of everything but the motion of air being pushed in and out of her body.

The nausea passed.

Mark had left some packages of crackers and another sandwich. Only one.

Tilly thought about Hannah and her heart ached. Given how weak and tired Tilly felt, she wondered how Hannah could have possibly made it to safety. She pictured the girl lying alone in the desert and wondered, not for the first time, if she'd made a mistake sending her away.

Two bottles of water and some bread. Not enough to sustain life in the desert. Especially given the effort it had taken Hannah to climb out that window.

The door would have been easier.

The fog of despair she'd been living under lifted, and suddenly Tilly became acutely aware that the door was unlocked. Or it could be. It was hard to think about what was real and what was just her imagination. Had Mark really walked out with locking it?

She reached up from where she sat and slowly turned the knob, surprised when it gave no resistance even though she hadn't expected it to. For a few minutes, she sat paralyzed. Had Mark forgotten to lock the door, or had he left it open for her? Was he trying to help her?

She remembered the sound of desperation in his voice as he tried to make her drink water. Maybe he was scared that if she died, he'd be held accountable for her death. Or maybe he didn't want her to die. Maybe that had never been part of the plan.

Good people sometimes do bad things. Her mother's voice echoed in her mind as she used the wall to pull herself back up to a standing position. It was harder this time. One bottle of water wasn't going to miraculously revitalize her. And yet this door might not remain unlocked.

She had to move.

CHAPTER 24
KATE

Detective Angie Lopez walked into the waiting room, followed by several uniformed officers. Roman and Kate met her at the door.

"You look better," Roman said awkwardly.

Angie laughed. "Most people look better when they're not in the hospital." She gave Kate a hug. "You both look like you need more sleep."

"I'll sleep for a week when my sister is home safe," Kate replied, far more snappishly than she'd intended. She grinned sheepishly. "Point taken."

"Where's the sheriff?" Angie asked,

"He's upstairs with Dan. Let me call him down." Roman stepped away and made the call. When the sheriff appeared, he introduced himself to Angie and the other officers.

"There's a conference room around the corner," he said, pointing. "The hospital has given us permission to use it for a while."

The whole group made their way down a side hallway to

a conference room. Everyone took a seat, while the sheriff pulled the cap off a dry erase marker and stationed himself at the white board. He drew a vertical line.

"This is I-25. We're here." He drew a dot. "We picked up Hannah here." Another dot. "According to her story, we think she might have been held here." He drew a large circle around the place where Hannah had emerged on the highway.

"How many structures are in that area?" Angie asked.

"The search area covers about eight to ten square miles. The county assessor's office has listings for eleven homes and several outbuildings, some of which have been abandoned for many years. We'll start with those and work our way out."

He passed them each a printed map of the area, a more detailed version of the sketch on the board. "Now, some of these properties are kind of off the grid. We're not sure about how well the dirt roads have been maintained. And we have to assume that the kidnappers are armed and dangerous. You can canvass the registered homeowners, but if you see signs of life at any of the abandoned properties do not approach. Right now, we're just looking for signs of life or any information that might narrow the search."

Angie turned to her officers. "Call in at every stop. The sheriff and I will set up operations here."

There was some hurried discussion as each group was assigned a search area within the larger grid.

"What can we do?" Kate asked, hoping they weren't just expecting her to sit around.

Angie took a breath. "When we find Tilly and the men who abducted her, we're going to make arrests. And maybe one of them will give us some names, help us unravel the rest of this ring. But we have to assume that they're prepared to lie to protect whoever is giving the orders."

"And?" Kate was losing patience.

"We need to connect Tilly's abduction to the investigation," Roman said, jumping in where Angie had left off. Like he was finishing her sentence. But as the words left his mouth, his expression soured.

"This move is an escalation, and it's unlike anything the group has done in the past. From what you said about your conversation with Ruth Flores, there's some kind of power struggle taking place."

Kate thought about this for a moment, and then understood. "We want me to try and get Ruth on our side?"

"Basically," Angie said. "I don't think she will. If what she said is true she's at the head of the operation, which makes her culpable. I don't see her giving herself up, and quite frankly I don't think cutting her a deal is in anyone's best interest."

"I'll go with you," Roman said quietly.

Roman was already standing when Angie interrupted. "No, I need you to get Dan up to speed on what's going on here, and then we might need you to go out and help with the search."

Roman's face turned to stone. "I'm not one of your officers, Detective. You don't give me orders. I'm not on duty here."

Kate was taken aback by the anger in his voice. The sheriff seemed confused as well. "Is there something I need to know?"

Kate wondered how Roman would answer his question.

He and Angie were staring each other down like they were preparing for a duel.

"Not at all," Roman said, his tone shifting back to neutral. "I'm happy to lend a hand with the investigation, but considering that Kate's sister has been taken I don't feel that it's either safe or wise to send her into the lion's den alone."

Angie looked ashen, but she stayed quiet. "Understood," she said, turning her attention to shuffling papers. Another look passed between Roman and the sheriff, but he didn't press the issue.

"We'd better head out," Kate said uncomfortably. Roman followed her out of the conference room and out to her car.

"I'm sorry. That was uncalled for," Roman said when they were seated.

"I'm not the one you should be apologizing to," Kate replied, then added, "But I know how you feel. It's only been two days since she was the one in the hospital. I know you're still processing a lot."

Roman looked at her, a question in his expression.

She said, "Sometimes you guys are in sync, and it makes me feel crazy. I don't know if it'll always be this uncomfortable working with Angie. I hope not." Kate sighed. "As much as I want everyone out there looking for Tilly, I feel better having you with me."

Roman smiled. He started the car and they headed back to Alamogordo.

————

Two hours later, they pulled up in front of the hacienda. Kate could hear Rusty barking frantically from the house.

"We can't both be gone all the time," she said. "After we talk to Ruth, I need to spend some time here."

During the drive home, Kate had been thinking a lot about what to say to Ruth. Did she really expect the woman to tell her anything? Roman kept Rusty out in the courtyard to play while Kate made a call.

"Hello?"

"Yes, may I speak to Ruth?" Kate had been certain that Ruth lived alone, so she was confused by the strange voice answering.

"She's resting. Can I give her a message?"

"Yes, thank you. Can you tell her that Kate Medina called? I need to speak with her and it's urgent. Any time she's available."

The person paused. "I'll give her the message, but she may not be up to visiting for a few days."

"Is she all right?"

"She had an incident yesterday."

When the woman did not elaborate, Kate pressed. "What kind of incident? Does she need to see a doctor?"

"I'm a home health nurse, ma'am." The woman was beginning to sound annoyed. "I'll have her call you when and if she can."

The call disconnected.

"Roman?" Kate called, rushing to the door. She stepped out onto the porch.

"What is it?"

"Something happened to Ruth. There's a nurse at her house."

"Did she say what happened?"

"No, she wouldn't tell me. Something about an incident." Kate's mind was racing. Ruth was an old woman. Any number of things could be wrong with her, and yet the timing seemed too coincidental.

"Should we just drive over to her house and see if we can get in?" Kate asked.

"We'll get flowers at the store," Roman said. "Just concerned friends stopping by. That shouldn't cause too much trouble."

Rusty was not happy to be left at home again, and Kate definitely felt some guilt. She grabbed her purse and they headed to the store. Half an hour later, they were standing at Ruth's door.

A woman in scrubs answered the door. "Can I help you?"

Roman answered. "We heard Ruth wasn't feeling well, so we wanted to stop by and check on her." He beamed, holding out the flowers, and Kate almost laughed at the earnest expression on his face. She hung back, hoping he'd charm his way through the door.

The nurse smiled and opened the door. "Come on in. She just woke up from a nap." She took the flowers and led them into the foyer. "Let me check and see if she's up for visitors. What are your names?"

"Roman and Kate."

When the nurse returned, she did not look happy. "She'll see you," she said, looking at Kate. Then she turned to Roman, "You can wait in the living room."

Roman chuckled, but he turned and walked to the couch, taking the seat where Ruth had been sitting just days ago. The memory felt foreboding.

As Kate followed the nurse, the woman turned and hissed, "Next time, I won't open the door."

"What's your problem?" Kate asked.

"I was clear on the phone when you called. No visitors. I don't know why Mrs. Flores agreed to see you."

"What do you think I'm going to do to her?"

The nurse turned on her heel and led Kate to the door at the end of the hall. "You can have five minutes. Then she needs to rest."

Kate stepped into Ruth's bedroom. The nurse shut the door behind her rather loudly. Ruth was sitting propped up on pillows. She looked pale, but really no worse than she had the day Kate met with her. The flowers Roman brought were in a vase on a bureau nearby.

"Give Agent Aguilar my regards," Ruth said, gesturing at the flowers. "No one knows I'm sick, so they're the first I've received. A nice touch."

"What's wrong with you?" Kate asked flatly. "Nurse Friendly out there was sure in a mood."

Ruth frowned. "She's keeping an eye on me."

"She's a nurse. I'm pretty sure that's her job."

"She's not a nurse," Ruth said, and suddenly Kate understood.

"What's going on, Ruth?" Kate walked over toward the bed, taking a seat in the chair nearby. She looked around the room for cameras or listening devices. "Are we safe to talk in here?"

Ruth laughed. "It's not a spy movie, Kate." She struggled to catch her breath. "I've had a heart condition for years. Yesterday, I had a mild heart attack."

"So, what's with her?" Kate gestured to the door.

"She was sent over by the respite agency, but I've seen her around. She's not one of my girls, but she's one of his."

"Whose?" Kate narrowed her eyes.

"Bill Gunnison," Ruth said plainly. "After all these years, he's decided he's the one running the show."

If they'd been talking about a regular business Kate might have been sympathetic, but the casual way that Ruth referred to human trafficking made her want to vomit. "Imagine that," she said sarcastically. "Two criminals vying for power."

"Sarcasm isn't really you, Kate. I much prefer the valiant warrior fighting for women's rights and the end of sex slavery in our town." Ruth's words cut Kate like a knife, but her expression didn't match the edge to her voice. She began to cough and didn't stop.

The nurse came in. "All right, that's enough. Mrs. Flores needs to rest now."

Ruth waved her hand. "I'm fine, Claudia. I just need water. Can you please bring me a glass?"

Reluctantly, the nurse left the room. She returned a minute later with a glass of water, and though she gave Kate a harsh look she left the room again, closing the door behind her.

"No doubt, Bill already knows you're here. It's good that you brought a bodyguard. That'll most likely keep him away, at least until you're gone."

Ruth's tone was completely flat, but Kate felt the threat in those words. "Can he hurt you?"

"He already has," Ruth said. "I've had a heart issue for a long time, Kate. I've been feeling worse lately. My doctor can't seem to pin it down."

"Are you saying he's doing something to make your heart condition worse?" Kate asked incredulously.

"Maybe. I doubt we'll ever know for sure." Ruth coughed again, taking a sip of water to calm down her respirations. "I have a feeling I'm not long for this world. Especially after this visit."

"You can report him," Kate said, but with Bill Gunnison as the Chief of Police, she knew that wouldn't help. She'd known that Gunnison's involvement in the trafficking ring was hindering the investigation, but the reality that he was leading the criminal activity weighed heavily. How could they ever hope to stop the abuse with the chief standing in their way?

Ruth sighed. "I expect you'll fill Roman in. Probably the State Police, too. That's one reason I agreed to talk to you."

"One reason?" Kate asked.

"I'm dying, Kate. And I'm ready. I've lived a long, hard life and I'm ready to rest."

Kate wanted to scoff, but she sensed that whatever Ruth wanted to tell her, there was only this one opportunity to hear it.

"I know what you think of me, Kate. A monster. That's what you called me. And maybe you're right. When my father's friend came to my bedroom at night, he was a monster. And my father, the way he treated my mother. I suppose I learned the hard way how the world works."

"And you justify your actions by looking back at all the abuse you've suffered." Kate's voice was hard.

"I never think of it like that," Ruth said simply. "My husband took advantage of the girls working in his office, but he never hurt them. He garnered political power by sharing his deviance with his friends, but he never saw the potential. I did what I had to do to survive, and then I found a way to live comfortably."

"On the backs of teenage girls."

Ruth sighed. "I'm not asking for forgiveness. I don't need your absolution, and I certainly don't care what you think about it. I'm not telling you this so you'll understand."

"Then why are you telling me?"

"Because times have changed. Women have more rights and opportunities. And the man who worked beside me all these years is trying to take my power." Ruth took another deep breath, as if every word wore her down.

"You can't possibly be surprised," Kate scolded.

"No," Ruth replied with a cold, predatory smile. "But I'm not going to give up my power. Not without taking him down with me."

CHAPTER 25
TILLY

As Tilly placed her hand on the doorknob with the intention to open it—to walk through it— she hesitated. Her body was weak with exhaustion. Would she be strong enough to fight? If she ran, how far could she make it?

Where was that knife?

She staggered to the mat as fast as she could, digging around the edges until her fingers slipped over the blade.

"Fuck!" A trickle of blood began to run down her hand, but she grabbed the knife handle and walked back to the door. She held the blade close to her side and slowly turned the knob until it clicked. Then she froze, listening hard for any sign of movement above.

When she finally felt confident that all was quiet, she pushed the door open. It didn't creak, for which she was thankful. She took a tentative step forward, and then another, pausing as her foot hit the first step. Nothing moved in the house above, but every step made Tilly's heart skip a beat.

The stairs creaked softly under her weight, so she took each step slowly, gingerly—pausing to listen between each movement. Her progress was painstakingly slow, and the exertion was taking its toll.

At the top of the landing was another door, but this door was ajar. Tilly fought to slow her breathing. Then she pushed the door open an inch. This time she heard some movement, but it was muffled as if coming from far away. She took a deep breath and pushed the door open in one smooth motion.

When no one jumped out at her she eased herself around the door, leading with the knife. As she cleared the door she closed it behind her, turning the knob so the door shut quietly.

Tilly heard footsteps coming toward her. She scanned the room, a rundown kitchen with no appliances. She kicked herself for assuming that someone was staying in the house. Maybe they were camping out, but there was no way this house was inhabited.

She backed into the corner, adjusting her grip.

She saw him before he saw her.

"Hey, Rick," she growled. He stopped short. His momentary pause gave Tilly a chance to study his features. He clearly hadn't been expecting to find anyone in the room. His cap and bandana were gone, and he was sporting a fat lip from where Hannah head-butted him.

He was holding a gas station fountain drink, which he dropped, splashing the liquid onto his jeans.

"Dammit!" He shook off his leg, but kept his eyes trained on Tilly. His confusion was short-lived, and his eyes reflected hatred and malice. He smirked. "What do you think you're going to do with that tiny little blade, bitch?"

Tilly checked her grip on the knife. She scanned the countertop nearby, looking for anything that might give her an advantage.

Rick laughed. "There's nothing for you to use. Nobody's lived here for years. No neighbors. It's a long way to the highway." His voice radiated confidence and his whole body relaxed, putting Tilly's nerves on edge. He took a step toward her. "You shoulda stayed downstairs. No one was going to give me a shot at you, but no one's here to save you."

The excitement on Rick's face was plain, and it was all Tilly could do to keep her body ready and her grip tight. She watched Rick move toward her, waiting for a moment to strike. Channeling all the fear and rage she could muster into her focus.

"You can scream all you want. Ain't no one to hear," Rick mocked.

Tilly froze. *No one to hear.* She realized what Rick was telling her. They were completely alone. Mark wasn't here to stop Rick, but no one was here to back him up either. She could run. If she could get past him, she could get away. A surge of strength fortified her, and she suddenly felt calm.

She smiled.

"What're you smiling at?" Rick had stopped his approach and was scowling. Despite his bravado, Tilly could see that she made him nervous. He wasn't sure how she'd gotten out of the basement, and he was wary.

Tilly stepped sideways, keeping the table between herself

and Rick. "What's the matter? Never seen a woman smile at you?"

Rick's scowl deepened with confusion. Something had shifted between them, but he didn't seem to have worked out what it was. Tilly took the opportunity to get into a better position. She took another step toward the door.

"You know there's something wrong with you," Tilly goaded. "Raping a defenseless girl."

"That bitch wasn't defenseless," he said, his anger returning. His hand traveled up to the scar near his lip.

"Right," Tilly purred. "She really roughed you up." Rick's posture had gone rigid, and Tilly sensed the growing danger. She wanted to make him angry, but she knew the situation was growing more dangerous by the minute. He might want to rape her, but she wanted him to want to kill her.

She'd nearly reached the edge of the table, and so far Rick was still standing in place. He didn't have a weapon that she could see.

All she had was this one chance. She said a silent prayer, conjuring images of Kate, Dan, Hannah—Jim, her parents—and then letting them all go, allowing all her focus to return to the task at hand.

She looked Rick in the eye, holding his gaze. His eyes were black and unfeeling. For a moment they were frozen in that space, locked in their individual positions, predator and prey. It seemed unclear who was which even to Tilly, who was single-minded in that moment.

Tilly lunged.

Shock registered in Rick's eyes, but he was fast. He threw up an arm to protect himself from Tilly's blade, but he didn't expect her knee. Using all her forward momentum, she swung her knee up into his crotch, As he buckled the knife sliced into his arm and drove hard into his now unprotected face, narrowly missing his eye.

He landed on the floor with a thud and curled up, all the while shouting obscenities at Tilly. Blood gushed from the wound to his face. He'd fallen in between her and the door, but it didn't matter. None of the wounds she'd inflicted would keep him down long—he was reacting more from shock than injury. She had to incapacitate him if she was going to make a run for it.

An old cast-iron skillet that looked like it hadn't been used in a hundred years sat on the counter near the door. Tilly grabbed it and, with all her remaining strength, brought the pan down on the side of Rick's head. The sound of the metal hitting his skull was sickening.

Rick's movements slowed, and Tilly raised her arm for another blow. She repeated her attack. All rational thought had left her, replaced by a feral rage that she couldn't contain. When Rick's body was still, she dropped the pan beside him and walked to the door.

Outside, the sun blazed bright, sending waves of heat onto the desert floor. As Tilly stepped out into the light and let her eyes adjust, her heart plummeted.

There was nothing. For miles.

The dusty landscape was covered in cacti and brush, but even the mountains seemed out of reach. A dirt driveway ran off into the distance, but there was no car.

She looked back at the house, calculating her options, and with each realization she felt despair take her. No car meant someone would be coming to join Rick, or to relieve him. How soon? She had no way of knowing.

Tilly walked back into the house and searched for supplies, coming up empty. There was still a little bit of water and half a sandwich, but not enough to keep her from dying of exposure, especially in this heat.

Any satisfaction she got from seeing Rick's form on the floor was overshadowed by the reality of her situation. She could try crossing the desert in the direction she thought Hannah went, but she was already feeling lightheaded from her altercation with Rick. And she was pretty sure she didn't have the stamina to make it far without water and rest. The sun was nearly directly overhead, so the hottest part of the day was yet to come.

And how long did she have before whoever was working with Rick returned? Maybe if it was Mark he'd just let her go, but there was no way to be sure.

And where would she go?

She pictured Hannah's prone figure lying somewhere among the bushes, baking in the sun. How could she have ever thought they'd be able to escape?

At the time, she'd been so certain that the threat of sexual assault, and maybe even death, was enough to justify trying. But when she looked out into the vast nothingness, she realized how foolhardy her plans had been. She'd most likely sent Hannah to her death by exposure. Was that really more merciful? What if their captors had been planning on letting them go?

Paralyzed by the hopelessness of her situation, Tilly sank to the porch and pulled her knees up to her chest. All the effort and she was still going to lose. She felt hot tears begin streaming down her face, and though she found the whole notion of crying at this point futile she couldn't seem to stop.

So, for the second time in as many days, Tilly Medina cried. As the hot afternoon breeze dried her tears into tacky trails on her cheeks, she leaned her head back and allowed herself to fully grieve for all that she'd lost and all the things she'd never know. Soon she rolled to her side, unable to fight the fatigue that was pulling her under.

All this effort, and she was still going to die.

CHAPTER 26
KATE

Kate was still sitting at Ruth's bedside when Roman walked in.

"We have to go," Roman said, not stopping to acknowledge Ruth where she lay. He looked worried, which put Kate on high alert. "Right now, Kate."

Ruth reached out a hand to Kate. "I guess the troops are on their way—looks like having your bodyguard here wasn't enough to keep them away. You'd better leave before they get here."

Kate looked over at Roman. He nodded.

"Here," Ruth said, putting something into Kate's hand. "Now go."

As she exited the room, Kate looked down at the object she was holding. A thumb drive.

"Shit," Roman mumbled. The nurse was nowhere to be seen, but a quick look out the front window revealed three APD police cruisers pulling up in the drive. Roman grabbed Kate's hand and pulled her to the right into the kitchen.

"Why are they here?" Kate whispered.

"The nurse called them. She was trying to be discreet, but I heard Gunnison's name. In here."

Roman had opened a door which led to a laundry room that connected to the garage.

"Are we in danger?" Kate asked, following blindly as Roman led her through the garage and out the back door. In the backyard, they slipped around the side of the house.

"We shouldn't be, but I get the feeling it would be better not to have a run-in with APD today." Across the yard was a gate leading into the alleyway, but getting there meant crossing directly behind the house and being seen by anyone inside.

"I don't think she'll tell them where we are," Kate said quietly. Roman gave her a skeptical look. "I'm serious. Maybe we can just lay low until they leave."

"What did she give you?" Roman asked. Kate showed him the thumb drive, and Roman frowned. "Yeah, we definitely don't want to get caught with that."

With his back against the wall, Roman inched along until he could see around the corner of the house. A metal gate separated them from the driveway.

"I don't see anyone outside," he said. "When I open the gate, we need to go right and see if we can get into the alley. There's a hedge running alongside the house. Maybe we can skirt along that. Just keep low."

Kate nodded and then crept through the open gate. Roman followed, closing the gate as quietly as possible, but Kate's heart still jumped at the sound. The space between the wall and the hedge was narrow. As they inched along Kate felt her back scraping against the stucco of the fence, while her arms and hands were getting scratched up on the hedge.

Her legs were starting to cramp, and they could hear the sound of voices in Ruth's yard. They moved slowly.

Finally the hedge ended, dumping them into the back alley. Roman slouched as he led them away from Ruth's property, hoping that no barking dogs would give away their location. After four houses, the alley emptied into a paved street.

Kate's legs screamed in relief when she straightened up and sprinted after Roman down the street.

———

A few blocks over, Kate and Roman found a community park with a shaded bench.

"We'll have to go back for your car," Kate said, realizing that the police had boxed in their car in Ruth's driveway.

Roman pulled out his phone. He spoke in low tones, and then disconnected. "Help is on the way."

Kate pulled the thumb drive out of her pocket. "What do you think this is?"

"I have no idea," Roman answered. "What did she say to you?'

Kate thought about Ruth's story. "She confessed."

"Are you serious?" Roman's tone was a mixture of confusion and indignation. "Confessed to what?"

"It was all her. She took her husband's side hustle and turned it into an empire." Kate described the conversation, noting Ruth's total lack of remorse. "She's a sociopath."

"So why would she give you this?" Roman asked, pointing at the drive in Kate's hand.

Kate thought for a moment. "If she can't be in charge, no one can. That's basically what she said to me." Kate looked at the tiny piece of plastic and circuits in her palm and wondered what kind of revenge a woman like Ruth could take on her enemies.

The thought was chilling.

They sat in silence until a car pulled up across the park.

"That's our ride," Roman said. Kate looked up to see Angie Lopez gesturing for them to get in. Roman took the back seat, leaving Kate up front. Angie pulled away from the curb and began driving in the opposite direction.

"Where are we going?" Kate asked.

"Up to the coffee shop. We'll circle back to grab Roman's car when the coast is clear."

"How will you know?"

Angie smiled. "We have an unmarked car parked nearby. They have a good view of everyone at Mrs. Flores' house."

Kate sat back and tried to relax. "I think we should do a welfare check after they leave."

"Why?" Angie's tone was sharp.

"What else did she tell you?" Roman was leaning forward in his seat, giving Kate his full attention. She'd filled him in on Ruth's confession, but not why she was ill.

"She thinks they're poisoning her. At least that's what she implied," Kate said. "She has some kind of chronic heart condition, but she said her health has been declining rapidly. I'm not sure if the nurse was actually a medical professional or not."

"Why do you say that?" Angie asked.

"The nurse works for Ruth's partner, which appears to be Chief Gunnison."

Roman groaned. "He's trying to get her out of the way."

Kate nodded. "Ruth gave me the rundown on how she got into the trafficking business. I wouldn't be surprised if she sped up her husband's demise—they weren't married very long before he died. I think Gunnison has been working with her for years, but it sounds like a shift in management is taking place." Kate hated how cold that statement sounded.

"We've definitely seen an escalation in violence lately," Roman said.

"Yes, and she claimed that the violence is not her doing," Kate replied. "But I don't entirely buy it. Or at least she sees the violence as an unfortunate side effect of routine business operations which, if I'm being honest, makes me want to vomit."

"On the other hand," Angie interjected, "this ring has been doing business for years. Right now the violence is leading to arrests, bringing things out into the open. It's definitely a change in direction, and if Ruth is losing control over the operation that would make sense."

"So she really might not know where they took Tilly." Kate's voice trembled. Now that she knew the full extent of Ruth's betrayal, it seemed ridiculous to think that Ruth ever could have helped her. And yet she couldn't deny that she'd been holding out some hope.

"She may not. I'm sorry, Kate," Angie replied.

"We're going to get Tilly back," Roman said, leaving no room for argument. Kate took some comfort in his confidence, but she couldn't muster her own.

CHAPTER 27
TILLY

Tilly spent a long time wallowing in her misery, until it occurred to her that no one had come. Rick was dead, and no one had shown up at the house. How long would she be alone?

Fueled by her growing thirst, she began to panic. She hoisted herself up to standing, and walked back into the house. Avoiding the pool of blood around Rick's head, Tilly ambled to the faucet. She wasn't surprised when a turn of the handle had no effect.

She searched every room, looking for the stash of water bottles that had been parceled out to them. Nothing.

Were her captors bringing it in with them?

Probably. It made sense. Out here in the middle of nowhere, amassing supplies seemed pointless.

The fatigue Tilly felt from searching the house was crippling. She stumbled back out onto the porch. The upper part of the house was beginning to swelter, making the breeze on the porch attractive. It was either that or return to the cool basement, and that wasn't really an option.

Tilly leaned against the doorframe, catching her breath. She looked out into the great expanse of desert that surrounded her. Then she walked down the steps and around the house to survey the path that Hannah had taken.

Hannah's description had been accurate. Creosote and other desert plants had grown right up to the side of the house, leaving only a narrow clearing to walk around. Spotting the basement window, Tilly looked out into the distance. A faint set of footprints was visible leading away from the house.

Tilly shook with relief and sadness. She wondered if she would ever see Hannah again. The view on this side of the house was the same. The outline of mountain ranges in the distance provided something to focus on, but not knowing where she was made it difficult to guess which mountains she was looking at.

If she tried to walk out, should she follow the trail Hannah left? Or head toward the mountains?

Either way, the task seemed insurmountable. As Tilly made her way back to the porch, she could feel herself losing strength. She sat on the steps, contemplating her options. Closing her eyes, she listened to the sounds of crickets and cicadas in the brush. Not a hint of civilization floated on the breeze.

Lying back, Tilly wondered how far she could make it. The effects of dehydration combined with the beatings she'd taken left her weak and vulnerable. Would it be wiser to take her chances with nature?

She thought about the knife. Mark had left her a weapon

—a feeble but real attempt to aid Tilly. If Mark showed up alone, could she talk him into letting her go? Though she despised him, he seemed reluctant to do her any more harm. And with Rick dead, he could just say she escaped.

For a moment, she thought she was on to something. A plan. But there were so many ways it could go wrong, placing all her faith in a man who'd abducted her. A coward who had stood by while Hannah was raped. And what if Mark wasn't the first one to arrive?

Finally, Tilly came to a decision. While she still had breath in her lungs and the ability to stand, she'd take a chance on walking out. She looked at the dirt driveway. How long could it be before it reached a bigger road?

Only one way to find out, she thought.

———

Pulling herself up to stand, Tilly walked down onto the track. The sun was still working its way up into the sky and the breeze was gentle—not the hard, fierce winds that often kicked up dirt and pollen and made the air so hard to breathe.

Tilly walked clumsily down the driveway, passing the house and entering the open desert. Without the structure to moor her she began to feel untethered, like the walls and floors of that ramshackle building had been holding her bones together.

The sun, which had seemed friendly only moments ago, began to bear down on her, evaporating what little energy she had left. Her legs wobbled and she began to shuffle, unsure about whether her feet would do her bidding if she raised them from the ground.

Each footstep left a puff of dust in its wake, until finally she couldn't continue her forward momentum and stay upright simultaneously. She froze in place, hoping to find some hidden reserve of power and determination from a well that had been dry for days.

Turning her head, she saw how little progress she'd made, and she knew in that instant that whatever fate held in store, it was tied to that house. She turned slowly and forced herself back to the porch, painful step by painful step.

As soon as she arrived she collapsed, dragging herself the remaining feet to the wall and then passing out.

CHAPTER 28
KATE

When the all-clear call came Angie pulled into Ruth's drive, parking beside Roman's car. Another car pulled up behind Angie, and a man stepped out. He had the look of a police detective, which Angie confirmed when she greeted him.

"Thanks, Chris. Kate, Roman, this is Detective Chris Montoya. He works in the Las Cruces office with me and has been getting up to speed on the investigation."

They made introductions and then stood at the ready, waiting for Angie to give instructions.

"Chris and I will check on Ruth," she said. "Would you mind calling Dan and bringing him up to speed?"

Roman and Kate moved back behind the cars, and Kate dialed Dan while Roman watched Angie and her partner approach the front door.

"Detective Lopez is asking for a status update," Kate said to Dan when he answered, her jaw clenched. Angie knocked on Ruth's door and waited.

"Nothing new, but we're waiting for the patrols to check in. About 10 minutes."

Kate's spirits reached a new low. "It looks like a dead end. Ruth doesn't know where they took Tilly, and unless Hannah remembers something specific I'm not sure what else we can do."

"They gave Hannah some pain meds, so she's asleep again. I'm glad, because she was getting more anxious." Dan sighed loudly. "I'm worried."

The statement was so loaded that Kate felt like a rock had been lobbed right at her heart. "Me, too."

What else could she say?

"Ruth Flores! " Detective Montoya's voice boomed across the way. "This is the police. Please open the door."

"I've got to go, Dan. I'll call you back." Kate disconnected and joined Roman, who had already started walking toward the front door. He paused about ten feet back and they all waited, the tension growing with every passing second. Finally, Angie nodded to Chris and he twisted the doorknob. Thankfully, the door was unlocked.

It was a slow process, entering the house. The two detectives cleared rooms one by one as Roman and Kate trailed behind. No one expected to find anyone from APD in the house, but the fact that Ruth still hadn't answered their calls had everyone on edge. Roman's hand stayed at this side, ready to draw his weapon if needed, but the house was eerily quiet.

When they finally reached Ruth's bedroom, Kate prepared herself for the worst. But when she walked into the room, Ruth appeared to be sleeping. Angie was standing beside her, holding her fingers to Ruth's neck.

"She's alive, but her pulse is weak." She turned to Chris. "Call it in."

Chris stepped away to make the call. Angie pulled a glove out of her pocket and began to search the area around Ruth's bedside table. The cup from the water she'd asked for during Kate's visit was empty.

"You should test the glass," Kate said. "She thought she was being poisoned. Maybe there will be traces in the cup. It was full when I was here earlier."

Angie nodded, then opened the drawer in the table. She pulled several prescription drug bottles out and set them on top of the table. "Blood pressure. Cholesterol." She shook a bottle. "Sleeping pills. The bottle is almost empty."

"Check the date," Roman said. Angie scowled, but she kept what she was feeling to herself.

"Filled a week ago. Thirty pills, so I imagine we'll find those in her system."

"The ambulance is on its way," Chris said, returning to the room. They could hear the sirens in the distance.

Kate sat beside Ruth's bed and took the old woman's hand. As disgusted as Kate felt, she also felt a deep sadness and disappointment. She'd wanted Ruth to be held accountable for her unimaginable crimes, but the idea of poisoning someone didn't sit well with her. The contrast was nauseating, and all Kate could do was sit and breathe while they waited.

A few minutes later, the paramedics came in with a gurney. Kate watched, half-dazed, as Ruth was carried away. She felt heavy and dull as her hand slipped away from Ruth's.

She heard Angie talking—explaining the situation and

giving orders—but everything happening around her seemed distant. She felt someone's hand on her arm, and while she assumed it was Roman's she couldn't make herself focus enough to look.

Her vision started to cloud, dark spots pressing in around the edges.

"Kate?"

She heard her name on the wind, but it was muffled, far away. Somewhere else. Maybe with Tilly.

Tilly.

Her sister's face came to mind as the darkness spread and she lost consciousness.

———

Kate awoke with a jerk. Her limbs felt like they weighed a ton or were pinned to the floor. She thought about shifting her head, but couldn't manage it.

"Kate?"

She tried to open her eyes.

"There you go. Come on, look at me, Kate."

It was Angie's voice, which was confusing. Kate began to panic. Why was Angie in her bedroom? Why couldn't she move?

Her palm was touching something rough. She curled her fingers, noting that the tips and then her knuckles scraped against a surface that was both soft and scratchy at the same time.

Carpet.

Kate turned her head, glad that her muscles seemed to be

under her control again. She saw the legs of a bedframe and shoes. She was on the floor. Why?

It came back to her in bits.

"What happened?" she mumbled, noticing how slurred her words felt.

"You're going to be okay." This time it was Roman's voice. She turned her head to the other side. The movement made the room look strange—skewed, almost like looking into a funhouse mirror. She blinked several times, trying to make sense of it all. Roman knelt beside her and Angie was at his side.

The detective's face was absolutely pale. "Are you okay?" Kate asked. Her voice was still quiet, but the words came more easily this time.

Angie smiled wearily. "Funny you should ask. How do you feel?"

Kate sighed. "Tired." She paused. "Did I pass out?"

"I wish," Angie said. "Drugged, I think. I suspect there was fentanyl on something you touched. Probably Ruth's hand, since touching her neck didn't affect me. You went down pretty fast, but I carry Narcan and the paramedics are still here so we got you dosed up right away."

"Fentanyl?"

"It can be used for pain management, but I've looked through Ruth's medicine stashes and I don't see any sign of it. We'll take blood when we get you to the hospital."

"Did anyone else?"

"No," Roman interjected. "After taking Ruth's pulse, Angie had her gloves on and when we saw you start to wobble, everyone gloved up. Unfortunately fentanyl is a big problem on the streets right now, so there's a protocol for suspected exposure."

Kate followed along, realizing she had read about fentanyl addiction recently. The information they were sharing was starting to trigger more memories, but it was painfully slow. She was confused, but also strangely calm and content. It was hard to hold on to her thoughts.

"We need to get you to the hospital," Roman said, taking Kate's hand. His were covered in gloves.

"Is it dangerous to touch me?" Kate shuddered at the idea that simply being near her could put his health in jeopardy.

"No," Roman said gently. He smiled. "But we need to get you checked out. And since we can't be 100% sure where you made contact with the drug—or if that's even what happened, though the fact that you're awake now is proof enough for me—we're just being extra careful until we can get you cleaned up."

Kate struggled to sit up and Roman put an arm under her to help. "Let me help you up. You may be dizzy for a while."

"Not dizzy, but everything looks too bright and the edges are sharp. But moving. That doesn't make sense does it?" She groaned.

Roman lifted her to standing, and Angie held her other arm to steady her. They walked her to Roman's car.

"I'll be right behind you," Angie said. She closed Kate's door and headed back into Ruth's house.

"How long was I out?" Kate asked when Roman slid into the driver's seat.

"A few minutes. It doesn't take long for the antidote to take effect."

"Makes it sound like I was poisoned."

"You were," Roman said, and when she looked at him she could see the strain in his expression. "Fentanyl can kill you. That's why we carry Narcan. You don't have to inhale it or ingest it. Skin exposure is enough. If that had happened earlier while you were in with Ruth, I'm not sure what would have happened."

"She would have called out to you," Kate said, but even as she spoke the words she wasn't sure if she believed them. Now that she knew the truth, Ruth didn't seem like the type of woman who would save anyone but herself.

And yet she'd handed Kate the thumb drive. Kate's hand moved toward her pocket, but she stopped short. Ruth needed Kate to exact revenge on her enemies. She might have intervened if Kate had been poisoned, but only to suit her own plans.

Kate returned her hand to her lap, trying not to touch anything.

"Your car will have to be scrubbed down."

It seemed like such a simple task compared to the insurmountable work that lay ahead. Tilly was still missing. Ruth may very well be dying. And Kate had nearly been killed. Kate had been scared before; worried, anxious. Now she was utterly terrified.

CHAPTER 29
TILLY

Tilly drifted in and out of consciousness as the hours passed. Though the porch shielded her from some of the sun's rays, any exposed flesh began to look red. By the time the sun was high overhead, there wasn't a single spot on Tilly's body that didn't cry out in pain when she moved. Even breathing was agony.

As her dehydration got worse, Tilly started seeing things in the desert. First, she saw coyotes and snakes and things you might actually see, but soon the visions turned fantastical.

Tilly saw her mother and father walking down the road toward her. Hand in hand, they appeared out of nowhere and their somewhat translucent shapes shifted in and out of focus, never coming any nearer. Her heart ached, and she convulsed with sobs that were dry.

She thought about death. About how her grandmother had reached out for her grandfather in the hours before she passed away. Tilly wondered if her mother and father had come to take her home.

The desert stretched out for miles in every direction—the dirt driveway the only sign that human life ever entered the area. Occasionally, Tilly caught sight of a jackrabbit scurrying from one bush to another. She imagined cozy burrows underneath the creosotes where baby rabbits took refuge until they were ready to enter the unforgiving landscape.

As a child, Tilly had loved seeing the rabbits at the county fair. She'd often begged her mother for a pet rabbit, one she could raise and show. A big, floppy-eared rabbit that would win blue ribbons.

Blue ribbons like the sky.

Tilly shook her head. Her thoughts were all jumbled, a mix of memories, hallucinations—maybe wishful thinking. As soon as she refocused on the desert, her mind began to wander again.

She remembered a morning a few years ago, before she'd moved away from Colorado Springs. After a long night at the hospital, she woke up in a sun-filled room to the smell of coffee. Or maybe it was rainy. The details didn't really matter, did they?

Jim handed her a cup of coffee. "Wake up, sweetie."

She blinked a few times, The image flickered and faded. Jim was smiling. He reached for her cheek. Then his hand turned to dust.

Was she dreaming? It was so hard to tell.

Wind kicked up the dirt, sending it flying over the porch where she sat, coating her already-parched lips with a layer of grit.

She was going to die here, right on this porch. With

Rick's dead body only a few feet away. Would Kate ever know what happened to her? If Mark found her here, dead, would he bury her? Or would he leave her there, on the porch to be scavenged?

The thought was less chilling than Tilly thought it should have been. With her body shutting down, she couldn't muster much feeling. She closed her eyes, hoping she'd fall asleep and fade away.

———

When she woke again the sun had moved, leaving her in shadow. The malaise that had fallen over her was also gone. She woke up in a complete panic. With the little energy she could muster she pushed her hands against the dusty boards, becoming more agitated every time her fingers slipped and she failed to gain purchase.

"Aghhh!" she screamed, the effort burning her throat but producing little sound. "Why? What did I do to deserve this shit life!" She was filled with rage and, lacking the energy to stand, or run, or fight, she thrashed around, waging a battle of will with herself.

Her mind was crystal clear. No hallucinations. No delusion. Just the cold realization that she deserved a better outcome. That she wanted a better outcome. A future. A life. The one she'd been refusing to live for nearly thirty years.

It had come to her in an instant, like an arrow shot directly into her brain. And it was Hannah, and Dan, and Kate—their faces in her mind. The idea that with all that love, with their support and care, she'd seen a glimmer of what life could be like. Of the life she could have.

And she was angry with every fiber of her being that that chance was being stripped away from her. Like every other good thing in her life–her family, her relationship with Jim, her childhood. Raw fury pulsed through her body, seeking release.

"Why?" she screamed again. Croaked. Over and over until her voice was barely a gravelly wisp of air over her raw vocal cords. Finally she closed her mouth, receding into her thoughts.

Please. Please let me go home, she pleaded silently.

She'd reached the point where she was so physically and psychologically drained that all she could do was wait, and sleep.

CHAPTER 30
KATE

THE AFTER-EFFECTS of being drugged kept Kate subdued physically, but that only made her anxiety worse. The feelings of euphoria were long gone and her mind was in full downward spiral, even if her body couldn't keep up. She pulled the blanket up to her chin, but she still felt the chill of the hospital room.

"When can we go?"

Roman had been dozing in the chair beside her, and she felt a twinge of guilt at waking him up. Again. With the same question she'd been asking for the past few hours.

"Hopefully soon." Roman sounded tired. "At least they agreed not to keep you overnight."

"Yeah." Kate sighed. She was so tired, but she knew that she needed to be where the investigation was. She wanted to be nearby if they found Tilly. "Maybe you should head back over to Socorro."

"If something changes, they'll call me." Roman took Kate's hand. "You could have died, Kate. I know it's got to be hell for you, just sitting here, but I'm not leaving your side. Ever."

Kate smiled and squeezed his hand. "Thank you." She took a breath and tried to calm her nerves. She was on her second breath when Roman's phone started buzzing, putting her back on high alert.

"Yeah." He spoke only a few words, but his expression darkened. When he disconnected, Kate tried to prepare for bad news as best she could.

"Ruth is dead," he said solemnly. It was not the news she was expecting. Such a mix of emotions overwhelmed her, bringing tears to her eyes. She suffered in silence as her thoughts and feelings spiraled out of control.

"That's not justice." Kate sighed. "It makes me angry how easily she left this world, when she's caused so much grief to so many."

"I agree," Roman replied. "But she was never going to face justice the way things were going. As brutal as it sounds, whoever killed her did us a favor. Ruth wanted revenge, so she gave us the tools we need to finish the job we've been doing."

Kate perked up. "What was on the drive?" She had a vague memory of handing the thumb drive over to Roman after reaching the hospital.

"Videos." The look on Roman's face told her just how bad the contents were. Kate was well-versed in things you couldn't unsee. She reached out to give his hand another squeeze.

"I'm sorry you had to watch."

"I'm glad you didn't," he said. "It's with the State Police

now and it looks like there's enough detail to identify everyone involved, victims and perpetrators alike."

Kate shuddered. "I hope there aren't copies."

"I'm sure there are," Roman said with a grimace. "Given how calculating Ruth was, I imagine she made sure there were backups. Angie got a search warrant for her home and office, so hopefully we'll be able to find them."

The idea of video footage featuring underage girls being raped was enough to turn Kate's stomach. She prayed that what Ruth said was ultimately true, that her intention wasn't to harm the girls. It was an equivocation, given that these girls had been injured—in some cases even killed—all under her watch.

But on some level, Kate didn't think Ruth would be foolish enough to use the videos unless there was something to gain. Her longevity in the organization had been based on discretion and stealth. Making those videos public added a whole level of complexity that Kate wasn't sure Ruth would have seen as good business.

"Ruth mentioned the chief by name. I wonder if he'll be in those videos."

Roman sighed. "I hope so, but I've known him for a long time. He's an asshole, but he's smart."

"I guess we'll just have to wait and see."

The nurse walked in with a stack of papers. "Looks like you're good to go," she said, handing Kate a clipboard. "I need you to sign this one. And then make sure you follow all the discharge instructions. Stay hydrated, and if you start feeling any new symptoms come back in immediately."

Kate agreed. A few minutes later, she was dressed and following Roman to his car. Still under a cloud of fatigue,

Kate prayed that she would be back up to speed sooner rather than later. The case was cracking wide open, and with Tilly still missing she worried what her sister's abductors would do if the situation became really desperate.

————

The hospital conference room was overflowing with people. Kate and Roman had returned to Socorro during a shift change. Worn and deflated, the first search teams were ready to call it a night, handing over notes and debriefing the relief teams.

The two State Police detectives, Angie and Chris, were directing traffic. Dan checked in when they all arrived, but retreated to Hannah's room when it was clear there was no news. After a while, the glaring fluorescent lights and noise of all the chatter was too much for Kate. She excused herself, smiling thinly at Roman's concerned expression, and made her way upstairs.

She knocked lightly on Hannah's door and then entered.

Dan was sitting in the armchair with his eyes closed. Hannah slept peacefully in her bed. Kate started to back out, when Dan said quietly, "It's okay. I'm awake."

He stood and ushered Kate out into the hallway. They walked down to the small waiting room that served as a quiet space for the families of patients on the floor.

Helping himself to some coffee, Dan joined Kate on the couch in the corner. The softer lighting and comfortable furniture made it hard for Kate to stay awake.

"What happened?" Dan asked.

Kate rubbed her temples. "Ruth Flores is dead. They

almost managed to kill me, too." Roman had filled Dan in on their hospital visit in broad strokes. "We got a big lead on the trafficking ring, but nothing on Tilly."

When Kate peeked at Dan's face, she wasn't surprised that it was blank. And while she knew how that felt—emptiness in the face of trauma—she felt uneasy. She waited for him to comment, but when it was clear he wasn't going to talk she jumped back in.

"What's on your mind, Dan?" Hoping to jog him out of whatever stupor he'd fallen into, she threw the question out as casually as possible.

The silence that followed was full of tension. Kate's heart began to pound in her chest despite her weakened condition. The numbness of the fentanyl was gone, leaving her vulnerable to a panic attack. She tried to slow her breathing.

"I don't know if I'm strong enough to do this," Dan finally said. He didn't have to elaborate. He had already borne witness to Tilly's reckless behavior—her penchant for diving head-first into danger with little regard for her own safety. And though this situation was most certainly not Tilly's fault, Dan and Hannah had already been through so much.

Dan looked up at Kate, tears glistening in his eyes. "The cases that come across my desk every day are enough to make me want to lock Hannah in her room forever." He smiled, but his eyes were sad. "Even when my wife got sick, I felt like we were lucky. Like the trouble we dealt with was normal." He shook his head. "What a stupid way to look at things."

"Not at all," Kate said, patting his arm. "My life hasn't been easy, but until my dad died and Tilly came back into my life I'd been operating under the totally false notion that my life had been normal. Even after the attack when I worked at the prison, I felt like I was coming home to normal."

Dan leaned his head against the wall. "Last year, when Tilly…" His voice cracked, but Kate knew what he was referring to. Before they'd really even known each other Tilly had landed herself in danger, using herself as bait in the case of a serial rapist. Dan's tenacity and desire for justice had put him in the right place at the right time. He'd saved Tilly's life, and through grief their relationship had grown.

"She was in a bad place," Kate interjected. "Honestly, when Jim died, I saw her starting to self-destruct."

"But that's just it," Dan cut in. "I saw that, too, but her drive mirrored my own. It was the first time I'd met someone who was as determined as me. She did things I couldn't do, and I admired her. Maybe even envied her."

Kate laughed. "Tilly's always had that fire."

"I didn't think twice," Dan's voice had grown quiet. "I knew she was the person I wanted to spend the rest of my life with. And given everything Hannah and I had been through, that's saying a lot. But then I saw Hannah on that gurney."

Kate felt her eyes begin to tear up. It was one of her worst nightmares, one that had tugged at the edges of her relationship with Roman. The idea that no matter how much you loved someone, it might not be enough.

In that moment, watching Dan teeter on the edge, she finally understood something that had been eluding her all her adult life.

"Here's the thing, Dan." She sat up straighter, letting the

swell of emotion fuel her words. "I've been fighting against being happy my whole life. I didn't see it. And when Roman and I reconnected, I had one foot out the door. Right up until this moment, when it finally dawned on me that we don't get to choose what makes us happy. And we can't control life. We can make decisions, hope for the best, but we can't avoid trouble. Or pain. Or death."

Tears were streaming down Dan's face, but Kate had to finish. She owed it to her sister. "Life with Tilly is never going to be easy," she said, trying not to wonder if Tilly was even still alive. "You've seen how trauma affects people. Families. She's going to be working on herself forever, and she's probably going to try and sabotage her happiness at every turn, because that's what we do when we're scared. When we're vulnerable."

Dan nodded, his head hanging down. "I know." He looked up. "If she doesn't make it…"

It was Kate's turn to let the tears fall. "If she doesn't make it, yours won't be the only heart that's broken."

"I'm sorry, Kate. It was awful of me to lay this on you."

Kate smiled through her tears. "Actually, I'm kind of glad you did. It really made me see how lucky I am. I've been feeling guilty for putting Tilly in this situation." Dan made an attempt at protest, but Kate held up a hand to stop him. "I know the drill. It's the bad guys, not us. But you know how hard it is to believe that, right? And I'm sorry that Hannah got dragged into it, and that her life is going to be different than it might have been."

Dan grimaced.

"But it doesn't have to be bad, Dan. When Tilly was raped, she had no one to believe her. To help her. When I was raped, I hid from the truth. Tried to avoid it so it would go away. Hannah's got a whole army around her, ready to help her through this. She'll be okay."

"I will." Hannah's voice drifted into the room from the doorway where she stood. She walked over to Dan and sat beside him. "I'll be okay, Dad. And Tilly fought so hard for me. She risked everything for me. So we have to be here for her, too."

Kate wondered how much Hannah had overheard, but she was so humbled by the warmth and love radiating from this beautiful girl. She reached over to take Hannah's hand and the three of them sat together, enjoying a peaceful moment of being together.

CHAPTER 31
TILLY

"Hᴇʏ!"

Tilly felt a stab of pain in her side where someone's boot was connecting with her already bruised, probably broken, ribs.

"Hey! Wake up." The kicks were becoming more insistent. And more painful. A searing-hot pain shot up her side. She opened her eyes and was surprised to be looking out into the desert. It was near sunset and she had to blink to focus in the dim light.

She looked up at her attacker. Mark. His face was uncovered and he wore a panicked expression.

"What the fuck happened?" he asked, peering over his shoulder.

Tilly took her time getting into a sitting position. She leaned her aching body against the side of the house, wincing as every moment brought a new level of pain and discomfort. Her vision swam as she settled into being upright. Her lips were dry and cracked, and her skin felt gritty.

"You have to get out of here," Mark pleaded. "You killed Rick and they're going to be here in a few minutes. If you don't get out of here, they're going to kill you."

"What if they do?" Tilly asked coldly. "You're the one who brought me here in the first place."

Mark paced in front of her, nervously running his hand through his hair. "Fuck!"

She watched him without much interest. Her body was racked with dehydration and exposure, making it nearly impossible to keep herself upright. If she tried to run now, she would fall two steps into the desert and be hauled right back down to her basement dungeon.

What difference did any of it make? Mark had given her a knife. She'd managed to kill Rick. But she never had a chance at escaping. Not really.

"Listen, maybe if you go back downstairs…"

"What?" she asked, unable to hide the mocking tone in her voice. "They'll think Rick accidentally bashed his brains in? Or that you did it? What could possibly happen to me if I just stay here that won't happen downstairs. Besides, I can't move."

"Shit!" Mark kicked one of the posts holding up the porch, which creaked unhappily. She could see sweat on his face. "I didn't sign up for this," he muttered.

Tilly laughed. "Oh, I see. You thought you'd kidnap two women—one of whom is a teenage girl—and then let us go, right? Y'all would get what you wanted and then we'd all just stroll away like nothing ever happened?"

It was remarkable how completely clueless this man was.

She thought about the trafficking ring and how many of those men really didn't have a grasp on the repercussions of their actions. That was the problem. People never thought about the consequences until it was too late.

She wasn't immune.

As a teenager, there had been moments when Tilly wished she was dead. That she had never been born. As an adult, she'd buried herself so deep in work that she didn't have time to care about what happened to her. It was only now—when her death was an inevitability—that she understood wanting to live, desperately.

The irony was suffocating.

And bearing witness to all this violence, knowing that people like Mark were aiding and participating, all the while thinking that they were somehow not accountable for the terrible things that happened under their watch made her question everything.

What was the point of living through this situation, knowing that the cycle would continue, no matter how hard she, or Kate, or anyone else worked against it?

Mark had stopped pacing and was standing with his forehead pressed against the post. Suddenly, he straightened. "Oh fuck!"

In the distance, headlights signaled the approach of a vehicle. Mark ran out into the drive, frantic. Tilly wondered what his colleagues would do to him. For letting her escape. For what happened to Rick. She felt a certain satisfaction in the idea of vengeance. She wondered if the same thought was occurring to Mark. He looked like a man sentenced to death.

Mark hesitated in the driveway, but only for a moment.

Then he turned and ran, not toward his car but straight into the desert. In the fading light, he was gone from sight in a manner of seconds. Tilly watched in disbelief as the headlights grew brighter. Whoever was driving was taking their time on the bumpy road, as if they'd never been this way before. Confusion took over.

The incoming vehicle pulled to a stop, leaving the headlights shining brightly on the area in front of it, making it hard for Tilly to make out any details.

Both the driver's-side and passenger door opened and two people stood, but kept themselves behind the open doors. "Police!"

"Help!" Tilly croaked from her position on the porch. A flashlight beam appeared near her and then shone into her eyes. She threw up a hand to shield them.

"Ms. Medina?" a woman's voice projected from the passenger side of the car.

"Yes!" Tilly said as loudly as she could, feeling breathless from the effort. She gathered her strength and shouted, "There's only one guy! He ran into the desert!" She pointed in the direction Mark had gone.

The driver reached in and turned off the headlights, allowing Tilly a better look. It was a State Police car. The female officer holstered her weapon and made her way over to Tilly, while the driver—a tall, wiry male—covered her.

"There's no one inside?" she asked.

"The other man is dead. I killed him." Tilly gestured to the door. "Mark said he's dead."

The officer walked over to the door, drawing her weapon. She peered around the threshold and then made her way into the house with her gun at her side. A moment later, she was back.

"Amos, call it in. We have two men: one deceased in the house, and the runner. We'll need backup to pursue. We need an ambulance now."

The officer knelt next to Tilly. "Are you okay?"

Tilly smiled. "Not even remotely," she whispered. "But I'm glad you're here. I'm not going to make it much longer." She'd begun to shake, from cold or from shock it was hard to say.

"My name is Linda," the officer said. "I'm going to go get you a blanket and some water while we wait for the ambulance."

Tilly nodded. She leaned her head against the wall and was asleep before the officer returned.

It was a long time before they drove away from the house.

Officer Linda Becker explained that their location was nearly thirty miles away from the hospital. She'd shaken Tilly awake numerous times, forcing her to take sips, though much of the water she offered dribbled down Tilly's front, creating a muddy riverbed on her shirt. She'd answered Tilly's questions, but once she told Tilly that Hannah had made it to safety Tilly had stopped listening entirely. The blanket and water couldn't come close to the comfort that news provided her.

Backup arrived, but the darkness complicated the situation. It would be dangerous to pursue Mark on foot, so there was a lot of movement as more backup was called in. Tilly thought she heard something about air support, but she couldn't keep her mind focused on any one thing. Her thoughts were slippery.

When the ambulance finally arrived, a quick assessment confirmed what Tilly already knew—severe dehydration, hypothermia, and the possibility of a few broken ribs. In the back of the ambulance, they piled warming blankets on her and started an IV.

As she was transported to the hospital, she surrendered to fatigue. Whatever happened now, Dan would have his daughter. Kate and Roman had each other. Everything was as it should be.

CHAPTER 32
KATE

TAKING time for only a small layover at her house to change clothes, Kate and Roman returned to the hospital in Socorro.

Kate wanted to sleep, but every time she closed her eyes visions of Tilly's face filled every corner of her mind—sometimes gray and cold, sometimes bloodied and bruised, but always anguished. Each time she nodded off, she jerked herself awake again.

Roman was still downstairs with the other law enforcement officers. Dan had taken Hannah back to her room. All was quiet in the waiting area, and a nurse had come by to offer Kate a blanket. She wanted to sleep so badly, but she couldn't.

After her talk with Dan, Kate realized how close they all were to giving up on finding her sister alive—maybe at all. Would she have been punished for helping Hannah escape? She'd seen what this organization would do to cover its tracks. Kate wanted to get Tilly back, but couldn't help worrying about the condition she'd be in.

"Ms. Medina?" A young nurse peeked around the doorway before walking into the room. "Can I grab your vitals?"

"I'm sorry, what?" Kate's mind was still moving slowly. She must have looked completely confused, because the nurse smiled as she pulled a cart over to where Kate was sitting.

"Your fiancé told us about the fentanyl exposure. I just wanted to make sure you're doing okay."

Kate laughed. "Sounds about right. He's not even here but he's checking in on me."

"Men," the woman said conspiratorially. She finished her assessment quickly, and then packed up the cart. "Your oxygen sat looks good. My name's Gail. If you need anything let me know. I'll be on shift all night."

"Sounds grueling."

"It's not bad," Gail said. "You get used to it. And getting good patient outcomes outweighs a lot of the bad."

"You sound just like my sister," Kate said, unsurprised when a tear slid down her face. "She's been a nurse for more than twenty years and she loves it."

Gail walked back over and took a seat beside Kate. "I've heard a little bit about what's going on. People talk and it's a small hospital really. From what I understand, your sister saved the girl in 409. And from the way she looks, I'm guessing that wasn't an easy task. I hope she makes it back safely."

Kate took Gail's hand and squeezed it. "Thank you. I was starting to feel a little bit hopeless. I need to remember that Tilly is strong and brave. She'll figure out how to live through this."

Gail smiled again and then made her way back to the nurse's station. Kate laid her head down on the arm of the couch, pulled the blanket to her chin and closed her eyes, seeking rest for her weary soul.

———

Kate woke with her head on Roman's lap. She didn't remember him coming in.

"Hey," he said gently. "Looks like you finally got a nap."

"What about you?" Kate said as she sat up, rubbing sleep from her eyes. "What time is it?"

"Around midnight. I came up a few hours ago and got a little bit of sleep, too."

"And Angie?"

Roman sighed. "Couldn't talk her into taking a break, but she looks rough. I can't believe she's working right now, having been in the hospital two days ago." He paused. "Hell, I can't believe you're lounging here instead of in a hospital room in Alamogordo." His tone was playful, but she knew just how worried he was.

"The nurse you sicced on me says I'm on the mend. She was very sweet. I'm thankful that the exposure wasn't worse. I've read all the articles about fentanyl overdoses in schools. Nasty stuff." Kate stretched. "I feel bone-tired—the worst fatigue I've ever had. But otherwise not too bad."

Silence filled the space between them.

"How long can this go on?" Kate let the question hang in the air. There wasn't an answer, and she didn't expect one.

Dan walked into the room and made his way over.

"When the doctor did rounds earlier, he said Hannah should be good to go home tomorrow."

"That's great," Kate said, though the idea of Dan leaving made her uneasy. "It's a lot easier to sleep in your own bed."

"She's still restless when she sleeps, but her spirits are high when she's awake." Dan sounded like a normal father describing a sick child, but they all knew the road ahead of Hannah would be long. Especially emotionally. Kate remembered the first year after her assault. She'd barely left the house, and that was after running home to live with her dad.

"I'm sure you've got contacts in Las Cruces, but if you need help finding a therapist for her let me know," Kate offered.

"Will you stay here?" Dan asked, not making eye contact. It seemed to be tearing him up, thinking about leaving.

"I'm staying," Roman said. "And I wouldn't dare suggest that Kate leave—not that I don't think she needs to rest, too."

Kate smiled. "Yeah, I'm not moving until we get some news."

Roman and Kate's phones pinged, with Dan's following a few seconds later. For a second, they all froze. Then Kate looked at her phone. Her breath caught in her chest as she whispered, "They found her."

CHAPTER 33
TILLY

For some indeterminable amount of time, Tilly drifted in and out of consciousness. She didn't remember much of the ambulance, and felt a twinge of surprise when she heard the familiar beeping sounds of a hospital room, not having any memory of how she got there.

Every time she awoke, the blankets on her bed were warm. The IV pushed a steady stream of hydration into her body. She felt peaceful. In her lucid moments, she longed to return to the warm, soothing oblivion of sleep.

When her periods of wakefulness began to gain mass, she realized she wasn't alone in the room. Her body seized up in fear, suddenly afraid she was back in the basement even though she could see that she wasn't. The visceral response only abated when she recognized her sister's face.

"Kate." Her voice was just a breath. Her throat felt raw, and the effort it took to speak that one word was exhausting.

Kate scooted her chair closer to Tilly's bed. Tilly heard the crunch and slush of crushed ice, which Kate spooned into her mouth. The ice temporarily numbed her throat, making it easier to breathe.

Kate's relief was practically palpable. "Do you want me to get the nurse?"

Tilly shook her head the tiniest bit. There was so much to say, but she couldn't muster the energy. As the silence grew, Kate's expression became worried.

"Just need sleep," Tilly managed. Seeing her sister beside her completed her feeling of safety. The ordeal was over. Kate would watch over her until she was stronger. She smiled at Kate, and then allowed herself to let go of her lucidity and slide back into the warmth and comfort of sleep.

———

The next time she woke, a nurse was changing her IV and taking vitals. "Nice to see you alert," she said, smiling. "There are going to be a lot of happy faces."

The nurse used the remote control to move Tilly's bed into a more upright position. The cannula pumping oxygen into her nose pulled against her cheek, causing some discomfort. The nurse held a cup of water to Tilly's lips.

"Let's start with a few sips. The doctor wants to get you drinking. We'll tackle food a little later."

Tilly's stomach growled loudly, causing the nurse to laugh. "Or maybe sooner."

As the liquid calmed the scratchiness in her throat, Tilly tried out her voice. "Where's Kate?" She was pleased that she managed to project more, though it left her feeling breathless.

"She's in the cafeteria. I pretty much had to throw her out

of here, but luckily her friends took over. I don't think she's eaten much since she got here last night, and she's still pretty weak."

"Why?" Tilly hadn't noticed anything wrong with Kate earlier, but she'd been pretty out of it.

The nurse seemed to realize that she'd overstepped. "They'll be back soon. Let's order you some lunch, probably soup until we see how it's going to settle. Are you in any pain?"

"Not really. Just achy."

"That's good. You've got a good number of abrasions and a broken rib, but the dehydration and hypothermia were pretty serious. You may start feeling the rib as you move more, and it'll make breathing a little bit tricky for a while. When you need to use the bathroom, have your sister help you. Or give me a call if she's not here."

Tilly took a breath and sighed, paying attention to the pain and stiffness in her chest. It wasn't bad, but she wasn't looking forward to getting out of bed.

The nurse pulled the mobile table over Tilly's bed. "Food will be here in about fifteen minutes. My name is Karen. I'll be back in a bit to check on you."

As Karen exited the room, Kate walked in with Roman on her heels. Kate sped up when she saw that Tilly was awake. "Damn, I wanted to be here when you woke up!"

Tilly smiled. "You only missed the big event by about five minutes." She took another few sips of water before continuing. "Hi, Roman."

Roman smiled. "How are you feeling?"

"Like I got hit by a truck."

Kate frowned.

"I'm okay," Tilly said. Kate's hand rested on Tilly's arm. Tilly pulled her arm out and took Kate's hand, giving it a tentative squeeze. "How do I look?"

"Like you got hit by a truck," Roman said, earning a glare from Kate. Tilly laughed, then groaned.

"Okay, maybe no laughing for the moment." She felt around her sore rib, locating the wrapping that was probably keeping her pain at bay. She could now feel bandages on her cheek, chin, and forehead. The edges tugged at her skin.

Tilly's stomach growled again. "So, who's going to give me the rundown on what's been happening?" She saw Kate start to protest, so she added, "Keeping me in the dark does not protect me, Kate."

"I know," Kate said reluctantly. "It's just hard to want to jump right into everything when you're only just finally waking up."

Tilly sympathized, but not enough to stop her line of questioning. "How's Hannah?"

"She's good," Roman answered. "She was dehydrated when she got picked up, but a truck driver noticed her on an early-morning run to Albuquerque, so she wasn't in the desert for long."

A weight lifted from Tilly's chest. "Is she still speaking to me?"

This time Kate smiled. "Oh, I imagine she has a lot to say to you." Tilly frowned. "Don't worry, she's just working through things like the rest of us."

"What they did to her..." Tilly's voice dropped off and she had to fight to maintain her composure. "I killed him, Kate."

A look of shock crossed both Kate and Roman's faces.

"It was that same bastard who attacked you last year. Rick. When I got free, I killed him." When Tilly spoke about Rick venom filled her voice, but as she talked about killing him she relaxed. For a moment she wondered if having no feelings about Rick's death was wrong, but she couldn't force herself to feel remorse. Not yet, anyway.

"The State Police have taken over the investigation," Roman said. "Rick's body is at the ME's office, and they caught Mark Arroyo a few hours after they found you. He's in custody."

"Good," Tilly said. She turned her gaze to Kate. "Now tell me what happened to you, and don't try to tell me nothing. The nurse let it slip." Tilly waited to see if Kate would call her bluff.

Kate sighed. "I confronted Ruth Flores. She doesn't appear to have had anything to do with your abduction. After I left Ruth was killed and I, unfortunately, was exposed to the fentanyl they used to kill her."

Tilly's eyes were wide. "I don't understand. Why did you go back?"

"Ruth told us that Chief Gunnison has been her partner. We're pretty sure he killed her so he could take over the organization."

Tilly shook her head. "I'm still confused."

"It's a mess," Roman said. "We were in Ruth's house when a bunch of cars pulled up. She told us to get out. She was barely alive when we came back."

The anxiety and dread that pulsed through Tilly's body were making her feel lightheaded.

"Let's take a minute," Kate said. Tilly slowed her breathing and tried to empty her mind. Any time her eyes closed she felt fatigue swoop in, so she fought to keep her eyes open.

A knock at the door broke the tension. A hospital employee delivered a tray with soup, bread, Jello, and a few choices of drinks. After he left, Tilly picked up the bread and began to take tiny bites, allowing herself time in between to make sure it stayed down.

Kate and Roman settled into the visitor chairs, seeming relieved to have a break in the conversation. Tilly knew that eating was going to take some effort, so she didn't protest.

Tilly took the cover off of her soup. The steam that crept up to her nose was like a balm to her soul. Her mind wandered to her childhood. If she or Kate woke up with a cold, her abuela would bring over a big pot of homemade chicken soup with big chunks of veggies and green chiles.

A tear rolled down her cheek as she let those memories wrap themselves around her heart, giving her strength.

"What is it?" Kate had moved to Tilly's side.

"I was just thinking about family," Tilly replied quietly.

"'Buela's soup?" Kate asked, smiling when Tilly nodded. "I could smell it, too. Just needs some green chiles. I'm guessing they don't spice it up at the hospital."

"I agree." Tilly took a spoonful and closed her eyes. "But this isn't too bad." They made small talk while Tilly finished her lunch. When the nurse took away her tray, she leaned back into her pillow and relaxed. She'd almost dozed off, when a quiet knock at her door startled her. Dan slipped inside, closing the door behind him.

Tilly didn't miss the look Kate gave Roman. Her stomach clenched. She'd spent so much time imagining how angry Dan would be—how quickly he'd want to sever ties with someone so prone to reckless behavior and danger—that the outcome of this visit seemed inevitable. And while she understood, the idea of losing Dan ripped her heart in two.

"We're going to go check in with Angie." Kate and Roman filed out of the room, taking all the oxygen with them. Dan looked like he'd aged about ten years, and Tilly braced herself for whatever might come. She pictured Hannah's pale, ravaged body and knew that, whatever he had to say, she deserved it.

Dan pulled a chair over to the side of Tilly's bed and sat down. She could see tears glistening in his eyes.

"I'm sorry." Tilly heard the anguish in her voice, and as she watched Dan's face contort another wave of guilt washed over her. She reached for his hand, trying to console him—waiting for him to give her bad news. A goodbye. "It's okay, Dan. I understand."

Dan let his head hang, his shoulders shaking. But when he raised his head he was laughing, tears streaming down his face. "I don't think you do."

Tilly frowned. "What's funny about this?" She was surprised at how angry she sounded.

He leaned forward, resting his head on the arm of her bed. He wiped at his eyes as he slowed his breathing. "You're a fighter, Tilly Medina. The first time I met you, I saw it—that ferocity. And even though it was aimed at me that time, there's always been something about you."

"Hannah wouldn't have been in that house if it weren't for me. She'd be whole and okay."

Dan raised an eyebrow. "You're absolutely right. Hannah wouldn't have been in that house if she weren't with you. But she also got out of that house because of you. And honestly, if you're telling me she's not going to be okay because of this, maybe you're not the woman I thought you were."

"Of course she'll be okay! But I'm a walking disaster. All the time. And now you and your daughter have been sucked right into all the trouble."

Dan chuckled, which further annoyed Tilly. "I'll admit these last few days have had me questioning a lot of things. And you're not wrong—life has been a lot more, um, turbulent with you in it."

A tear slid down Tilly's cheek. "She could have lived her whole life without having to experience this kind of violence. She deserves better."

"You all do, Tilly. Every victim deserves better. You can't change what's happened, only how you react to it. How you move forward. Hannah will be okay. She'll be different, but she'll find a way through this. Like you have."

Tilly frowned, thinking about all the times she'd sabotaged her own life over the years. She didn't want that for Hannah, but Dan was right. She couldn't change what had happened. But she didn't have to like it. And she wasn't sure how she would forgive herself.

Dan let go of her hand and gently cradled her cheek. "I knew you'd blame yourself for this whole situation, even if you'd never allow another victim to do so. Whatever you thought I was going to say when I came here, well, you're probably wrong. And it's certainly not the last time. But there's no one I'd rather prove wrong."

CHAPTER 34
KATE

DOWN IN THE hospital conference room, the State Police had cleared out their temporary war room. The investigation would be moving to the Las Cruces headquarters, and the detectives were ready to head out.

Angie and Chris were seated on one side of the table, with Roman and Kate across from them. Angie had her laptop in front of her.

"We've identified nine of the thirteen suspects on the videos provided by Mrs. Flores. We'll be starting our arrests tomorrow."

"Was Sam Garrett one of them?" Kate asked.

"He was. The videos only date back to 2002, so something must have made Ruth nervous. But we're still talking about two decades and only thirteen faces." Angie sighed.

"I know how you're feeling," Kate said. "Both relieved and disgusted."

"Pretty much," Angie replied. "Benny Parks is in the mix, but not his uncle, so we already know this isn't a complete list. Ruth may have only handed over the videos for men she perceived as a threat."

"Was Gunnison on the videos?" Roman asked through gritted teeth.

"Unfortunately, no."

Kate took Roman's hand. She could feel him shaking with anger.

"We have to get him," Kate said, knowing how futile saying it out loud was. "Ruth said Gunnison is taking over the show, and I believe her. I think that she was self-serving to her very last breath. She chose what information to share with me. What evidence to hand over. And there's got to be more out there."

Chris spoke up for the first time. "We need to get back to Cruces and start sorting things out, and we need to talk with your sister before we go. Is she alert?"

"She was a few minutes ago," Kate replied. "Dan was with her and she was eating. She looked pretty worn down, so you should probably get up there."

Angie nodded. "How's Hannah?"

"Dan says she's doing better," Roman answered. "They should release her today. We'll go up and see her now."

They all stood.

"Roman, can I talk to you for a moment?" Angie had her eyes down on her computer, but her voice was tense.

Roman looked at Kate. "I'll meet you up there."

Chris held the door for Kate and she walked toward the elevator, wondering what new bombshell Angie would drop into their lives.

Kate met Dan in the hallway outside Hannah's room.

"We have to stop meeting like this," Dan said. He looked tired, but more hopeful than he had in days.

"I take it the chat with Tilly went well? Did she try to throw herself under the bus?"

"As well as can be expected. Your sister is one stubborn woman." Dan chuckled. "I want to thank you for letting me vent and be a total asshole."

"You weren't," Kate said, smiling. "And you're welcome. It's been a hard road, Dan. I wonder if Tilly will ever forgive me for dragging her into all this. She's had so much trauma already."

"She made the same argument with me about Hannah. And it's so easy to blame ourselves. I kept asking myself why I hadn't just told Hannah to wait for me. Tilly over-heard them saying she was an unexpected complication. But eventually I came to the conclusion that they could have aborted. When they saw Hannah, they could have waited for another opportunity. But they didn't. And that's the bottom line. These people are reckless, and they don't care who gets hurt."

They approached Hannah's door. "We all work hard to prevent this kind of crime from happening. Every day we know that for every person we help or save, there's someone else we can't reach. We have to keep trying. But we also have to remember to be gentle with ourselves."

"Wise words, Counselor." Kate knocked on Hannah's door and then walked in. Hannah was sitting up in bed, picking at the tray of food in front of her. The TV was on, but the volume was down.

"What did they bring you?" Dan asked, taking a seat beside her.

"A weird sandwich and Jello. Blech."

Kate laughed. "Sounds awful. I can go get you something from the cafeteria."

"That's okay. The nurse was just in and she said they're discharging me after lunch." Hannah smiled at her dad. "Hoping Dad will agree to a drive-thru pit stop on the way home. I've been craving a milkshake ever since I turned on the TV. I had to mute it because my mouth kept watering at every commercial."

"I think I can be talked into it," Dan said.

Kate marveled at how normal Hannah sounded. She wasn't naive enough to think that Hannah would bounce right back from her assault, but she knew it would be easier with so much love and support.

"Did you talk to Tilly?" Hannah was looking at Dan with a very serious expression.

"I did," he said. "She's awake and eating, so that's a good sign. I think she liked her lunch better than you did."

"It probably wasn't a sandwich," Hannah said, wrinkling her nose. "I only had a few rounds of the gross sandwiches they fed us, and I could live my whole life without seeing another one."

The nurse came in, followed by the attending physician. "Looks like you're ready to head home." The nurse handed Dan a stack of papers. "This is the discharge paperwork. She'll need to follow up with her PCP in a few days."

"Got it," Dan said.

After they left, Kate and Dan stepped out so that Hannah could change into her clothes. The outfit she'd been wearing when she was abducted had been taken as evidence, but her bag had been recovered from Tilly's car, untouched.

Kate remembered her own assault, and having to change into donated clothes after. It wasn't a memory she liked to relive. The minute she'd gotten to her apartment, she'd peeled them off and thrown them away.

"Where's Roman?" Dan asked as they walked down the hall.

"We got an update on the case, and then Angie pulled him aside. The detectives are heading back tonight, but they'll talk to Tilly first."

Kate realized she hadn't actually answered his question, because she really didn't know the answer. It had been twenty minutes, and Kate just hoped they'd gotten to Tilly's room before she fell asleep again.

Her irritation must have been obvious, because Dan stopped her. "What's going on with you and Roman? And Angie?"

"Nothing. Everything is fine," Kate replied unconvincingly. When Dan gave her a look, she sighed. "It's complicated. You know that Angie and Roman dated seriously. Recently she's been ill and Roman is feeling a lot of things, mostly angry that she never told him about her illness."

"But you two are okay?"

"We will be. Once we get past all this and have a chance to sort things out. We haven't really had a chance to talk about it. It's not a priority right now, but there's a lot of tension there and I'm not sure what to do with it." Kate sighed. "We'll talk through it."

Dan nodded. "I get what you're saying, but don't let it go too long. I doubt this will all just resolve itself quickly, and I would hate to see you two divided when you're basically the best couple I know."

Kate smiled, and as if on cue Roman stepped off the elevator and walked down the hall toward them. Kate studied him. He had that carefully crafted expression that revealed nothing, but Kate knew it meant trouble.

"Are you guys heading home?" he asked when he got to them. He sidled up close to Kate, putting his arm around her shoulder. Whatever had happened had him seeking comfort, another clue to Kate that something was up.

"Hannah's getting changed now," Dan said. "I'll take her down to see Tilly before we go. You'll keep me posted?"

"Of course," Kate replied. Dan walked back down the hall and disappeared into Hannah's room.

"Do you want to talk about it?" Kate asked Roman, turning to face him. From the look on his face she didn't really want to know what Angie had said, but her anxiety was growing.

"No." His tone was even. She wondered how much effort it was taking him to keep from breaking down.

"I'm probably going to stay the night with Tilly, if that's okay," she said. "You should probably go home and get some sleep."

"Kate," he started, but then he took a deep breath, as if rebuilding the structure that was holding him together, brick by brick. Kate couldn't help feeling fear, but she knew that fear didn't serve her and it wouldn't fix whatever had just been broken.

"It's okay, Roman. I'm here for you whenever you're ready. And right now I think we could all just use sleep. One night of solid sleep sounds like a miracle."

"I'll be back in the morning," he said. He leaned down and kissed Kate with so much intensity that it left her breathless.

As she watched him walk away she told herself it would be okay, and then prayed that she was right.

CHAPTER 35
TILLY

TILLY WATCHED Angie walk out the door, contemplating the task she'd been given. She couldn't even imagine getting out of bed, but Angie had placed the fate of the entire investigation in her hands.

Sort of.

They now had enough evidence to take down at least half a dozen members of the trafficking ring, but not a shred that tied the Chief of Police to any criminal activity. He and Ruth had been very careful.

They all knew what that meant—things would go quiet for a while and then right back to where they were before. Maybe worse, since Gunnison seemed less cautious than Ruth had been. Maybe he'd make a mistake, but how many more girls would suffer before that happened?

"You look like you're about to walk in front of a firing squad." Hannah was standing at Tilly's door. Seeing Hannah alive made Tilly's heart swell, but almost instantly that joyous feeling was replaced by guilt. Hannah's beautiful face, the part that wasn't covered in bandages, looked like she'd been fighting a mountain lion. One eye was swollen, and the bruising was turning ghastly shades of purple and yellow.

But she was alive. That's all that mattered.

Hannah walked across the room and sat near Tilly's bed. "It's better to be on this side of the bed."

"Agreed," Tilly said. "Are you guys heading home?"

"Yes, thank God! I need real food." She sounded so much like her old self that Tilly laughed, and allowed herself a tiny bit of hope. "When are they going to spring you?"

"Not sure, but I'm guessing it'll be a day or two. I'm still feeling the effects of dehydration. They'll make sure I'm stable before letting me go."

"Then why do you look like something bad has happened?"

"Things just got complicated," Tilly said. When Hannah frowned, she continued. Given everything they'd been through, it didn't even occur to Tilly to hide things from Hannah. "I'm not in great shape, but it looks like Mark is asking to talk to me."

Hannah's face went ashen. "You're not seriously going to."

"He's in custody. He can't hurt me. And he may be the only person who can give the police the information they need for their investigation."

When Angie dropped the news Tilly had begun to shake, her emotions still raw. Now, seeing the fear and pain on Hannah's face, she tried to pull herself together.

"I don't want to, Hannah, trust me. I would rather go my whole life without seeing any of those men again." Tilly inhaled slowly. "But if it means saving even one person from what you and I have experienced, it's worth it."

"Why can't they bring him here? How can they even think about letting you go anywhere?"

"It's important, Hannah. It has to be done, and I'm the only one he'll talk to."

Hannah didn't look convinced, but Tilly saw something hard in her expression. It was definitely something Tilly was familiar with.

"Are you coming home after?"

"Eventually. I have no idea when I'm going to get the doctor's okay to actually go home, and I may need to stay with Kate for a while. My broken rib is going to keep me out of work, and I'll probably need help getting dressed and showering." She was trying to keep her voice light, but the uncertainty of it all weighed heavily on her heart.

Hannah's eyes glistened. Tilly took her hand, searching for the right thing to say to reassure her without making promises she couldn't keep.

"You don't have to lie to me, Tilly." Hannah's words tore at her heart.

"I would never lie to you," Tilly said, and she meant it.

"Good. Then I want to know two things."

Tilly had a sinking feeling.

"Are you and my dad okay?"

Tilly smiled. "I think so. I'm not in a great frame of mind right now, and this has been really stressful for him. I can't even imagine how he must have felt."

"Yeah, I know," Hannah said. "I'm getting a new phone right away, and I swear I will never give him a hard time about wanting me to check in again."

"A silver lining for sure," Tilly teased. "So, what's your second question?"

"Did you kill Rick?"

The question was like a blow to her heart, but she didn't hesitate. "Yes."

"Good," Hannah said. She grew silent, and her eyes seemed dark and distant. Hadn't Tilly imagined killing her abusers? Getting revenge? But that hatred had eaten away at her. And now, being responsible for Rick's death, no matter how despicable he might have been, would weigh on her conscience.

"Ready to go?" Dan was at the door with Hannah's backpack in hand. Hannah's expression relaxed.

"Absolutely. Can we stop somewhere for a milkshake and then something when we get home, too?" Hannah's voice returned to its usual cheerful tone. The moment had passed, but Tilly was sure it would come again.

Dan chuckled. "Sure. And when you're throwing it up because you over-ate, I'll hold your hair back."

"Charming," Tilly said, but her smile was wide. "Can I have one more minute with Hannah?"

"Sure," Dan said. He kissed Tilly on the cheek and then went back out into the hall.

"Hannah, I have to ask you a favor, and I don't want to."

Hannah squinted at Tilly for a moment and then her expression turned neutral. "You don't want me to tell Dad about what you're about to do."

"If he asks you, don't lie. But right now you're the only person who knows about this besides me and Angie. He's been through so much. I just don't want to add more to his plate. Not right now."

"When he finds out you didn't tell him, he's going to be mad." Tilly knew she was right, but she knew that Dan needed to be home with Hannah. She needed him, and Tilly didn't want to be the reason his loyalties were any more divided.

"I love you and your father, Hannah."

"We love you, too, Tilly. It goes both ways." Hannah leaned over to give Tilly a gentle hug. "Be careful."

———

A few hours passed. Kate dozed in the armchair in Tilly's hospital room. Tilly had done her best to rest, but each time she drifted off she had visions of blood pooling around Rick's head. She didn't regret killing Rick, but she didn't feel good about it either. Telling Hannah had unleashed all the feelings she'd been avoiding.

"What's wrong?" Kate's voice was soft and sleepy. Tilly hadn't realized she was awake.

"I'm all right. Just having trouble getting any rest."

"Is it time for more pain meds?"

"Pain isn't the problem." Kate met her gaze, and Tilly could see that her sister understood. It was something they had in common, with each other and with so many other women and men and children. She let out a huge sigh and then groaned at the pain it caused. "How are you?"

Kate stretched and yawned. "Tired mostly. Roman let the nurses know about the fentanyl poisoning, so they've been checking on me. I swear every time I nod off, they're in here. I'm not even a patient!"

Tilly laughed at Kate's exasperation. "Good! I always knew Roman was going to be an excellent brother-in-law."

When Kate's face darkened, Tilly felt her own heart fall. "What's going on, Kate?"

"I don't know," Kate said. "First we find out Angie's sick. Then you're taken and we spend the next three days working with her. She took Roman aside after our briefing this afternoon and something is up. I don't know what it is, but I'm worried."

"You're always worried, Kate. You came into this world worrying." She softened her tone. "But I don't think you need to worry about Roman. He's loved you pretty much his whole life. I doubt that's going to stop now, no matter what happens."

Kate wiped at a tear that was leaving a trail down her cheek." I know. But you should have seen his face, Til. He looked so...devastated. I can't imagine what she told him that would leave him that upset." Kate paused. "I can actually imagine a lot of things, but it's probably best not to let my imagination take the wheel."

"Maybe you should go home and sort things out. Figure out what's going on."

"And leave you?"

Tilly laughed. "What? You think these guys can't take care of me?"

"Oh, believe me, they'll take care of you whether you like it or not," Kate huffed, but she couldn't keep up the charade for long. "I'm scared, Tilly."

"I know you are. And I wish I could tell you everything will be okay, but I would never try to placate you like that.

You and Roman will have all kinds of trials, but you'll get through them together."

Kate reached over and squeezed Tilly's hand. "Thank you. I'm so glad you're okay and I'm so, so sorry that this happened to you. And Hannah."

"Find me a milkshake and we'll call it even," Tilly said with a smile. "Hannah was talking about milkshakes, and now that's all I want."

"You got it, sis," Kate got up and stretched some more. "I'm going to go grab some dinner in the cafeteria and then hunt you down the biggest milkshake I can find. You're sure you're okay?"

"Absolutely. Get out of here." After Kate closed the door, Tilly took a breath and relaxed back into her pillow. She'd started to doze, when her door opened.

"Tilly?" Angie walked in. "Where's Kate?"

"Hunting me down something ice-cream-based, I hope. I thought you guys headed back to Las Cruces."

"The team went back, but they're keeping Mark Arroyo here in Socorro. You and I need to see him before he's transported."

Tilly sat up uneasily. "Now? I'm not even off my IVs."

Angie shifted uncomfortably. "You'll have to leave against medical advice. We can't wait any longer."

"I'm not going without Kate," Tilly said, ready to dig in her heels. Angie must have recognized the defiance in her gaze, because she didn't protest.

"I'll call her."

A nurse walked in, forcing Angie outside. This particular nurse had been with Tilly all day and they'd developed a rapport. Tilly hoped it was enough to gain an ally in what she knew was a risky mission, given her current condition.

"Charlotte, I need you to unhook me."

The nurse looked at her like she was crazy. "Are you feeling all right?"

Tilly smiled wearily. "As well as can be expected, I guess. But there's something I need to do, and it can't wait. The detective who just walked out the door needs me to go talk with the man who helped me escape."

"The man who helped you escape? You mean the man who abducted you?"

Tilly could see that Charlotte wasn't going to budge. Her voice became urgent. "You have to understand. These men were working for someone else, and unless we can find out who it'll happen again. We have this one chance. I wouldn't even consider it if it weren't this serious."

"You've been on pain meds all day. I'm not sure you should even be on your feet, much less go anywhere."

Tilly could see a small crack in Charlotte's armor.

"Hannah Bross, the girl who was with me… Charlotte, she's just one of dozens, probably more, of girls who've had their lives irrevocably changed by this organization. Please help me help them."

Charlotte was silent for a moment. Tilly could barely breathe, and when Angie opened the door she jumped. Nurse and detective were locked in a tense glare. Finally, Charlotte turned to Tilly.

"The doctor already did his rotation for the night, so I may be able to cover for you while you're gone. But you need to come back so we can continue to monitor you, Tilly.

You have no idea how close to death you were when you came in last night."

Charlotte was wrong. Tilly had felt death's door within reach. She'd even welcomed the end a time or two.

As Charlotte began taking out Tilly's IV, Angie murmured, "Thank you." The nurse didn't acknowledge her.

Kate walked in a few minutes later, wearing an expression that could kill. "Let me help her get dressed."

When the sisters were alone, Kate said, "If something happens to you tonight, I will never forgive her for asking you to do this."

"Fair enough," Tilly said. "But Kate, maybe she's right. Maybe this is the one thing that will bring Gunnison down."

"That's the only reason I'm agreeing to go along with you." Kate said. "And don't think it hasn't occurred to me that you knew about this earlier and didn't say anything."

Kate helped Tilly into some loose-fitting sweatpants and a t-shirt. By the time she was dressed, sweat was forming on her forehead.

"Let's get this over with," Tilly said, and with Kate's arm wrapped around her shoulder they met Angie in the hallway and made the slow, painful journey out of the safety of the hospital.

CHAPTER 36
KATE

Exhausted from the walk out to Angie's vehicle, Tilly had dozed off almost immediately after snapping her seat belt, leaving Kate and Angie alone. Without Tilly as a buffer, the tension between them grew uncomfortable.

"How are you feeling?" Kate asked. She looked over at Angie, who was driving, watching for any indication that she didn't want to talk. Angie's expression, which was usually unreadable in professional situations, was now awash with barely concealed anger.

Kate was angry, too. They were springing Tilly against medical advice, to talk to one of the men who'd not only abducted her but had also been responsible for many of the bruises and abrasions Tilly was sporting.

"I'm fine."

Something about the way she said it not only confirmed that Angie was not fine, but also that some of her anger seemed to be pointed at Kate.

"Did I do something?" Kate asked, unable to hide the bite in her question.

Angie took a big breath, blowing it out slowly and dramatically. But she kept silent, spiking Kate's anxiety.

"You might as well just say what's on your mind," Kate said, switching on the non-emotional tone she reserved for sensitive or hostile patients.

"I'm focused on driving. Since I'm sure Roman has filled you in on my medical situation, you can probably guess that I'm not feeling well. I don't have the energy to talk about it."

Under any other circumstances, it would have been a reasonable statement. Kate would have leaned back into her seat and stayed silent, allowing Angie the space she needed to safely get them to the jail. But this situation was anything but normal, and the memory of the pained look on Roman's face was still fresh in Kate's mind.

"I'm sorry you're not doing well health-wise, Angie. I really am. But we both know that's not the whole story. Dragging Tilly out of the hospital for this interview? And whatever went down with you and Roman? You don't have to talk to me, but don't pretend that I don't know what's going on."

"You tell me, Kate. What's going on?" Angie had lightened her tone into something almost playful, but there was an edge that made Kate shiver.

"I don't know what you want me to say. I'm sorry, Angie. I know that my relationship with Roman isn't fair to you."

Angie laughed. "It's not that, Kate. When I met Roman, I knew he was hung up on someone. Yeah, I'm not happy that my plans got completely derailed by your relationship, but what really pisses me off is how flaky you are. He's so committed to you but you're always cautious, like you're ready to run. Add to that the fact that I've had to watch that for a whole year. I can't cut ties because we're all working together on this case, and Tilly is in Las Cruces, and I'm just so fucking mad that you get to have the life I wanted!"

The strain in her voice was evident. Angie was barely holding herself together. Kate peeked back over her shoulder to where Tilly was still sleeping. When she looked back at Angie, she could see the slump in her shoulders—the fire she'd had was gone.

"I know," Kate said quietly. "I'm jealous of the time you had with him. The time I wasted by leaving and cutting ties. And I know how much he cares about you. And I wonder, more often than I'd like to admit, whether I should have just walked away. I don't want to hurt him. Or you."

"Then don't," Angie said. "He's made a choice, and even if I hate it, you won."

"It's not a competition."

"Not anymore," Angie said with a smile that made Kate immensely uncomfortable. "The issue for me is that I like you. And I really like Tilly. So I've been lingering, trying to convince myself that I'll eventually be okay seeing you two together. And the stress is killing me. Literally. My doctor told me that if I don't make a huge change in my life, I could be facing permanent damage and disability."

"I'm sorry…"

"Don't." Angie's jaw was clenched tightly. "Don't you dare feel sorry for me, Kate."

An uneasy silence followed.

———

Kate leaned back in her seat, trying to sort through her emotions. She'd always suspected that Angie resented her, maybe even hated her, but to have that confirmed was a shock.

Kate thought she'd feel worse, but for the first time in her personal life she felt resolute. Maybe Angie was right. Maybe they'd been competing this whole time, unintentionally. Even as their relationship grew more solid, more stable, Kate had been waiting for Roman to leave. Sure, it might have been her own insecurities, but she'd always seen Angie as a threat.

And every subsequent action and reaction had been a move in a game Kate didn't know she was playing.

Kate tried to convince herself that Angie had made peace with the situation, but she'd known, hadn't she? She'd known that Angie was not okay, because she herself would be crushed if Roman left her.

Now, in a matter of minutes, the veil had been lifted. Angie had been honest with Kate about her feelings, and the relief from hearing that truth set Kate free. She realized that her intuition had been correct. She'd been doubting herself unnecessarily.

More than that, she realized that she could feel empathy for Angie's loss without feeling undeserving of her own gain. By feeling so insecure about her place in Roman's life, she'd been unfair to all three of them. To Roman, who was so happy in the direction their life was going. To Angie, whose life had been upended by her break-up with Roman.

And also to herself. Every moment she spent waiting for the other shoe to drop kept her from being fully present in their relationship, and in her own life.

CHAPTER 37
TILLY

AT THE JAIL, Tilly and Angie went through the check-in process, leaving Kate in the lobby to wait. She felt groggy and dazed, not quite coherent and certainly not ready to face the task ahead. Nonetheless, she gritted her teeth and submitted to a search before following Angie and the guard into the secure area.

"It's highly irregular to allow anyone but an attorney to see prisoners at this stage." This was the third time the guard had repeated this concern, making it clear that he did not approve and reinforcing Tilly's anxiety.

"I understand," Angie said stonily. "We wouldn't be inconveniencing you if this wasn't absolutely critical to our investigation."

Once again, the guard eyed Tilly. "She doesn't look very good."

Tilly laughed at Angie's scowl. "You're a real charmer," she muttered, earning herself a glare from the guard, but he unlocked a door and ushered them inside.

Mark Arroyo was in a prison jumpsuit and shackles. He looked gray and there were scratches all over his face, including one nasty-looking gash that went into one eyelid.

Angie took a seat across from Mark, giving Tilly the chance to sit farther away from her attacker. They sat for a few minutes, studying one another in silence.

"Why did you ask to see Ms. Medina?" Angie asked finally.

Tilly looked at Mark, but he kept his gaze trained on the table in front of him. The atmosphere was tense and sad. Mark looked utterly defeated, and Tilly regretted coming. At the moment, she had no room for sympathy.

"Look, Mark," Tilly said. "I don't really care why you asked to see me. I'm here for one reason and that's to find out who you're working for. If you can't tell me that, we're done here."

When he didn't respond, Tilly was afraid she'd blown it. Finally, Mark looked up at her and said, "I'm sorry."

"That's all you have to say?" Angie's voice was so full of vitriol, it caught Tilly off-guard. "You abducted two women, held them prisoner for days, and are responsible for the rape of a teenage girl. You really are a worthless piece of shit."

The words tore at Tilly's heart. Despite everything she'd been through, Angie's venom was more painful to hear than any physical injury she'd suffered.

"Stop," Tilly whispered.

Angie looked at her, startled. "What?"

"I said stop." Tilly's voice was gaining volume. "Mark knows he's fucked. There's no reason to tear him down."

Mark looked just as surprised as Angie.

"I believe that you're sorry," Tilly said, looking Mark in

the eyes. "I don't think you knew what you were getting yourself into, and so I believe you. But what you did is unforgivable. Hannah's life will never be the same. My life will never be the same. Rick is dead. You're going to prison."

Tilly could see tears forming in Mark's eyes. She took a breath and went in for the kill.

"The only thing you can do right now to make it right, even a little bit, is help us take down the bastards who are throwing you under the bus."

Angie sat back in her chair. Tilly could see her shoulders relax as she let Tilly take the lead.

"They're not going to save you, Mark. They let Benny Parks go to prison. They killed Sam Garrett. Or maybe that was you?"

The look on Mark's face said no, making Tilly wonder just how many thugs Ruth and the chief had steamrolled into taking the fall for them. She felt bile rise in her throat.

"Are you okay?" Angie whispered, looking concerned.

"Not really," Tilly said. Then she turned her attention back to Mark. "I have to go back. If you're not willing to talk, then we're done here."

"It's not that easy," Mark said. His voice shook. "They were careful not to let us know too much." He hesitated.

"But you know something," Tilly interjected.

Mark nodded. "After Rick… the girl…"

"Raped her," Tilly said harshly. "Let's call it what it is, Mark. And her name is Hannah."

A tear slid down his cheek. "After Rick raped Hannah, I heard him arguing with one of the guys we worked with. They usually talked in code, but I heard him say that Bill wasn't going to be happy about it."

"Bill?" Angie looked at Tilly. "Was that it?"

"He also called him 'the chief'." Mark hung his head. "I live in Alamogordo. I knew who he meant. And he'll find out I talked to you, so I'm probably dead."

"We'll do what we can to protect you," Angie said, pulling out her phone and furiously typing on the screen.

Tilly felt like her heart had stopped. She had to remind herself that she could breathe, nudging her body back into motion.

"Let's go, Tilly," Angie said as she stood. She reached down to take Tilly's arm, but Tilly stayed glued to the chair. She'd never actually expected to get anything out of Mark. She'd hauled herself out of bed, bruised and broken, so that she could say she'd done everything in her power.

She'd never expected this. The whole situation was surreal, like a dream. She felt like her grasp on reality was getting more tenuous, more slippery.

As Tilly turned her head to Angie, her vision started to blur.

"Whoa," Angie said, reaching down to steady Tilly where she sat. "Take a breath, Tilly. You're not breathing."

Tilly tried, but her lungs felt stiff and stalled, unwilling to perform their most basic function. Every time she tried to inhale pain shot through her midsection, cutting off the intake of breath before it made it to her lungs.

"We need a medic," Angie said to the guard, who grabbed his phone and made a call.

Tilly's ears rang and her head swam. She leaned her cheek against Angie's body, feeling herself being pulled away from her body, and wondered if any of this had been real.

CHAPTER 38
KATE

Kate's feet tapped the floor at a frantic pace as she waited for news. At the jail, the medic was able to revive Tilly, and somehow Kate and Angie got her back to her hospital room, in her gown and in bed.

Angie had run to the nurses' station, and within minutes the room was buzzing with activity. Someone nudged Kate and Angie out the door, but Kate had retreated into her own protective inner world. The sight of Tilly unconscious again, when her health was so precarious, left Kate in a dark place.

"Kate? Kate, what happened?" Roman's voice pierced a hole in her cocoon.

He'd showered and changed, but she could still see the dark circles under his eyes. Then she realized it had only been a few hours since he'd gone home—not enough time to sleep.

"What are you doing here?"

Roman sat down beside her. "I almost didn't leave." He ran a hand through his hair and then tangled his fingers through Kate's. "The last week has been a nightmare, and I haven't been at my best. I shouldn't have left you here. I'm so sorry, Kate."

Kate tucked those words safely in her heart. "Tilly's blood pressure dropped really low. They're trying to get her stabilized."

"What happened?"

She'd gone through the story she was supposed to tell Roman repeatedly—a story concocted by Angie and Tilly on the way to the jail. But when she looked into his eyes, she knew with certainty that she would never lie to this man again.

"Mark Arroyo asked to see Tilly. We took her to the jail."

Roman sighed. "We?"

"Angie and I. Apparently they'd talked about it earlier in the day. Angie tried to round her up when I was out of the room, but Tilly refused to go without me. And before you ask, I would have tried to talk Tilly out of it. But it was clear she wasn't going to take no for an answer."

Kate watched his reaction closely, waiting for anger. What she saw instead was resolution. About what, she wasn't sure. He took a few deep breaths, his hand still warm in Kate's.

"Did he talk to Tilly then?"

"Yeah. From what Angie said, I think he wanted to apologize to her. But Tilly wasn't having it. She told him that if he didn't reveal who he was working for, his apology meant nothing. It was brilliant."

Roman straightened. "Did he tell her?"

"Sort of." Kate paused. "He wasn't privy to much information—he was just a hired gun. But he did overhear a few things that seem to point to the chief."

"Angie was there?"

"Yeah. I stayed in the lobby, so I'm basically telling you what Angie told me. Tilly passed out at the end. We barely got her back here." Kate looked around. "Wait. Where *is* Angie? She was in the room with me a minute ago."

Roman frowned. "I didn't see her when I came in."

The door to Tilly's room opened and people began spilling out, heading in various directions. The doctor walked over to Kate.

"She's stable. Did you see her pull her IV out?"

"No," Kate said. "I was out of the room for a while and didn't really notice anything when I came back in. Just that she was really pale again and sweaty."

"She's still dehydrated, and she may be having some complications related to that. I've ordered some more blood work, but if her BP falls again we'll move her into the ICU."

Kate felt cold. "Can I go see her?"

"She's sleeping right now. I'd suggest waiting until morning. Right now what she needs most is rest, and from the looks of it so do you."

Kate nodded, knowing she must look as defeated as she felt. Roman helped her to her feet, and they headed home.

———

When Kate opened the front door, Rusty practically bowled her over. She patted his head and walked to her bedroom, leaving Roman downstairs to get the dog settled down. Peeling off her clothes, she started the shower in their master bathroom and stepped in, barely feeling the heat of the water.

The whole shower may have lasted an hour, or maybe only a few minutes. She couldn't really remember if she washed her hair or her face, but soon the feel of the water began to irritate her skin. She dried off, pulled her wet hair into a braid, and put on some pajamas.

Roman was changing when she came out of the bathroom. "I've set my alarm for five in case we sleep in."

"I'll leave my ringer on in case the hospital calls." Kate put her phone on the bedside table and pulled down the covers. She wearily lowered herself into bed. Roman lay down beside her and took her hand.

"Angie's moving," Roman said. "That's what she wanted to tell me, after the briefing."

"Oh." The relief that Kate felt was tempered by guilt and worry. "Why?"

Roman hesitated. "Easier access to doctors."

"And farther away from you and me," Kate finished. Roman's silence was confirmation. "So why all the theatrics? She could have just told us both."

As soon as the words left her mouth, she knew the answer.

"She asked you to go with her?" Anger swelled in her chest.

"Yes." His voice sounded strained. "I'm not surprised, really, but I've never hated her as much as I did at that moment."

Kate sat up and looked at him.

Roman's face was unreadable, the way it got when he was working hard to hold himself together. "I admit, when you and I first reconnected I had moments of hesitation. It hasn't been easy, and I imagine we'll have lots of bumps ahead, even without the insanity of the world we live in." The look he gave her was fierce. "It wasn't even a possibility, Kate. I hope you know that. And given where we were and what had happened…I kind of get it, why she asked. But I still can't believe she thought I might say yes."

"Maybe she didn't," Kate said softly. "Maybe it wasn't about you saying yes. Maybe she just needed to say goodbye."

Roman nodded slowly. "Then she took Tilly to see Mark Arroyo and nearly killed her."

A dozen arguments entered her mind, but there was nothing she could say that Roman hadn't considered, she was sure. It stung a bit that Roman's reaction to Angie was often intense, belying a connection that would probably always be there.

And yet the loyalty that he showed Angie was no less than the devotion he showed Kate. That was Roman. And ultimately it was one of the things that made Kate feel confident in their future, even with her tendency to wobble.

"When is she leaving?"

"She's gone." Now Kate felt uneasy.

"What do you mean? I was with her two hours ago."

"Detective Montoya is taking over the investigation."

"How could she?" Kate felt herself becoming hysterical. "We're so close! How could she just dump this on someone who hasn't been involved?"

"I asked the same thing, but she shut me down with a standard answer about him being up to speed."

Kate felt sick. "I can't believe this." She thought about

Tilly lying in her hospital bed. Angie had made the call, putting Tilly's health at risk, knowing that she would be leaving them. Kate tried to stop herself from thinking the worst of the detective, but so many of her actions in the past few days had been rash and reckless; something Angie had accused Tilly of being. And Kate, for that matter.

Kate had met Angie's replacement. He seemed competent, but she wondered if he'd take the case as seriously as Angie had. Then again, had Angie's interest been more about Roman?

"I'm sorry, Kate. It doesn't mean we'll stop fighting." He pulled her over where she could rest her head on his chest, interrupting the torrent of unpleasant thoughts swirling around in her mind.

It was a while before she could relax. Kate listened to the beat of Roman's heart and the sound of his breath as it slowed. She tried to imagine herself in a different place—a place where life was peaceful. But she knew in her heart that that place was one she would have to create herself.

CHAPTER 39
TILLY

After another day in the hospital, Tilly was finally released. The doctor couldn't explain her setback; Charlotte didn't mention Tilly's trip to the jail, though she did seem extra bossy for the duration of Tilly's stay. Tilly took it in stride.

Kate offered to take Tilly back to her apartment in Las Cruces, but Tilly wasn't ready to go home yet. Instead, she talked her way into staying with Kate for an unspecified duration. Not that Kate put up any argument. Even Roman seemed relieved that Tilly was staying around, probably so that he could keep an eye on her.

It was Tuesday morning. Kate and Tilly were sitting on the couch, when the doorbell rang. Rusty leapt up out of a dead sleep and barked ferociously.

Kate picked up her phone and opened the security app. "It's Detective Montoya."

A few minutes later, Kate led him into the living room. He took a seat across from Tilly. Kate's whole demeanor had changed, and Tilly watched her sister perch tensely on the edge of the coffee table.

"What's going on with the investigation, Chris?" Kate's tone was barely civil.

To his credit, the detective remained calm. "Listen, Kate. I'm sorry that Angie left in such a hurry. I don't agree with the way she handled things. All I can do is try to keep the momentum going."

"We appreciate that," Tilly said when Kate remained silent. Kate had updated her on the whole situation with Angie. Tilly didn't expect her to let go of that anger for some time. "So tell us what's going on."

"Our tech department identified all the people in the videos. We've examined the meta data and there are some irregularities that may cause issues in court."

Tilly wanted to know more about the videos, but Kate interrupted.

"What about Chief Gunnison?" The question hung in the air like a poisonous gas.

Chris sighed. "The information Mark Arroyo provided isn't enough for an arrest, but we're hoping we can get at least one of the other men to turn on him."

"Where is Mark now?"

"Detention center in Las Cruces."

"Under guard?" Tilly pictured the lengths these people had gone to in order to silence Kate. She had no doubt that Gunnison would do anything to keep himself out of the crosshairs.

"Yes, though he really doesn't have much to offer. If we manage to arrest Gunnison and then make it to court, maybe. It's going to be an uphill battle."

"This is bullshit!" Kate shouted. She was up on her feet, and Tilly swore she could feel the rage radiating off her sister. "That thumb drive can't be the only evidence there is."

"I agree, but we've searched Ruth Flores' house and office. We're actively searching the homes and offices of each of the men we have under arrest. It will take some time, but hopefully we'll find more that we can use."

"What about the victims?" Tilly interjected, causing both Kate and Chris to turn their attention to her. "Have you interviewed the victims?'

"What victims?" Chris asked. "The only person I'm aware of was groomed but never assaulted, as I understand it. We haven't identified any other victims."

Tilly turned to Kate. "What about Mandy? What was her last name…Garcia? Right? She was the reason Benny Parks was arrested."

"Mandy Garcia?"

Kate jumped in. "She's living in Albuquerque now. Or was the last time I heard from her."

"Didn't she tell you the Chief of Police was involved?"

"She did, but…"

"Call her," Tilly said. "You have to call her, Kate. If she has first-hand knowledge of Gunnison's involvement, maybe she can help end this."

Kate pulled out her cell phone and excused herself to the kitchen.

"She doesn't want to make that call," Chris noted.

"She's afraid," Tilly replied, guessing how her sister must be feeling. "Mandy barely got out of town alive. Benny Parks ripped her family apart, not to mention the abuse she suffered because of him. Kate's never been big on revictimization."

"I understand, but she has to know how high the stakes are."

Tilly smiled. "She knows. That's why she's making the call." Chris looked away, seeming to realize how ridiculous his statement had been. Kate and Tilly had suffered unspeakable loss as a result of this whole operation. Hannah and Tilly's abduction was just the most recent tragedy.

"How's Miss Bross doing?" Chris asked, changing the subject.

"You tell me," Tilly said. "I've been out of the hospital for about three hours. I haven't had time to check in with anyone."

Not entirely a lie, but not truthful either. When Tilly arrived at Kate's her sister had urged her to call Dan, but Tilly put it off. She had a lot to think about, and she needed time and space to do that.

"I spoke with Dan yesterday. She seems to be doing well."

"That's good," Tilly said softly, hoping Chris would change the subject. Thankfully, Kate walked back into the room.

"What did she say?" Chris asked.

When Kate sighed Tilly wanted to cry, but she tried to rein in her emotions long enough to hear what Mandy had to say.

"She wants to help," Kate said, then paused. Tilly was waiting for the *but*, but it never came. "Gunnison was around when Mandy was being abused. She saw him."

Chris' jaw dropped. "Oh. Well then we need to get a statement right away. She'll have to testify."

"She knows," Kate said warily. Tilly understood Kate's feelings on a visceral level. A week ago, she'd testified in a sexual assault trial. Watching a victim go through a brutal cross-examination with her attacker in the room staring at her was a harrowing experience for everyone. It wasn't something you ever wanted to put someone through, even if it was necessary.

———

Later, while Kate worked, Tilly sat listlessly on the couch trying to rest, but her mind wouldn't give her a moment's peace. In the course of one week, so much had happened. So much had changed.

She thought about Dan, who she still wasn't ready to call. Tilly wondered if she could ever ease the guilt she felt about Hannah's experience—the abduction, the assault, her escape across the desert, not knowing whether Tilly was alive or dead. How could she look Dan in the eye every day, or ever again, knowing what she'd cost him?

"You know better," Kate said, making Tilly jump.

"You scared me half to death."

Kate sat down beside Tilly and smiled. "I know that look, Til. It's the 'I'm about to sabotage my happiness forever' look that you're always calling me on."

Tilly grinned ruefully. "You're pretty observant for a therapist." It was an old joke, stemming from a playful argument they'd had as teenagers.

"And you're pretty feely for a nurse." Kate put her arm

through Tilly's. "I apologize in advance, but I'm putting my psychologist hat on right now. You know you cannot change what happened. Not by avoiding Dan. Not by hiding out in my house, though I do love having you here and you're welcome to stay as long as you want to."

Tilly scowled, railing against what she knew was 100% true. "Intellectually, I know that. It's harder to convince my damn emotions."

"I'd be out of a job if emotions were easy," Kate teased. "But seriously, what did Dan say to you before he took Hannah home?"

"That he loves me, basically."

"And what did you tell me when I was ready to bail on Roman, even though I knew he loved me?"

Tilly smiled. "That you were an idiot."

"There you go," Kate said. She patted Tilly's hand and went back into the kitchen to work.

Tilly picked up her phone and dialed.

"I'm shocked. I expected this to take a lot longer," Dan said when he answered. His tone was playful, but there was a hint of something else.

"Me, too," Tilly replied. "Luckily, my sister is unwilling to allow me to wallow in self-pity."

"Good." This time she heard the smile in his voice.

"How's Hannah?"

"She's doing pretty well. I got her a new phone. She says if you don't text her right after we hang up, you're in big trouble."

Tilly laughed. "Aye-aye, Captain. Listen, Dan. I'm not going to pretend that I'm okay. It'll be a while, and probably a whole lot of therapy to process everything."

"I know," Dan said. "All I'm asking is that you stay open to me. To us."

Tilly pictured Hannah beside him. He was making space for her in his family, despite everything that had happened. Tilly's heart felt so full it ached.

"I love you, Dan."

She heard him suck in a big breath, and for a moment the line was completely silent.

Tilly smiled. "Heavens! Have I rendered you speechless, Counselor?"

Dan laughed. "I didn't even know that was possible. Thank you for that."

They talked a few more minutes, and when Tilly disconnected she felt more at peace. She tried to ride that high as long as she could. There on Kate's couch she could wrap herself in love, away from the harsh realities that awaited them all.

CHAPTER 40
KATE

It had only been a year, but Mandy looked much older than her eighteen years. She'd graduated high school and finished her first year of college since Kate had last seen her.

When Kate opened the door, Mandy stepped right up and wrapped her arms around her.

"It sucks that we're here, but I'm also just so grateful to see you." Mandy's eyes sparkled with life, something that had been distinctly missing when she'd been a student at Kate's high school. It gave Kate hope.

"Come on in," Kate said, making way for Mandy and her father to enter the house. She showed them to their rooms and then returned to the kitchen to make some iced tea.

A few minutes later, Mandy came downstairs and took a seat at the table. "Dad's taking a nap," she said. "He didn't sleep much last night."

"I can imagine." Kate sat down across from her. "How's your sister?"

Mandy smiled kindly. "It was a rough year for her. She

doesn't completely understand everything that happened, and she's angry that she can't see Mom. But all in all, we're doing okay."

"I'm sorry I had to drag you back into this, Mandy."

"None of this is your fault, Ms. Medina." Even Mandy's voice sounded more mature. She was growing up, but trauma had a way of stalling that part of life or speeding it up, and Kate couldn't help but mourn the carefree girl that she'd never known.

"I've been seeing a therapist, and I talked to her yesterday after you called. Back when we left, I couldn't even think about coming back here. I remember when Chief Gunnison came into your office and threatened you, Ms. Medina. That day, after school, Benny took me aside and told me that if I ever said anything to you about what was going on, the chief would have me killed. At the time, I thought that's what had happened to Gabby. And I was terrified."

"Now I can see how they've made us all so afraid. That's how they've stayed off the radar for so long. I know that going through this process is going to be hard, but I've got support and I'm ready."

Kate smiled, even though her heart felt heavy. "Thank you. You have no idea how much I didn't want to call you, but you may be the only person who has first-hand knowledge of Chief Gunnison's involvement."

A shadow flickered over Mandy's face, so quickly that Kate might not have caught it if she hadn't been looking at that precise moment. Despite the brave front Mandy was putting on, she was still afraid. And after everything they'd all been through, Kate knew she had every reason to be.

———

Over the next few days, Kate's house became a base of operations for the investigation. Detective Montoya wanted to keep Mandy's presence under wraps—a goal that they all shared. Interviews were conducted. Statements taken.

In between the bustle of activity Mandy and her father David shared stories about their lives in Albuquerque, though he was often quiet. Kate wondered if he'd been seeing someone to help him grapple with the trauma they'd all endured.

"I took a class last semester in physical anthropology. It was so interesting," Mandy said enthusiastically. "We did labs where we got to look at bones and tell the sex, how old they were… It's so cool how much information you can get from a couple of old bones."

Kate smiled. "You sound like Tilly."

"I loved anthropology in college," Tilly confessed. "And for a while there I was binging episodes of *Bones*. Forensic anthropology is fascinating, but I think I like working with people who are alive more than I would like spending all my time with skeletons."

"The books are better than the show. Have you read them?"

Tilly laughed. "I haven't done much reading lately, but I admit I do love crime fiction. Police procedurals and books heavy in forensic science used to be my go-to when I wasn't reading textbooks."

"The nice thing about college is that you get to take so many different kinds of classes."

Mandy nodded. "I'm really not sure what I want to major

in. They make you put something down when you register. I chose business, but those classes put me to sleep. I think I'll start taking more science courses." She turned to Kate. "When did you know you wanted to be a psychologist?"

"When I was in high school," Kate said, giving Tilly a knowing look. "I remember seeing troubled teens and wishing there was more help out there."

Tilly smiled. "She means me, by the way."

"Not just you," Kate said. "Though there were times I wished I knew how to help you. I've always loved trying to figure out what makes people behave the way they do. Which is why it's so hard for me to forgive myself for missing all the clues with you, Tilly."

"We were kids," Tilly said soothingly. "I used to wonder what would have happened if I'd thought to tell you instead of Dad."

"I'd like to think I would have protected you." Kate had been so wrapped up in her own life as a teenager. She hoped she would have helped her sister. "Can't turn back the clock, though. So I'll just keep trying to help this generation be more aware and learn to intervene."

"You saved my life, Ms. Medina. You protected me."

"Mine, too," Tilly said softly.

The room grew quiet. Mandy's father excused himself, leaving the three women to contemplate their lives and the trauma that bound them together. Talking about that bond was soothing, but it also reminded Kate how important it was to look beyond the trauma—to see people as they were and as they could be.

CHAPTER 41
TILLY

IN THE WEE hours of the morning, Tilly gave up trying to sleep and walked quietly to the kitchen to make herself some tea. She padded along the cool tile, trailing a hand along the wall to avoid turning on any lights that might disturb the sleeping house.

As she rounded the corner, a soft beam of light glowed into the hallway. Kate was sitting at the table, staring into space. Tilly wasn't surprised. Sleep would be elusive for a while, maybe for all of them.

"Want me to make you some tea?" Tilly asked. Kate turned her head toward her sister, her glazed stare betraying just how exhausted she was.

"No. Thanks."

Tilly put a mug of water in the microwave and rifled through Kate's stash of teas. Deciding on some soothing chamomile she retrieved her mug, plunked the tea bag into the steaming water, and lowered herself into the chair across from Kate at the kitchen table. Her sore ribs ached, but Kate had helped her tighten the bindings before they'd finally retired, which took some of the pressure off.

"I didn't think I'd be able to let my mind settle, you know?" Kate murmured. "And I fell asleep, but it didn't last. Now I just feel like a zombie."

"Understandable. A lot has happened in a very short amount of time."

Kate looked at Tilly, eyes wide and shimmering with tears that were gathering around whatever thought had just gripped her. "I'm so sorry, Tilly."

"Kate, don't. You know this isn't your fault."

"I know," Kate said. "But the guilt of it all is crushing. When Dan showed up on my doorstep and you were gone— I have never felt grief like that, Til. Not when Mom died. Or Dad."

The words tore at Tilly's heart, making her feel dizzy with emotion. Her hands shook as she lifted her mug to her mouth.

"Sorry, Tilly. I know this is too much right now. I have to work through the guilt without making it a burden to you." Kate smiled. "But I love you. And I wanted you to know how much I need you in my life. Even though it took a lot of grief to get to where we are."

Tilly nodded. "Me, too."

She hoped it was enough, because between her exhaustion and her ribs talking seemed like too much. The problem with the fatigue she was feeling was that it made her struggle to stay upright, but she knew the moment she went back to bed she'd be wide awake again.

After a few silent moments, Kate said, "It's hard to believe that this might all be over soon."

Tilly wished it were that easy. In reality, taking Ruth and Gunnison and the current trafficking operation out of commission would leave a vacuum, and there were always those who were happy to step in. It was one of the hardest things about working to end this kind of violence—knowing that the battle would never be over.

Still, Tilly wouldn't choose another profession, and every victory, no matter how small, was a cause for celebration.

———

The nervous energy emanating from Mandy's father was palpable. Tilly watched him pace and then sit, shifting around until he finally got back up to his feet. When Tilly caught Mandy watching him, she couldn't resist asking her, "I was wondering, why not give your statement in Albuquerque? Seems like it would have been safer and easier."

Mandy smiled ruefully. "Do you really not know?"

Given everything they'd talked about last night, there was no doubt in Tilly's mind why Mandy would choose to walk right back into the lion's den—though she hadn't been privy to Kate and Mandy's conversation prior to her coming. But she wondered if hearing the reason might help her father find some peace in what they were doing.

"I have an idea, but I'm thinking that it might be important for you to explain." Tilly gestured over her shoulder toward Mandy's father, who'd stopped near a window and was peering out, clearly listening to the exchange.

Mandy nodded. "Moving to Albuquerque was the right thing to do. But I don't want to spend my life hiding out. I wanted to face this head on, so that I know I can. And then, maybe, I can really start to move forward."

"I wish I had been that courageous when I was younger," Tilly said wistfully. "When my father didn't believe me I just assumed no one would, so it made sense to get as far away as I could."

David finally came and sat down beside them. "I know this conversation is for me." He smiled at Tilly, the first genuine smile she'd seen since they arrived at Kate's house. "Thank you. When Mandy told me she wanted to do this, I panicked. But I do understand why we're here. It just makes me nervous."

"Sorry for the subterfuge, but I hope you know how critical it is to Mandy's recovery that she has you. Kate and I both see a lot of victims who have no one, and it's a hard journey back without a support system."

"What did I miss?" Kate queried, rounding the corner. Tilly had gone back to bed after their middle-of-the-night kitchen chat and slept like a rock for a few hours. It looked like Kate might've gotten some rest, too.

"Your sister was trying out some of your fancy psychology tricks on my dad," Mandy said, grinning.

Kate cocked her head sideways as she looked at Tilly, which made Tilly laugh. Which led to a cough. Which led to a whole lot of moaning as her ribs protested.

"Sorry," Mandy said sheepishly. Tilly resisted the urge to laugh again.

Roman had entered the room in the middle of all the drama. "Are you all right, Til?"

"Broken ribs are a beast," she replied.

"Agreed," Roman said, taking a seat beside David. "How is everyone this morning?"

David and Mandy exchanged a look, and finally David answered. "We're good. When are we getting started today?"

"Detective Montoya will be here around ten. He called a little while ago. Based on yesterday's discussion and the videos we received from Ruth Flores, they were able to issue four more arrest warrants." Roman spoke to the whole group, but his gaze rested on Mandy. "Our whole focus today is on Chief Gunnison. And then we want to get you guys back home."

Tilly saw Kate flinch. It was brief, almost imperceptible, but that one movement communicated a mouthful. Someone knew that Mandy was here. And what she was doing.

CHAPTER 42
KATE

As she watched the tail lights of Mandy's car fade away in the distance, Kate released the breath she felt she'd been holding all week. Since the moment she'd spoken to her former student on the phone, Kate had been bracing for something terrible to happen. But for the first time in a long time, everything went according to plan.

When Mandy and her father drove into town, the focus of the whole investigation shifted. While they tried not to place too much responsibility on Mandy's shoulders, her participation provided the spark that fueled their work. In the safety of the hacienda, Kate had seen a side of Mandy she'd never known—a girl so full of life, dreams, and ambition. Now that they'd left the sanctuary of Kate's desert fortress, her fear for the girl's safety had returned in full force.

"Do you think they'll be okay?" Kate asked for the hundredth time.

"They have a police escort to Socorro, and the State Police will be making their arrest tonight."

Kate followed Roman back into the house, locking the gate behind her. With Tilly and Mandy as guests, Kate's paranoia had taken hold. She'd gone from simply arming the alarm system to checking the security apps relentlessly.

"You're like a teenager on her phone," Tilly teased when she caught Kate looking again. "You literally just set the alarm."

Roman gave Kate a look and then headed upstairs for a shower.

Tilly filled up two cups with tea, handing one to Kate. "So now we wait."

"Now we wait," Kate agreed. She took her cup to the living room and got comfortable on the couch.

"Marie called today." Tilly sat down next to Kate. "She wants to know when, or if, I'm coming back to work."

Kate frowned. "What did you tell her?"

After a pause, Tilly said, "I didn't." She leaned back. "I've got an appointment with a counselor on Tuesday. I think I need to get my head on straight before I start taking cases again. And my rib needs to heal a bit more before I even return to the office. I told her I'd call her mid-week."

"Sounds healthy." Kate smiled. "We're adulting much better these days, eh?"

"We have our moments."

Kate looked up toward the sound of Roman's footsteps coming down the hall. When he appeared, she stopped breathing. His phone hung down in his hand—his hair was still dripping wet, leaving patches on his gray shirt.

"Is it Mandy?" Kate's voice shook.

"No," Roman said. "They went to arrest Gunnison. He's holed up in his house, armed, with hostages. He's not going down without a fight."

"Hostages?" Tilly's voice was barely a whisper.

"His neighbors." Disgust was written all over Roman's face. "He invited them over for drinks, apparently. An elderly couple."

"What an unbelievable bastard!" Kate's voice approached shouting volume. Blood was coursing through her veins at breakneck speed, and she knew what it meant to see red.

Roman and Tilly were talking quietly but Kate was trapped in her anger, unable to move or think. She'd experienced a whole range of emotions throughout the investigation, but nothing compared to the raw fury that now consumed her.

"Whoa, Kate. Breathe." Roman was at her side, and she felt like she'd lost time. Tilly was standing nearby, a look of near panic on her face. "Til, can you grab me some water?"

"Yeah," Tilly murmured as she hurried away.

"Are you okay?" Roman asked. His voice, which was normally soothing, sparked another flare of rage.

"No!" she screeched. "I am not okay. Nothing about this is okay!" Her breaths were coming fast—too fast. As her vision dimmed at the edges, she prayed for release from the anguish she was feeling.

Movement happened all around her. She felt Roman's hand on her arm. The cool water she sipped sliding down her throat. The feel of the couch cushions as someone guided her into a sitting position. But everything felt far away —detached.

Kate wasn't a stranger to panic attacks, having struggled with them for years. She'd kept herself together for more than a week, and it became clear that her body had had enough. Her pulse raced. She felt sweat forming all over her body. Breathing took so much effort. She closed her eyes, unable to ward off the impending attack.

In a hell of her own making, Kate withdrew as far into herself as she could.

———

It was dark outside when Kate came around. She was lying on the couch, a blanket tucked around her. The house was quiet, but the kitchen light created a path of light into the shadowy living room. Tilly was wrapped up in a blanket, snoring softly in the armchair.

Kate's mind was muddled. As she tried to piece together why she wasn't in her bed, anxiety began to build again.

"Tilly?" Kate didn't want to startle her sister, but keeping her voice steady and quiet was a challenge. "Tilly? Wake up."

Tilly stirred, and then sat straight up. "Kate? Are you all right?"

Tilly's reaction only fanned the flames of Kate's mounting panic. "Um, I'm okay. My head feels foggy, like it did with the fentanyl. But I'm pretty sure I'm also about to have another panic attack. What's going on?"

"You need to drink," Tilly said, ignoring her question. "Dehydration can cause drowsiness and confusion. I don't remember seeing you drink anything before you fell asleep."

"Was I sleeping?" Kate struggled to remember. She sat up

on the couch and took the cup of water Tilly handed her. Minutes passed. The cup grew lighter. And suddenly the news—Gunnison, hostages—all came back to her like a punch to the gut.

"Where's Roman?" Kate's heart began to race.

"Calm down," Tilly said. "Roman got called in to work."

"At the stand-off?" Kate was approaching hysteria. "When did he leave?"

"A couple of hours ago. He tried to wake you up, but you were pretty out of it." Tilly had moved to sit beside Kate and was pressing her fingers against Kate's wrist. Kate jerked away, but Tilly held on tight. "Let me check your vitals. Are you feeling any more clear-headed?"

"The water helped," Kate grudgingly admitted. Thankfully her anger began to dissipate, so she focused on slowing her breathing while Tilly took her pulse and felt her forehead.

"What happened before?" Tilly asked quietly. "I was worried you'd gone into shock. Not completely convinced we shouldn't have taken you to the hospital."

"Maybe I *was* in shock," Kate muttered. "I couldn't get the picture of that couple out of my mind. It was like having a panic attack, but the anger was so intense. I've never felt anything like it."

Tilly sighed. "We're going to need a lot of help working through all of this, Kate. Starting with Dad's death and then everything that followed."

"It's hard to picture being okay in a world that's just so awful."

"It's not all terrible," Tilly said. "That's what you told me, and you were right." She took a deep breath. "When I was in that basement, I didn't care what happened to me as long as Hannah got out. And I was angry just for being there. And scared. I said my goodbyes to you, to Dan. I was ready to be done."

Kate turned her full attention to Tilly. Looking into her sister's eyes, she was reminded of their mother. Addy Medina's face had been so easy to read, every emotion reflected in her expressive eyes. Tilly inherited that trait, while Kate was much like their father Frank—able to hide her feelings behind a neutral expression.

"When I close my eyes, I see so many horrors. I'm not even ready to go home, to sleep in my own apartment alone, much less consider going back to work where every single moment will be triggering." Tilly paused. "But then I think about all the people who walk through the doors of our clinic. I've never tried to convince myself that I can save the world, but I know that if I make a difference in one person's life all the pain is worth it."

Kate nodded. "I know. I know you're right. And when Roman walks back through that door, I'll probably have an easier time believing it."

"He's a cop," Tilly said in a somber tone. "You know as well as I do that he's at risk every time he walks out that door. Today is no different. And you know that Roman is always going to do everything he can to come home to you."

Everything she said was true, but she would never feel safe with Chief Gunnison on the loose. For now, all she could do was wait—and pray that they managed to apprehend him without any more loss of life.

CHAPTER 43
TILLY

In the early morning hours, the gate alarm rang. Kate and Tilly both froze in place. Unable to sleep, they'd been sitting vigil in the living room all night. Tilly watched Kate's hand hover over her phone, but she didn't touch it.

Instead, their attention turned to Rusty, who had jumped up and was wagging his tail. A minute later, Roman's key turned in the door. Kate launched herself off the couch and into his arms.

Roman looked weary, but no worse than when he'd left the previous afternoon. His relief at seeing Kate upright was unmistakable. Tilly whispered a silent prayer of thanks.

"I'm okay," Roman said, holding tightly to Kate's trembling frame. "It's over." He led her back to the couch and sat down. "The hostages are safe."

"Is the chief in jail?" Tilly asked.

"Dead," Roman said. "I don't know if he had a change of heart or what, but at some point in the night he went into his bedroom and OD'd—probably fentanyl. SWAT found him after freeing the hostages. They'd been tied up, but that's it. They've been taken to the hospital to get checked out."

"Mandy won't have to testify," Kate said with relief.

"Do you think there's anyone else who can keep the organization running?" Tilly asked.

Roman shook his head. "We may not know for sure. But they'll be tearing apart Gunnison's house, so maybe we'll get lucky and find something that proves one thing or another. Hopefully there will be enough pressure to keep anyone from trying to follow in his footsteps."

Tilly let the news sink in. She was relieved that Gunnison was gone, that the hostages were okay. But she was conflicted. His death was too easy. Too clean. Fentanyl caused feelings of euphoria. Gunnison had probably died peacefully, like falling asleep. Quick. Painless.

She thought about Rick, about how good it felt in that moment to see him bleed. He'd suffered, and somewhere inside her Tilly had felt a sense of satisfaction. It was that feeling—not the trauma of her abuse or the injuries she'd sustained at the hands of violent men—that made her fearful.

Once upon a time, she'd believed that there was nothing worse than surviving and then trying to integrate and over-come trauma. She'd fought hard for the victims she helped, but she'd been seeking justice. Revenge was a much more frightening aim.

As Kate breathed a sigh of relief, murmuring "It's over" into Roman's chest, Tilly knew that nothing could be further from the truth.

EPILOGUE

THE GATES at the hacienda stood wide open for the first time in a long time. Streamers flew in the hot summer breeze. Cars lined the road nearly all the way out to the highway. It was the grand opening of the safe house—the official start for Kate's passion project.

Roman and Dan stood in a group of FBI agents, talking animatedly.

Kate was flitting about, talking to her guests and refilling pitchers and bowls.

Tilly sat in the shade, watching the party without joining in. It had only been a few months since the abduction and all that happened in its aftermath. Tilly's physical wounds were healed, but it would take time for the emotional and psychological scars to fade.

Hannah walked over to where Tilly was sitting and noisily pulled a chair up beside her.

"It's hard to be in the middle of the crowd," Hannah said, echoing Tilly's thoughts. Tilly had gone back to work as an administrator, but she hadn't made her way back into an exam room.

Every victim needed something different to heal. She needed time.

Hannah's healing journey seemed to be smoother. She'd finished out the school year, and was getting ready to spend the summer working as a camp counselor. The boy who'd taken her to homecoming, and then prom, was now officially her boyfriend.

But at times Tilly saw the wariness in Hannah's otherwise bright eyes. The abduction, the assault, and what followed would stay with them both forever. Tilly hoped Hannah would find her way back to something more normal.

Tilly watched as Dan broke away from his conversation and headed toward where she and Hannah were sitting.

"Ready to go?"

"I am," Hannah said with a sigh. "I think I'm maxed out on people for the moment. And I start my job on Monday, so I'd love to just relax the rest of the weekend."

"Me, too." Tilly smiled. "Let's go find Kate and say our goodbyes."

"You found me." Kate had popped up beside Dan. Roman followed, putting arm around her waist. The summer promised happy times, including a much anticipated wedding. Despite all the recent trauma, Kate seemed more grounded than ever. More sure of herself.

Tilly was a little bit jealous, but her joy at Kate's happiness outweighed her moments of envy.

"We're going to head home." Tilly stood up to give Kate a hug. "See you next weekend?"

"Absolutely. I'll be wearing my grubby clothes. Be afraid." They all laughed. Dan looked at Tilly and smiled warmly.

Tilly spent the first few months alone in her apartment, grappling with her nightmares and seeing a therapist twice a week. She dealt with grief, with fear, and with an all-consuming anger that crushed her chest. So she'd sought release. All the old temptations—alcohol, violence, self-harm, self-sabotage—sometimes haunted her days and her nights, holding her in a fierce battle for her own sanity and for the health of her relationships.

It would be an undertaking—a journey through life that she had never anticipated. And yet there were moments so sweet it made the whole thing worthwhile.

A few weeks in, she returned to work. A month or two later, she decided it was time to deconstruct the barriers between herself and Dan. He'd promised to wait for her, and he had.

Hannah slipped an arm around Tilly on one side and Dan on the other. "I'll have everything ready at the house."

"What are you up to?" Tilly asked, giving Hannah the side-eye.

Hannah grinned. "Dad and I have been doing some cleaning and decluttering, that's all. After all, you'll be bringing a bunch of stuff with you when you move in."

"I told you not to do anything special. Kate's taking a few things, and I can put the rest in storage." Tilly's protests were met with a squeeze from Hannah.

"Nope. A wise woman once told me that sometimes you have to jump in with both feet."

Tilly blushed. She hated having her own advice thrown

at her, but hearing it from Hannah made her smile. If things worked out, Tilly might be a stepmother—not a role she ever expected to have.

Kate leaned in and whispered. "Family."

Tilly's eyes began to mist. "Love you, Kate."

"Right back atcha," Kate said. "I'll see you Saturday. Have coffee ready."

Dan took Tilly's hand and they followed Hannah through the courtyard. Tilly glanced over her shoulder. Kate was smiling, Roman at her side, surrounded by community members who supported her mission. Some days, Tilly had to work hard to picture life as it was before her father died. Before she'd gotten her sister back.

Life moved forward. It was the one constant in all of this. Tilly knew there would be struggles. It was inevitable. But as she held Dan's hand, she felt the warmth and safety of home and family.

She breathed in, relishing the smell of desert flora.

ACKNOWLEDGMENTS

Writing about human trafficking can be harrowing. It's a topic people don't like to discuss and when you dig deep into the details–the staggering number of victims, the truly disgusting amount of money that is generated by the sale of human beings, and the lasting impact to individuals, families, communities, and society as a whole–self care and emotional support are essential. I am truly grateful for my friends, family, and writing communities including Writing Heights Writers Association, Rocky Mountain Fiction Writers, and Sisters In Crime Colorado. Your support, love, encouragement, and understanding has been a vital gift for this author.

Writing any book does not happen in a vacuum, despite the stories you've probably heard about writers holed up in cabins writing feverishly with no contact from the outside world. Those quiet moments are lovely, but eventually we have to come out of our writing caves and get our creative works out into the hands of you wonderful readers. I am lucky to work with some awesome professionals who help make my books the best they can be. A huge thank you to Carl Graves for another stunning cover design and my fantastic editors Christina Kaye and Kimberly Huther for working out all the kinks and cleaning up my messes.

I couldn't do this work without the support and first-readership of my husband, and the unwavering love of my kids, who still think it's cool that their mom's an author. You guys are always there for me, and you've taught me so much about what it means to be present and authentic. I think you're all pretty cool, too.

To my mom, who is often both in wonder about and completely excited by my professional life. She loves being nearby at events so she can participate in the discussion, which is something I love. And to my dad, who doesn't read a lot but is making his way through this series. You're so much fun to travel with and I love seeing you laugh until you're wiping your eyes. I couldn't have asked for better parents.

To my sister. If even a fraction of the love that Kate and Tilly feel for one another came across in these pages, it's because of you. You are such an amazing woman and I'm so lucky to have you. Thanks for looking past all those bossy big sister moments and letting me be part of your life.

To my best friend Jessica. Honestly, you get more excited about my work than I do sometimes, and I appreciate that because it keeps me moving. We talk a lot about trauma and how it shapes people's lives. Thank you for wearing the "ask me about my best friend" t-shirt at events, and supporting me every step of the way. My life is better because you're in it. Squirrel!

There are so many people, past and present, who have made an impact on me, both personally and professionally. I've grown as a person, learned how to draw and enforce boundaries, followed my passion, learned how to let go, and accomplished so many extraordinary things. Thank you for being a part of this adventure.

And to you, dear readers. I know these stories can take you to some dark places–I'm right there with you. Thank you for supporting my efforts to make change through fiction by buying, reading, recommending, and reviewing my books. It is such a pleasure to talk with you on social media and to see you at events. You are the absolute heart and soul of the work I do, and I hope to keep creating stories for you that will both keep you turning the pages and also, maybe, change the world for the better.

ABOUT THE AUTHOR

Amy Rivers is an award-winning novelist, as well as the Director of Writing Heights Writers Association. She was named 2021 Indie Author of the Year by the Indie Author Project. Her psychological suspense novels incorporate important social issues with a focus on the complexities of human behavior. Amy was raised in New Mexico and now lives in Colorado with her husband and children.

ALSO BY AMY RIVERS

A LEGACY OF SILENCE SERIES

Complicit

Stumble & Fall

STANDALONE

All The Broken People